HALF MOON BAY

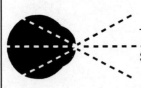

This Large Print Book carries the
Seal of Approval of N.A.V.H.

HALF MOON BAY

ALICE LAPLANTE

THORNDIKE PRESS

A part of Gale, a Cengage Company

Farmington Hills, Mich • San Francisco • New York • Waterville, Maine
Meriden, Conn • Mason, Ohio • Chicago

LIBRARY OF CONGRESS CIP DATA ON FILE.
CATALOGUING IN PUBLICATION FOR THIS BOOK
IS AVAILABLE FROM THE LIBRARY OF CONGRESS

ISBN-13: 978-1-4328-5625-0 (hardcover)

Published in 2018 by arrangement with Scribner, an imprint of Simon & Schuster, Inc.

Printed in Mexico
1 2 3 4 5 6 7 22 21 20 19 18

To my beloved friends and members of the Tramuntana Writers, in Pollensa, Spain, who supported me through the writing of this novel: Sarah Barnett-Benelli, Maureen Gallagher, Shirley Kerby James, Carol Jackson, Ann Morgan, Jeanette Russo, Nicole Szulc, and Danica Wilcox.

All I maintain is that on this earth there are pestilences and there are victims, and it's up to us, so far as possible, not to join forces with the pestilences.

— Albert Camus

PART I
LOSSES

Six p.m. Fog. Impenetrable, but not cold. Balmy, like Hawaii. That red cottage on the south side of Kauai, near Princeville. Shrouded by eucalyptus, so pungent after rain. Cockroaches scuttled when you pulled back the shower curtain. Where Jane and Rick and Angela stayed their last Christmas. The last year. The last vacation. Last things. So many last things.

As Jane steps outside into the Northern California evening, the fog's moist veil slaps her face, temporarily obscuring her vision. Dark things loom. Trees, cars. Jane takes off her jacket and tosses it back inside her cottage. The door closes with a click. She doesn't lock it behind her. No one does, here.

Jane can't see the ocean from her cottage, but she can hear it and, most important, smell it. She leaves her bedroom windows open when she leaves the house so that

11

when she returns, her pillows are damp and scented of seaweed. Of crabs and fish. Of the larger, mysterious things that swim in the depths. One of the reasons she moved here, to be closer to the sea, that deep insistent body of possibilities. Probabilities.

Once upon a time there was a woman. Actually, just a girl, when it begins. One of a family of ten children — first seven girls, then two boys, then a female caboose on the end. Jane is Number 3. Tragedy awaits, but she does not know it. She is being prepared. Everything in her life is building toward this moment. As she is hurt, as she is torn apart, she puts herself in a state of suspension, anything to dull the pain. *This is not true,* she says; *this is not my life.* It is her life.

Jane's cell phone rings from within the cottage. She'd set the ringtone, in a fit of rage one day, on the *Dies Irae* and never changed it back. *The day of wrath.* One of her sisters probably. Or a friend from Berkeley, checking in. Her people. Her community. Worried about her, as they should be. But no contact tonight. No.

Jane is haunted. Ghosts touch her but deign

not to speak. She wakes up in the middle of the night, cold fingers on her shoulder. Others on her arm. The laying on of hands, not to cure but to blame.

Jane walks toward the sea, avoiding the surfers' beach that borders Route 1. Despite the fog and the hour, two or three fanatically fit young men will inevitably be catching waves, sleek as seals in their glistening black suits. Instead, she heads over to Mavericks Beach, the home, when conditions are right, of towering eighty-foot waves, recently discovered by the international surfing set, a place so cool that Apple named an operating system after it. Jane's go-to place when she is in extremis.

It has now been one year, two weeks, and two days. She can calculate the hours too, if asked. Nobody asks. Nobody refers to it, out of . . . ? Kindness? Courtesy? Fear? It should be fear, fear of wakening the beast smoldering inside Jane.

Jane puts one foot in front of the other. That's how it works for her these days. The fog so thick she can see only a yard ahead, but she knows every step of this route. Right foot. Left foot. Right foot again. She loses herself in the rhythm. Nothing but the muffled sound of her own steps for a quarter

13

of an hour as she winds through the industrial district of Princeton-by-the-Sea. She is nearing her destination. She can smell the rotting seaweed, hear the plaintive calls of the ringtail harriers from the marsh. Then she stops. Something is wrong. Red and blue lights flicker through the mist. Voices, both men's and women's, jumbled and unintelligible. A crackling sound, as of an untuned radio.

Jane had lost people before. Joshua, her postcollege boyfriend. She noticed the lesions first. A beautiful bruised purple. Aubergine. On his back and his thighs. And then how thin he was getting. She'd originally thought he was looking good, more fit. She'd even complimented him. But the constant illnesses, colds, flus. And those lesions. One day she woke up before he did. He had his back to her. She couldn't see his face, but from the wasted body, she understood that she lay next to a dying man. How could she not have known? Her tears wet his shoulder blades, sticking out of his thin back like chicken wings. He had been so kind to her. She had felt safe with him, even loved. It wasn't until later that it occurred to her that she had been betrayed. She didn't feel betrayed but bereft. She might have known that this beautiful gift of this beautiful boy would have strings attached. *Oh, Janey,* he'd said. *Oh, Jane, don't cry.* But he had been crying himself.

A police car, she can see as it comes into focus. Its lights flashing. White with black geometric markings. And another. And another. A dark figure approaches, grows darker and more substantial as it gets closer.

May I help you, ma'am? When did she turn from a miss into a ma'am? The shift has been imperceptible. Yet it has happened. Maiden, mother, crone. She is no longer either of the first two, so that leaves the final stage. At thirty-nine, her red hair glints gray in direct light.

What's going on? Jane asks. Even her voice is muffled by the fog.

The figure comes closer. It is wearing a hat, a uniform with a badge on it. It is male, as she should have known from the voice. But somehow that surprises her. What did she expect? Something not quite of this earth. A hobgoblin. Bugbear. But this man seems solid, human. A policeman. The bearer of bad news.

It's a search party. You live near here?

A silly question. No one lives near Mavericks. To reach it, you have to wind your way

15

through the acres of rusting warehouses and grounded boats Jane has just navigated.

Over there. Jane motions with her head in the general direction of her cottage.

You know the McCreadys, then?

Just the name, Jane says. She tries to conjure up faces, fails.

They live up on the hill. He points into the darkness.

Oh. That explains it. Hill people. They're different. In another life, Jane would have been one of them. They live in the new houses clinging precipitously to the steep hill above Princeton-by-the-Sea. The ornate ones painted to look like Victorians from the last century. With balconies no one stepped onto, lounge chairs no one sat in. Hill people were the prosperous professionals: the doctors and lawyers and engineers who commuted every day over the hill to Silicon Valley. Another world from here, the San Mateo coast. Although it's a small community, Jane isn't on speaking terms with any of the people who live up the hill. Most of them belong to a different species altogether, with their business suits and BMWs that roar off at 7:00 a.m. to make it over Route 92 to Sunnyvale or Milpitas by the start of the workday. Programmers and project managers. Financial analysts, accountants. Men and women who spend more time on the road than at home. People capable of organizing their thoughts into logical code, Gantt charts of responsibility, and numbers that add up. Ambiguity banished from their lives during the day. Then back here, to the rolling sea and amorphous fog. A strange existence. It takes a certain kind of person to juggle the contrasts. Jane knows she sounds scornful, but really she is envious. They have found balance.

What about the McCreadys?

Their little girl, Heidi. She's wandered away.

Jane considers. *Why are you looking here?* she asks. It seems an implausible place and time.

This was her favorite spot. She'd been here with her parents this afternoon. The little girl lost her magic pebble. They thought she might have come back to look for it.

Jane considers. Magic pebbles. It hurts to remember. Magic string, magic pencils, even magic bugs. Jane had fixed up a cardboard box to contain the spiders and the roly-polies Angela captured from under the porch, but they all skittered away through the cracks. Jane's heart breaking to see Angela's tears of irrevocable loss. A child's grief, never to be trivialized.

How old was she? Jane asks.

Five.

Angela didn't speak until she was five. Jane and Rick had taught her sign language and communicated with their hands. *Eat. More? All gone.* Then, suddenly, out came everything in full sentences. Angela had kept it all inside until she burst. She learned that from Jane.

A long way to walk for a five-year-old, Jane says.

A missing girl. Police. This will end badly. Such things always end badly.

Your name? The policeman has taken out a pad. A pen. He looks at Jane, or at least she thinks he's looking at her. The fog so thick he no longer has a face.

Jane.

Your last name, ma'am?

O'Malley. Why is Jane so reluctant to give this information? She feels as though she is confessing to something, that he is writing an indictment with his pen right now.

And what are you doing here?

Just walking, Jane says, but it doesn't sound convincing. Alone, in the dark, in the fog, without a coat or a flashlight, striding along, hands in pockets. She should have brought her landlord's dog. No one questions you when you're walking a dog.

I'll be heading home now, she says, in a

voice that sounds deceitful, even to her.

You do that, ma'am, agrees the policeman, but she sees him circle her name on his pad before he turns away.

But Jane doesn't go home. Instead, she takes a few steps before doubling back and heading toward the sea. She circumvents the official vehicles and walks the dirt path alongside the base of the cliff. Even here she's not alone. Scores of flashlight beams scan the sand, the bay, the breakwater. The fog is now floating high above her head, wispy threads that glow in the light of the unblocked moon. If Jane were a child, this is exactly the kind of night she'd wander off, excited by the proximity of the sea and the moonlit strands of fog. She'd go straight into this enclosure between the fog and the sand. Straight toward the water. To sink in. To give in. Don't think she hasn't considered it.

A seabird calls. Another answers. The sea glows, gives off its own undulating light. Jane sees black heads, unblinking eyes, staring at her from the water. Seals. Selkies. The Celts thought them capable of taking on human form. If a woman wishes contact with a selkie male, she must shed seven tears into the sea. If a man steals a female selkie's skin, she is forced to become his wife. Selkie women make excellent wives but will always long for the sea. They will abandon everything — home, husband, and, especially, children — if given the chance to return to it.

The fog miraculously clears for a moment, and the stars are so clear Jane can see them twinkle. The air still. Satellites that carry voices and texts crawl slowly across the sky. The moon, full. You must be by the water on such nights. It is best to touch it. Bare flesh to cold water. Jane did this when Angela was small, only then it was the bay, not the ocean. The Golden Gate Bridge shining in the distance as they did their moon dances. Jane had taught Angela to moon-dance, as Jane's mother had taught Jane and her sisters. And as Jane expected, Angela to teach it to *her* daughters. Who had remained single little egglets, never united with sperm, unpenetrated, nestled in Angela's unstretched womb. Not that Angela had been a virgin. No. Just smart about birth control. Jane had taught her that too.

Jane reads. Jane goes to a shrink. Jane knows many facts. Are they helpful? No.

Approximately 19 percent of the U.S. population has experienced the death of a child. Almost 1 million deaths annually. This leaves 2 million bereaved parents every year.

The loss of a child triggers more intense grief than the death of a spouse or parent. After the death of a child, the divorce of the parents is a statistical probability. This is science.

Parents who experience the death of a child are more likely to suffer *complicated grief.* This is bereavement accompanied by feelings of separation and *trauma distress.* To earn this diagnosis, the person must experience extreme levels of three of the four *separation distress* symptoms — intrusive thoughts about the deceased, yearning for the deceased, searching for the deceased, and excessive loneliness since the death. They must also show "extreme" levels of four of the eight *traumatic distress* symptoms: purposelessness, numbness, or detachment, feeling that life is meaningless, feeling that a part of oneself has died, a shattered worldview, assuming behaviors of the deceased, and excessive irritability or anger.

Jane reads: *These symptoms result in significant functional impairment.*

She has to laugh. *No shit, Sherlock.*

Intrusive Thoughts of the Deceased.

Intrusive is a good word. Jane commends the psychologists who coined the phrase. Angela intrudes everywhere; each stone, each glass of water, each cup of coffee resonates with memories both bitter and sweet. Is anything just what it should be? A couch, a sweater, a doorknob? No. Angela inhabits every object on the planet that Jane encounters.

Yearning for the Deceased.

Oh, how Jane yearns! Even for the last, bad teen years, for the slammed doors and refused plates of food and terrifying nights when Angela borrowed the car. Jane would take any of it now. And the early years! She looks at the few photos she kept, and weeps — what she wouldn't do to trade places with that younger, more vibrant Jane! The busy and as-yet-uncomplicated mother.

Searching for the Deceased.

Jane searches for Angela everywhere. In the house: Is she in the kitchen, making a mess scrambling eggs with butter and leaving the perishables on the counter? In her room, with her earphones on, listening to retro seventies music? On the street Jane constantly sees Angela and hurries to catch up to her, turns corners only to accost startled strangers.

Excessive loneliness

Loneliness: affected with, characterized by, or causing a depressing feeling of being alone.
Excessive: an amount or degree too great to be reasonable or acceptable.

Jane *is* alone. Utterly alone. The suffering is great, but it is both completely reasonable and absolutely acceptable. She deserves it, after all.

★ ★ ★

Jane has traveled the world, drunk deeply of its joys and sorrows, and landed here, in Princeton-by-the-Sea, a small village on the Northern California coast, a mile north of Half Moon Bay. She is suffering from complicated grief. She is trying to build a life here. She *is* building a life here, she tells people. Those who know her from her previous life admire her spirit. They exclaim about her resilience. They call and offer their support, but don't talk about what drove her here. Those who don't know Jane from before see a sad-faced woman, late thirties, friendly enough although guarded. The most notable thing about her is her hair: a deep, true red. She wears it long and straight, over her shoulders. She is talked about. *That new red-haired woman. You know the one.*

Jane works in Smithson's Nursery in Half Moon Bay, the largest town on this stretch of the coast. Her fingernails are often dark from earth when she shops at the Safeway after the nursery closes, buying vegetables that are a riot of color: red peppers that match her hair, dark green cucumbers, light green lettuces, yellow squash, purple eggplants. She is an expert in native California plants, in which Smithson's specializes. She can tell you whether to plant Big Sur manzanita (*Arctostaphylos edmundsii*) or Heart's Desire (*Ceanothus gloriosus*) in that half-shaded alcove in your garden. If you speak to her, she startles. It is best to approach her gently, as you would a wild faun.

Half Moon Bay was once known as Spanishtown. The land was wrenched from the Costanoan Indians in the early 1800s, and

Routes 1 and 92 still follow the old Costanoan trails along the ocean and over the hills. A luxury campground, Costanoa, has been built on top of the creekside hollow that was the main Costanoan settlement. Today, tourists feast on roast buffalo and wild pig before going to their "tents," amid the sand dunes, really small ultraluxurious wooden houses on stilts with shiny bathrooms and king-size beds and down comforters. They do not think of the people they displaced. They do not know the old legends.* Like when the first person died and began to stink. The meadowlark smelled it. He did not like it. Coyote said: "I think I will make him get up." The meadowlark said: "No, do not. There will be too many. They will become so many that they will eat each other." Coyote said: "That is nothing. I do not like people to die." But the meadowlark told him: "No, it is not well to have too many. There will be others instead of those that die. A man will have many children. The old people will die but the young will live." Then Coyote said nothing more. So from that time on, people have always died. They are still being buried in the

* Source: A. L. Kroeber. "The Origin of Death." *Indian Myths of South Central California* (1907). http://www.sacred-texts.com/nam/ca/scc/scc11.htm. Accessed December 26, 2016.

cemetery at the corner of Main and Route 92, the evidence of Coyote's momentous decision the first thing tourists see as they enter the town.

After the Indians were vanquished, the first houses were raised in the 1840s by Mexican settlers given land grants. Whites began moving in after the Civil War, and after another kind of bloody resettlement, the town officially became Half Moon Bay in 1874, renamed for the perfect crescent-shaped harbor just north of town. Which brings us to one of the peculiarities of Half Moon Bay, and indeed many other Northern California coastal towns. Although situated in one of the most naturally stunning landscapes on the planet, the town center is set half a mile inland, its back to the ocean. The harbor itself is ugly, industrial, at the rear of a seedy mall with a Burger King and destitute variety shops. The town, really only Main Street, is itself quite quaint. Many of the original wood buildings still stand, although the adobes and early brick buildings were destroyed in the 1906 earthquake.

In 1907, the Ocean Shore Railroad was constructed along the shoreline from San Francisco to Tunitas Glen, south of Half Moon Bay. Developers had grand plans to turn Half Moon Bay and its environs into Atlantic City of the West. Plots were sold.

Prices soared. Posters depicting bathers venturing into sky blue waters were printed. The developers imagined large hotels, splendid avenues, swank shops. But they hadn't accounted for the freezing water and thick fog that covered the coast from June through August. No one came. Or if they came, they left hurriedly, shivering. Due to financial problems and the increasing popularity of the horseless carriage, the railroad ceased operation in 1920, the rails long ago ripped up and sold. Now all that remains are the broad streets laid out in large concentric circles facing the ocean in Jane's town, Princeton-by-the-Sea. The avenues of Monterey pine trees planted to line those streets are now majestic, fulfilling the long-ago vision of a sophisticated playground for tourists, but underneath them are small rotting wood-frame cottages like Jane's. The former train station is now a Chinese restaurant. It has a decent Mongolian beef, but do avoid the sweet-and-sour pork.

Who lives here? Who would choose this beautiful but remote spot? It isn't easy to get to where the jobs are — either the long trek up Route 1 to San Francisco or the dangerous trip up and down the steep hill to Silicon Valley. Still, people do live here and are mostly content. There are the farmers, large and small, mostly organic these days. The shop owners, optimistic and typically disappointed by the clientele, who look but do not buy. These come and go. Some stay after their shops close. They like the fact that everyone pretty much knows everyone else by sight and that it's a safe place to raise kids even though the schools are lousy. Water is scarce, so building new houses has been banned except for the Silicon Valley billionaires who buy up sections of the coastline and bribe the Coastal Commission for permits.

Take a walk now, down Main Street. See Marilyn Standish, the tough proprietor of the tiny coffee shop. She has had a mastectomy but without the reconstruction surgery. *That would be vanity,* she declared. She is a Seventh Day Adventist and doesn't let her daughters celebrate their birthdays, although they secretly defy her and eat birthday cake and accept presents in the cafeteria at school. Keep going. See Bob Orlando, who owns Bogies, the grocery store. Downstairs is the usual food and produce. But upstairs, a trove of oddities. You can buy kissing nun salt-and-pepper shakers, authentic fisherman's hats, books by local authors on the coastal flora and fauna. Everything jumbled in piles and seemingly forgotten for years. An Aladdin's cave. Joan Acuesta is there now, sifting through the piles of extra-large flannel shirts and pillbox hats from the 1930s for a gift for her niece, whom she has raised from a baby. Unbeknown to Joan, her niece in seven months will give birth to a child of her own. She will refuse to name a father. Such things happen here frequently.

Go downstairs again and out the door. One block to the left, and you get to the Three Sisters Café. Run by three sisters, naturally: twins and their younger sibling. Opened only one year ago, and now the heart of the town. This is where you go to get the best coffee on the coast, the most flavorful artichoke soup, the freshest and most titillating gossip. You can't see the walls of the café; they are covered with children's drawings, notices of births and deaths, advertisements for the Coastal Players' production of *My Fair Lady,* hot yoga classes by Martha, dog walking by Ian, and other essential services. You could spend a year reading those walls. By doing so, you don't feel alone. You understand that life is pulsing around you, that even on Sunday nights, when Main Street is deserted and the fog shadows the streetlights, other hearts are beating around you. The wall brings comfort to Jonathan Hummer, who lost his wife to a sudden heart attack in February.

He pulls off a paper tab containing a phone number for Ohlone Singles when he thinks no one is looking and puts it surreptitiously in his pocket. He will get a good one this time. He will get one who doesn't blow cigarette smoke in his face, who can tolerate having dog hair on the living room furniture. He will.

The Beach Belly Dancers are meeting in the assembly room of the old First Methodist Church two blocks south of Three Sisters. They are mostly women of a certain age who would never wear two-piece bathing suits, who make love with the lights out, who buy their clothes on the Internet. Yet here they are, dressed in gaudy silk-like ballooning trousers and sparkling bras, exposing their pudding-like bellies to the world as they shake and whoop and stop to drink some wine or taste one of Janet Thimble's homemade oatmeal cookies or plot a political coup on the town council. Together, they are a nation, and they are important. When they leave at 10:00 p.m., their shoulders are a little straighter, their steps a little faster. They return to their sleeping families feeling like army generals after a truce has been declared. What to do with all this energy? They sit at kitchen tables and write lengthy to-do lists and strident letters to the editor of the *Moon News.*

Darkness descends on Half Moon Bay. Fog mixed with smoke from wood stoves hovers above the houses. The surf pounds the sand, a full half-mile from Main Street, but the rhythm of the sea and its tantalizing scent permeate the porous window frames of the old wooden houses, soothing the inhabitants, luring them to their beds. They know they live in a bubble. They know that dark things, unimaginable things, wait in the wings for their turn to propagate and thrive. The Costanoa's Coyote, the trickster, will ascend again, in more alluring form, in retribution for past sins. But for now, the town sleeps, content in its innocent ignorance.

That night, Jane can't stop thinking about little Heidi. This is unusual. Jane has gotten good at not thinking. She has gotten very good about not feeling. She settles on her couch with a book, something a previous tenant left behind, the cover art portraying a bosomy sorceress fighting an army of horned beasts. But Jane can't concentrate. She's agitated. She thinks about the distraught parents. If she had sufficient generosity, she'd walk up the steep hill, offer to sit vigil with them. She'd tell her story. She'd reassure them that everything would almost certainly turn out all right. For them. And she'd be lying and secretly reveling in it. She considers the scenarios the parents are inevitably conjuring as they await news. Jane pictures Heidi as the little Swiss mountain girl in Angela's version of the book by that name, snub-nosed with blond braids, puffed-out white sleeves, and an embroidered dress. Jane goes to bed and dreams of Heidi, safe on her mountain picking bluebells.

There is little talk of anything but Heidi at the Three Sisters Café, where Jane gets her coffee the next morning.

Have you heard? asks one of the young café owners as she refills Jane's cup. Jane has finally gotten to where she can tell the sisters apart, they look so similar, even though only the two older ones are twins. They share a pale oval face with small dark eyes. They look like marmots, with their manes of dark hair caught up in ponytails, their large blue unblinking eyes. Somewhat feral, but nevertheless approachable. Sympathetic.

It is a closely knit community, and although this misfortune has hit outsider over-the-hill people, locals are feeling it deeply, Jane can tell. Voices are subdued. Children too young to be in school are being hugged close by their parents.

They're organizing a search party, said the sister, her name is Margaret, on her next trip around the tables. *Sign up at the sheriff's office.* Jane can't — she has a job to do; she is, despite her fragile state, gainfully employed — but she leaves Margaret an extragenerous tip in recompense. People nod to her as she leaves. It's that kind of place.

As it turns out, Heidi is dark-haired. She is not adorable. It is not an attractive photo that appears on the signs on the street, in the shop windows, in the *Moon News.* How can a five-year-old girl be so plain? Jane remembers Angela, her friends at that age, so heart-stoppingly lovely, the mothers universally convinced that strangers would be tempted to snatch them away if left unguarded for even a moment. So they weren't. A generation of tiny prisoners.

Sometimes Jane walks, and talks, and acts as if she were still a mother, still a woman with a family, not a woman alone. A mother walks slower. She has much on her mind. Where is the daughter? Who is she with?

What is she doing? And, most important, what could go wrong? A woman without a family is lighter on her feet, less distracted. She's not thinking, *Nearly dinnertime. What shall I feed her?* Or see a dress in a window and stop and think, *Wouldn't she look cute in that?* before reality sets in.

Two days pass. Three. People start shaking their heads in the Three Sisters Café. *This will end in tears,* Jane would tell Angela when, as a child, she played too roughly with her toy soldiers, her Barbie princesses, in an all-out war of the sexes, the pink bosomy Barbies overwhelming the small green plastic soldiers. Rick's idea of bringing Angela up without gender biases. Jane walks past the photos of the singularly unattractive Heidi papering the windows of the stores along Main Street. *This will end in tears.*

Jane is not a believer in Dr. Kübler-Ross. The five stages of grief do not exist. Or rather, they are not stages. Or rather, they are not grief. They are madnesses. Jane accepts the fact that denial, anger, bargaining, and depression are now her life. Acceptance is not, nor will it ever be. Always a maker of lists, Jane has created an Excel spreadsheet on her laptop. She checks off the madnesses as they engulf her minute by minute, day by day, on a scale of 1 to 10. Is what her shrink calls the *intensity* dissipating? Jane's shrink says yes; her spreadsheet says no.

Kübler-Ross missed some of the most important madnesses. *Shame. Guilt. Hope.* And yes, *ecstasy.* Sleep can bestow glorious gifts, as when Angela arises, whole and un-mangled, acting as though nothing has happened. *What's for dinner?* she asks. Or, *Can I have the car?* Or, worse, just a plain inquiring *Mom?* Then Jane wakes, and it is like hearing the news for the first time.

How do you define loss? Jane has posted Merriam-Webster's definition on her bedroom mirror. *Deprivation.* She has been grievously deprived.

Here's what Jane remembers. Heat. Even for July, it had been unusual. All the clima-tologists saying *Get used to it.* A hotter world. An increasingly inhospitable planet. Berkeley was certainly hostile that summer, if Jane remembers properly, if she is not *fantasizing,* if she is not *transforming emotions into facts,* as her shrink often accuses her of doing. *You are the unreliable narrator of your own life.* Yet surely it is true that at that time, the garbagemen are on strike, and stinking refuse is piling up on the street, overflowing onto sidewalks. Fans sell out at the hardware stores, as do rat traps. People stop picking up their dogs' poop. The homeless, who refuse to shed their layers of clothing no matter how hot the temperature, are passing out from heatstroke and dehydration. The university lets them bathe in the fountains, an unusual concession of humanity. And then there is that night, when Jane sits in her living room waiting and worrying. No, she is not psychic. This is simply what she does when Angela is out at night. Where does this fear come from? She had grown up in a middle-class family in a safe middle-class town. Was the word *fear*? No. *Terror.* She waits, terrified, night after night.

When the police car pulls up in front of the house — of course, her curtains are open, of course, she makes sure she had a clear view of the street and sidewalk — you could say she was prepared. Jane had anticipated this day from the moment of Angela's birth sixteen years ago. She hadn't known what the details would be, of course. There were so many possibilities! But the two uniformed men who tread heavily up to Jane's door fit in well enough with her fantasies. Yes. It could happen like this. Yes, it could. And then the knock on the door.

It is 2:00 p.m. at Smithson's Nursery, and no one has taken lunch yet. Mid-August, time to start gearing up for the annual Pumpkin Festival, the biggest weekend in Half Moon Bay, when people come from all over the state to get lost in corn mazes, drink local designer wines, and pick out their pumpkins for Halloween. Children choose their own pumpkins from the piles of small pumpkins. Parents look for the biggest and most symmetrical to carve into leering faces. At the end of the weekend, they drive home, a pumpkin nestled below each pair of feet like a small pet. Smithson's doesn't sell pumpkins, but from experience knows that tourists will also swoop on any plants that flower in autumn. There has been talk of canceling the Pumpkin Festival because little Heidi has not been found. But the talk is not serious. The Pumpkin Festival is essential to the health of the local economy.

Jane likes watching her colleague Adam as he digs up tiny shoots of pepperweed (*Lepidium lasiocarpum*) from a seedling tray. He is pleasant to look at, his fingers brushing dirt off the leaves, deftly inserting the tiny plants into the larger plastic pots. He's got one earpiece in, listening to dreamy neo-hippie music that would put Jane to sleep in a moment. Even half hearing it, combined with the somnolent humidity of the green-house, makes her drowsy. Adam's long body is bent over the rough wooden table, over the plants he has nurtured from seeds, his longish blondish hair brushing the green tops. They're among Smithson's best-selling ground cover. Suddenly he stands up straight. Dirt falls from his fingers. His eyes are wide. He presses the earpiece closer. *The Big Kahuna!* he says. *Surf's up!* He's already got one hand out to grab his jacket off the back of the chair and the other hand starting to unbutton his shirt.

Whoa there, cowboy, says Helen Smith-son, the owner of the nursery, but she's laughing like the rest of the staff. Adam keeps his wet suit and surf board in the back of his aging Volvo wagon, and he changes into it by semicrouching in the parking lot. If you think, as many of the staff do, that Adam looks good in his jeans and T-shirt, you should see him in his wet suit. You should see him out of his wet suit. He's oblivious to the attention.

Adam has been making noises lately that he wants to be friends with Jane. She hasn't decided if she's ready to let anyone into her life, especially someone as sunny and seemingly uncomplicated as Adam.

They find little Heidi McCready eight days after she disappeared. Her body discovered by the side of Route 1 just south of Montara, in a field of late-blooming tiger stripes (*Coreopsis tinctoria*).

She had been carefully, even lovingly, wrapped in a woven Indian-style blanket, the kind they sell at the San Gregorio Store and a thousand other places in the Bay Area. Nothing unique about it. Her black hair had been combed and tied back with a pink ribbon. Most disturbingly, her eyes were open, and she had been made up expertly with foundation, rouge, and lipstick, nothing excessive, but enough to make her appear still alive and blooming to the teenagers who'd found her. According to the *Moon News,* they'd tramped through the field on their way to a grove of Monterey pines that was a popular high school party site and literally stumbled across her, a small figure lying flat, peacefully contemplating the night sky.

What? Why? Who? There are nothing but questions. The town is horror-struck. But

Jane welcomes a sort of equilibrium: for once, the atmosphere in the external world mirrors her internal darkness. The weather cooperates, serving up wind and fog and pelting rain that feels like tiny bullets to the face. For the first time in more than a year, Jane feels human again, connected to others of her species by a common grief.

The loss goes forward as well as back. The loss of *what would have been* in addition to mourning *what was lost.* Today Angela would have been seventeen. She would have started her senior year in high school, would have been applying to college. Jane is looking ahead at grim milestones of this kind for decades. By now, Angela would be graduating from college. By now, advancing in her career. What would she have done? Jane would have bet on a scientist. Angela, underneath her teenage rebellion and emotionalism, possessed a fact-centric personality. Jane would never have dared to make an argument without backing it up with numbers. A data-driven girl.

- The average teenage hours per day spent goofing off: 5.81. (*See! I'm not weird!*)
- The most valued or essential relation-

ship for high school students: their mother (47 percent). (Angela hated that one.)

- Percentage of high schoolers who have had sex: 41.2 percent. (*So there.*)
- Twenty-nine percent of teens have posted mean info, embarrassing photos, or spread rumors about someone on Facebook. (*That doesn't make me feel any better.*)

Not that any of this helped much in the combative teenage years. But it held out hope for the future. A future that didn't exist anymore.

The *Moon News* says the police are not releasing the cause of death, but the buzz at Three Sisters, always on the money, is that there weren't any apparent wounds or injuries. Nothing that marred Heidi's appearance, as unprepossessing in death as it had been in life.

That poor kid, says Helen to Jane quietly the morning the news broke. *That poor poor family.* Already, a shrine has appeared, a large one, with a statue of Our Lady of Guadalupe and hundreds of bouquets of flowers strewn at her feet alongside Route 1 near the field where little Heidi was found. Half

41

Moon Bay has never experienced a child abduction, much less a child murder, in anyone's living memory.

Jane is conflicted. She should be ashamed to feel joy in someone else's misfortune, yet the inevitable schadenfreude has raised its ugly head. *I told you so.* The madnesses descend, one by one. Jane takes out her spreadsheet, and with shaking fingers, types 10s in all the cells. She calls her shrink for an unsatisfactory session of hand-holding. But the madnesses have taken over her world.

Naturally the teenagers who found Heidi documented the scene with their cell phones; that's what this generation does. They order a meal, they take a photo and post it. They find a dead body, they do the same. The police tried to clamp down on the distribution of the crime scene photos, but it was too late. Jane sees the phones being taken out at the Three Sisters, studied, handed around, but manages to decline with a semblance of sanity when someone offers to show her what's on one of them. She's seen it all already.

Jane held her own child like that, just so. What remained of Angela had also been carefully wrapped in a blanket. *We'll leave you alone, then,* said the doctor, and she and the nurses exited the room. Jane's daughter's upper torso was intact but cold. She had inherited Jane's bright red hair from some long-ago Irish ancestor. Her eyes so black you could barely see the irises. Yes, they were open too, Jane could see herself reflected in their dark depths. A modern *Pietà.* Jane did not look any place but Angela's face, miraculously unscathed. The doctors had been considerate. What was left of the lower body had been tightly wrapped in hospital linens. Jane remembers swaddling Angela as a colicky infant, wrapping the soft cotton blanket tightly around the small, furious, kicking red body. Jane knows she should be in sympathy with Heidi's parents, but she isn't. She has more in common with the murderers. She's killed, and then held the victim of her deed in her arms. Somehow Jane knew this had been the case with little Heidi as well. She had been loved to death.

Jane studies the photo of Heidi on the front page of *Moon News* — the same photo that was on the flyer distributed after her disappearance. *The parents were lucky,* Jane thinks, *that Heidi was taken at this age and not later.* The McCreadys' grief was pure, unblemished by disappointment or bitterness that would have inevitably arisen as Heidi grew older. None of Jane's friends with teenage children were altogether happy with their choice to reproduce. The ones with full-grown adult children even less so. The worry! The pain! *If I had known then what I know now,* they had told each other at book club meetings and coffeehouses, only half joking. *What an idiot I was, thinking I needed to have children to be whole,* they'd say. *I wish I could write a letter to my younger self, explaining how wrong she was.* Jane had been one of them, the regretful, complaining mothers. She had that on her conscience too.

The police are everywhere. Not just the limited Half Moon Bay police force, but San Mateo County sheriffs are making the rounds. They are interviewing everyone. There is word that the FBI will be coming in, forming a task force, because of the child kidnapping angle. Something about the Lindbergh Act. But the two men in uniform who come to Jane one afternoon at the nursery are locals.

Jane recognizes one of the cops by his voice. It is the one she'd spoken to the night Heidi disappeared, the one who circled her name on his pad. She can finally see his face clearly. He is much younger than she would have guessed. An unlined, untested face, and therefore one not to be trusted. Jane finds herself ill at ease these days with those inexperienced in life. Does that include children? It does.

You said you didn't know the McCreadys, the policeman begins abruptly. No social niceties.

Jane is carefully wiping the leaves of the lilyturf (*Liriope spicata*) plants to keep them moist. Each leaf coming out a deep pure green after her wet cloth passes over it. She continues what she is doing. She breathes in deeply, as she's been taught to do in times of stress.

I didn't. I mean, I don't, Jane says, finally. *I knew that people with that name lived up on the hill, but I've never spoken to them.*

But you have. This was the other cop, the one with the San Mateo Sheriff's Department patch sewn on the shoulder of his uniform. If it wasn't an interrogation, Jane would have warmed to this man. He reminds her of Rick, with his narrow blue eyes and sandy-colored hair that curls around his ears. A deep quietness that reassures.

They came here and bought some plants from you. Quite a large order. They remember

45

you distinctly. Your red hair. Your boss remem-
bers them too.

Jane feels trapped. She's never been good with authority figures. She invariably feels guilty of whatever has occurred. She is willing to admit to anything anyone accuses her of. In middle school, when her teacher called her to the front of the room to commend her on an essay she'd written, Jane blurted out, *I didn't plagiarize!* Which of course caused the teacher to treat her with suspicion thereafter. Jane learned not to say what she was thinking, instead tried hard to look nonchalant and innocent when lunch money went missing or obscene graffiti was scrawled on the gym walls. But she's not a good actress and can't always force herself to do what liars apparently did to convince people of their innocence. Look people in the eyes. Don't swallow. Don't put your hand near your face, especially don't hide your mouth or eyes. Don't make any grooming gestures. Jane had practiced not lying in the mirror. She was terrible at it. Her hand was always straying to her face, and she always hesitated and swallowed before answering even the simplest questions. Jane would appear a liar even if asked for her name, or her favorite color.

When was this? Jane knows it sounds like

she is buying time. She is.

Last January. January fifteenth, to be exact.

Jane considers what to say.

I was not . . . myself . . . back then, she says. *I had only just arrived here. A lot of things from that time are a blur.*

The nicer-looking policeman nods in what could be interpreted as a sympathetic manner.

Nevertheless, it was a little odd to find you wandering alone in the dark the night the little girl disappeared, he says. *At that place, at that time.*

I often wander in the dark. Especially to that place. Especially around that time of night.

Even though the beach closes at sundown?

Not to locals, Jane says. *Not to me.*

This makes both cops stop and look more closely at her.

You're somehow privileged? the friendly one finally asks without hostility, just interest, it seems to Jane.

You know you could be ticketed for trespassing after hours, says the other, at the same time. He *is* hostile, Jane decides.

Yes, and yes, says Jane. *But it's not patrolled, and everyone knows it.* Then, fiercely, *You're wasting my time.* She turns her back on the cops to tend to her lilyturfs. She's learned, over the last year, that being rude rather than polite, pushy rather than obsequious, gets her what she wants: to be left alone.

But it doesn't work. The questions continue.

Where were you earlier that evening? (Home.)

Can anyone vouch for you being there? (No.)

What were you doing? (Straightening up. Organizing stuff. Reading.)

Do you have a car? (No.)

How do you get around? (Motorbike.)

Her answers to the last questions seem to terminate their interest. *We might have more questions for you later,* the friendly cop says finally, and they turn to leave, but not before the unfriendly cop plucks a glorious white rose from one of Helen's prize bushes and holds it to his nose.

Why don't flowers smell like anything anymore? he asks no one in particular.

Jane considers this a victory.

Despite all the police activity, no plausible suspects emerge. No one is charged. *It must be a stranger,* people say. They view anyone who recently moved to the coast with suspicion. There haven't been many of them. The Schroeders, a boisterous family of six. The parents opened a frozen yogurt store on Main Street six months ago, are wonderfully patient with all the kids who hang out there. Greg and Jim, a young cohabiting couple, doing something in the arts scene up in San Francisco, and frequently away on trips. A few other unlikely persons. No single older men, normal or strange. Everyone in couples or families. No weirdos, unless you count the ones who have lived here for years. And Jane of course. Jane tries to look innocent. She tries to look concerned. She keeps her hands away from her face, doesn't pat her hair. But she feels the burden of the unasked questions. *Who are you really?*

The faces of the townspeople, the shopkeepers, are grim. This is when the coast typically gets its most beautiful weather, but even that isn't cooperating. The usually joyous preparation for the big Pumpkin Festival scheduled for the third weekend in October have begun, but sotto voce. Posters are being placed around town, fields mowed, pumpkins harvested. Local stores are gearing up for their busiest time of the year — pumpkin harvest brings in even more than Christmas — but everyone is subdued. Fewer families come to the beach on weekends, fewer customers from over the hill stop by Smithson's on their way home. The sky is a metal gray and the wind chills you even if you're wearing layers. Jane shivers as she rides her motorbike to and from work. Bad juju is in the air.

Jane is kneeling by the side of Route 84. Five hundred yards west of the old San Gregorio Store. Within spitting distance of the Pacific Ocean. Tending the roadside memorial that's been here for nearly a hundred years. A small wooden cross. A teddy bear and a companion stuffed rabbit. And always fresh flowers. This is one of Jane's secret places.

A child died on the road here, a long, long time ago. Whether in an accident involving an early automobile or an unfortunate fall from a horse and wagon, no one alive knows. Jane has asked, but people just shrug. Jane discovered the shrine soon after she arrived on the coast, in her meanderings during endless solitary weekends. A clandestine society to which she anonymously belongs tends the site, keeps the flowers fresh, and replaces the teddy bear and rabbit when they become wretched and stained from the rain and sun. A community that mourns together yet alone.

This memorial isn't the only one on Route 84. This road is hazardous, twisting as it snakes up the mountains that overlook Silicon Valley and then heaves over the summit and down through the redwoods onto the California coastal plain. Cars as well as bicycles and motorcycles go too fast around the blind curves. They crash into redwood trees, plunge off precipices, run headlong into deer. Drink is frequently involved. Fatalities galore. It's become a bit of a tradition for people around here to put up these crosses, leave flowers at these sites of conflagration and death.

Most of these homemade shrines don't last more than a couple of months before being vanquished by the elements. People lose interest. The memories fade, the urge to honor the dead dissipates. The flowers on little Heidi's memorial, over on Route 1, are already wilting.

Jane doesn't approve. She's seen too much death. She's smelled its breath. You can't — shouldn't — forget such things. Nine months ago, still mad with grief for Angela, Jane closed her mother's mouth, held it shut so that the face didn't freeze into an unsightly gape. They'd been warned by the funeral director to do this immediately after her last breath. He didn't want to have to break her jawbone to make her presentable for the viewing. Jane had taken the night shift at her mother's bedside with full knowledge of what might be expected of her.

It's heavy stuff. That's meant literally. The weight of your mother's chin in your palm, the upward pressure you exert to bring her lips together. The muffled click as her teeth meet. These are sensations Jane will remember forever. She holds the jaw in place for five long minutes. Then she says a quick prayer — although she's not a believer, not really — and releases, and to her relief, the mouth remains shut. Her mother will have nothing more to say now. Jane more or less successfully represses the impulse to laugh. The face was still warm. To caress a face is an intimate act, an intimacy her mother mostly denied Jane when alive. This thought does something to Jane. She decides she's had enough. She leaves the room, changes her plane ticket, and goes back to California early, skipping the wake and funeral.

She adopted this shrine in recompense, for that and other sins. She'd passed it numerous times before finally stopping, curious about a grief so fresh that someone placed fresh flowers here twice or even thrice weekly. That's when she saw the date:

October 18, 1917. The cross is white, and that too is constantly refreshed with new paint, but you can still read the d-a-r-l-i-n-g carved into it. Whose darling? *A mother, of course,* Jane thinks. Although her word for Angela when little was *sweetheart.* She didn't realize how much she used the endearment because it came so naturally. Sweet. Heart. Yes, of course, that is what you call your daughter. Jane had never used an endearment before in her life. She didn't realize the force of her habit until she understood Angela thought *sweetheart* a synonym for *child. Now I'll be the mommy, and you'll be the sweetheart,* she'd say in the car. Or, *Look! Sweethearts!* as they passed a playground with children on swings or seesaws.

Behavioral psychological studies have shown that if you intermittently reward rats with food pellets for pressing a lever, they will obsessively press that lever, even when nothing comes out for long periods of time. Hungry for pellets and not able to discern a pattern to their disbursement, a rat will press and press the lever until it dies of exhaustion. That was Jane in her previous life. Seeking emotional sustenance from unlikely places. And randomly getting it, occasionally being blissed out of her mind with it, which turned out to be considerably worse than never being rewarded at all. She remembers Tennyson from her undergraduate days: *'Tis better to have loved and lost than never to have loved at all.* Don't fall for that line. Tennyson was never in that cage pushing the lever.

The night Jane's husband told her he was leaving, she had just washed her hair. A new shampoo, one that smelled of peppermint. A rather momentous occasion. For the first time since Angela's death, Jane had showered. She had rubbed this new peppermint-scented shampoo into her hair. She had soaped her body with lavender body wash. She was trying to excite her senses. She was trying to bring herself to life again. She was going through the motions. Later, in the living room, toweling off her hair, she even smiled when Rick walked into the room, even grasped his hand when he placed it on her shoulder. The therapist had told them, *Touching is healing.* Then Rick said those words. *I'm in love with Clara.* Clara? Oh yes. Jane remembered. The girl at work, the one in HR. The one with the *big personality.* That of course had made Jane feel particularly small. The girl resembled a young

Charlotte Rampling. He'd laughed about it at first, telling Jane how all the men in the office were obsessed, how she'd charmed the head of IT to the point where he'd spontaneously invited her home for dinner, to the mystification of his wife. Then Rick had simply stopped talking about her, about this Clara. Jane should have guessed. But she had been at that point otherwise preoccupied, so she missed the signals, was stupidly blindsided. She supposed the faint sting of hearing Rick's words was good news of a sort: she was still alive. If you pricked her, she could still bleed. But there was surprisingly little pain. It hurt to breathe, but then it always hurt to breathe nowadays. Her mouth was dry, her skin numbed as if encased in rubber. The shower notwithstanding, Jane was not yet feeling things. So what did she do? She proceeded to comb the tangles out of her wet hair. And then took a steak knife from the kitchen drawer and made five precise incisions on her left wrist. Jane watched the blood well up from the cuts, then bent her head and licked it off her skin. A sweetish, slightly salty taste. From then on associated in her mind with betrayal.

Little Heidi's funeral is a bit of a circus.

Everyone in town attends, as do many, many strangers. Death attracts. Jane knows this from experience. Heidi's story is featured on CNN the night before the funeral, and the rest of the media come sniffing for something people will tune in to or read. Dead child as clickbait. Reporters from the major newspapers from San Francisco and San Jose and a dozen national media outlets show up. Titillating stuff, after all. Everyone of course wanting to know if little Heidi had been sexually violated, so much so that the police spokeswoman has to repeat *We found no evidence of sexual assault* throughout the press conference that preceded the funeral. Television vans with satellite dishes on top block Main Street near Our Lady of the Pillar, where the funeral service is held. Crime bloggers show up — Jane hadn't known such people existed until she meets one in Three Sisters. *We're better journalists than traditional journalists, and better detectives than the real ones,* the woman boasts. The bloggers even specialize: murder blogs, murder-of-children blogs, murder-of-little-girls blogs. This one, a woman in her fifties, dressed a little casually for a funeral in jeans and T-shirt, is a specialist in young girl abductions. Certainly she asks Jane more pointed questions than the local police had.

Are local children free to play outside by themselves? How vigilant are parents? Any strange characters living here? Jane notices the blogger surreptitiously tapping an icon on her phone before laying it on the table between them. Jane tries to leave. The woman puts a hand on Jane's arm. It is a seemingly casual gesture, but the pressure hurts. Jane shakes it off but sits down again. She is easily bullied.

Who do you think did it?

I have no idea, Jane says.

No rumors?

None, Jane says firmly. But in fact there have been. About Fred Barnes, the football coach for the Half Moon Bay Cougars, whose wife suddenly divorced him two years ago and left with their two little girls without saying anything. And Jim Yang, who runs the local lumberyard, who is married but childless and known to ogle younger teenage girls, offering them sugar-free chewing gum and cans of Diet Coke when they walk past in their groups of three or four, giggling and taking selfies. Both men. Both clearly needing something from the world that they weren't getting.

The blogger catches something in Jane's hesitation.

Tell me, she says.

But Jane resolutely shakes her head. Bad karma to snitch. Even if Jane had anything to say — she didn't — she would have kept her mouth shut. Jane learned that early in life.

She later sees the woman in Three Sisters and hears she was at the site where Heidi was found, casually stepping over the police tape that had been wound around the place to keep her ilk out. The *Moon News* includes a link to the woman's blog: *In Memory of Her.* EVERYTHING POINTS TO A LOCAL CONNECTION is the headline. POLICE HAVE A SHORT LIST OF SUSPECTS. In the blog is a list of locals, all men, Fred Barnes among them. The woman's name is Emma. Emma Jones, her byline almost as big as the headline. Jane wonders how this Emma found out who is on the list. Jane wonders how Emma can sleep at night, given her job.

After the funeral, the mood remains heavy in town. There is no sign of progress from police. But then, two days after the funeral, something happens. Something that perks people up. A certain vibe. Jane hears the news when she stops in at the Rite Aid to pick up some aspirin. She's been battling headaches lately, fierce ones that accompany nightmares. Not about Angela. And not about important things. In one, she loses her driver's license. In another, her keys. She wakes up weeping from the grief of these losses. Other dreams have more weight. In one, she kills a sister. She often kills sisters in her dreams.

Jane gets the news waiting in line at the checkout counter at Rite Aid. She senses a certain buzz. Two women ahead of her have the scoop. Nancy Oster and Susan McLean. They talk about new arrivals in town. Interesting people. Not tourists. Not transients. *They've got substance,* says Nancy. *A couple. She, an adjunct professor at Stanford. He, an environmental activist, setting up an office. YourBeaches.org.* Jane listens. She senses excitement coming from the women, especially when they talk about the man.

The timing is unfortunate, but they don't seem to be put off by it.

They're staying in the Coastal Cottage B&B until they find a permanent place to live.

He seems like kind of a jerk, Susan says, but she says it like she possesses a secret. She smiles in a curious way.

He can check out my beaches anytime, says a woman in line behind Jane who, like her, has been eavesdropping. Open laughter. A women's coffee klatch at the Rite Aid. The single man in line is looking down at his basket, pretending to tune out.

God knows we need a group like that to take interest in the overdevelopment.

This last is from Janet Holcomb, the mayor of Half Moon Bay. She is in the next line over. The owner of that rare thing, a successful clothing boutique on Main Street. A staunch opposer of new developments on the coast. The previous year, before Jane had arrived, some precious land adjacent to the surfer beach in Princeton-by-the-Sea had been developed into what the builders called an "aparthotel." Before completion, the place was torched and burned to the ground twice, and rebuilt each time, the third time with twenty-four-hour security guards stationed around the perimeter. The authorities never found out who was behind the fires. Now, farther south, near Secret Beach, a much more grandiose development is being planned, against the wishes of the locals, but very much to the liking of San Mateo County due to expected tax revenues. To everyone's surprise, the Coastal Commission signed off on it. There is much talk of money changing hands.

Jane listens to the chatter but feels only a great lethargy. Since the day of Heidi's funeral, she has found it difficult to raise herself from her pillow in the morning. Sleep crusts her eyes, which still look red and puffy when she gets to work. Oddly enough, her plants are doing extraordinarily well. Helen and Adam and the other nursery workers exclaim. The young plants have exhibited unusual growth spurts for no reason. The more mature ones bloom early and luxuriantly. But Jane herself is in a state of dread. This is not over. The proverbial other shoe has not dropped. *This will end in tears.*

Sleepy. So sleepy. The heavy air of the nursery is casting a spell over Jane. She can barely keep her eyes open as she checks on her seedlings. The dusky, seductive smell of damp earth. If she'd owned a car, she would have taken a nap in the backseat, the way she'd seen Adam doing in his Volvo, his surf board and wet suit in back. Adam. The man-child. Jane would have put his age at thirty or even younger, but was surprised when he told her he was thirty-eight. Just a year younger than she is. Still, she can't help treating him like a younger brother. With affection but no edge. For Jane, attraction has to have an edge to it. Not that she is in any shape to feel attracted. That part of her died with Angela.

■ ■ ■ ■

One week after Heidi's funeral, Jane encounters unexpected traffic on her way home from work. Driving north on the usually empty Route 1, she pulls up behind a long line of cars stretching at least half a mile ahead. As she inches closer, she sees that a large crowd has gathered at Surfers Beach, one block west of Jane's cottage. She has to wait ten minutes to turn onto her street, obstructed by gawkers as drivers pause to stare at whatever is causing the snarl. Jane gets a glimpse before she turns the corner. An astonishing sight. A whale has beached itself on the sand. People in official-looking emergency vests are gathered around it, with yellow police tape keeping the crowds at a distance from the huge gray mass. An alien in their midst.

Jane decides to check it out. She parks her motorbike in front of her cottage and heads toward the beach. The crowd is growing by the minute as cars pull over to the side of the road and people pile out to stare. Two trucks with satellite dishes park in the bicycle lane. The media have arrived. Or perhaps they never left. Jane can just see the headline: ANOTHER DEATH ON THE COAST.

Jane picks her way carefully down the rocks to Surfers Beach. It's not easy. No path exists, merely sharp-edged boulders piled on top of each other. You have to balance on odd surfaces to prevent yourself from falling. Surfers somehow manage it carrying six- and eight-foot boards, and look graceful to boot. Jane has always marveled at them.

Jane finally reaches the beach. In addition to the whale and the crowd, the water is full of surfers. It is a great day for the sport. The waves are perfect blue-green tunnels that roll in as if generated by a machine. The foam-topped water dotted with bobbing black bodies on boards. Otherwise the weather is mixed. The sun is shining through a low-hanging mist, too porous to be called a fog. It throws the entire scene into an unreal light.

The surfers come in and out of focus as they glide on top of the waves, the mist wafting around them. One especially is an object of beauty, his taut body in his black wet suit shining, his feet securely planted on the long surf board. The mist is inseparable from the white of the breaking wave, so it looks as if he is magically gliding above the water. Then he tumbles and comes down with a splash twenty feet from where Jane is standing. He stands up in water that comes up to his waist and effortlessly hops onto his board again, lying on his stomach this time, paddling toward shore. Five feet out from the edge of the water, he slides off the board, tucks it under his arm, and strides toward the beach. With a shock, Jane recognizes Adam, his wet hair long and lank behind his ears. He sees her and cracks a wide smile. He comes splashing through the shallow water at an easy trot.

Jane realizes she is pleased to see him. His uncomplicated face shines. A good sprite. He rests his board on the sand.

Can you believe this? he asks, pointing to the whale. It towers over the heads of the people in the crowd. But as Jane and Adam walk closer, Jane can see that something isn't right. On the whale's side are splashes of color, lines, and loops of red, blue, and green.

Some asshole, says Adam. *Last night.* At first Jane isn't sure what he's talking about, but now she can see that WE'RE ALL FUCKED has been spray-painted on the whale's enormous side. A majestic creature turned into a platform for obscenities. A smiley face has been added on the creature's tail.

Who would have done such a thing? Jane asks. Adam shrugs. He seems to have taken it in his stride. She would have thought it would have insulted his sense of cosmic justice.

It's worse than you think, he says. *The whale was still alive. The rangers had put wet blankets on it and were coming regularly to hose it down. They hoped it would go out in the second tide today, which is going to be a high one. But whoever did this also poured water into the whale's airhole. It drowned.*

Jane hadn't known whales could drown. *How horrible,* Jane says, and means it. So much killing, so much death. She shivers.

Do you think it's related? she asks. Adam knows exactly what she's talking about.

No, he says firmly. *This is the work of kids. Rotten kids, but kids. That Heidi thing . . . that's something else.*

And yet Jane felt the desecration of the whale is associated with the dead child in some way. As Adam would say, *Bad vibes.* And the wind chilling you through and through. Jane has never been as cold as when she first moved here, to the edge of the Pacific.

That last Christmas, in Hawaii, Angela

had reluctantly agreed to go on a whale watching trip with Jane and Rick. At the age when parents were toxic. She sat sullenly on the other side of the boat from Jane and Rick, her back to them, staring moodily out to the horizon. No whales. Nothing to see. Rick enjoyed himself by making friends with a couple from Ohio, trading work stories, recalling the horrors of the midwestern winters of his youth. Jane, who could not be happy if her child was unhappy, sat with her back to the boat railing, keeping an eye on Angela without being obvious. Then, suddenly, a whale leaped out of the water. Right next to the boat, next to where Angela was sitting, a spectacular full breach in which it flung its body twelve feet into the air and flipped its massive weight head over tail. It was at most five feet away from the boat.

Jane's first conscious thought was, *She's going overboard.* For Angela had stood up and now appeared to be standing directly under the arc of the descending whale. Her arms were raised above her head. She waved them up and down, something she did when terribly excited as a toddler. Then, a miracle. She turned her glowing face away from the whale toward Jane, who saw the raw joy of the child Angela had once been. Angela opened her mouth and called, *Look, Mom, look!* Jane felt a pleasure so intense her chest hurt. Her girl.

The people in Three Sisters are subdued by little Heidi's murder, but not so subdued that they can't talk about the new people in town. The woman, the physicist, seen purchasing tampons at the Rite Aid, the man, the environmentalist, at the hardware store purchasing a hammer, other tools. Exciting sightings, as of some fabulous creatures. Jane was curious about how they could make such a stir. Why?

They're something, Margaret, the youngest of the Three Sisters tells Jane. The couple had stopped by one morning right before official opening hours. She'd let them in early and served them black coffee, the only thing ready at the time. *The man, he was impatient,* she says. *But it was okay. I didn't mind.* She paused. Then she said, *They were beautiful. Just so beautiful.*

Jane continues to see Angela everywhere. On the street, in the grocery store. In the pages of magazines. Jane sees her as a baby being rolled down Main Street in her stroller. As a toddler, on the verge of falling as she staggers, naked, across the loose sand of the beach. Jane sees her as a teen, chattering on her cell phone, driving a car badly. As the adult she never became — a doctor at the clinic, a young mother with two squalling children. Jane talks to Angela constantly, as she used to keep up the running commentary when Angela was a baby riding on her right hip. *And now we buy some lettuce for our lunch! And here we look from left to right and back to left before we cross the street!*

But if this is madness, Jane is a high-functioning madwoman. She goes to work and plants seedlings of elegant *Brodiaea,* and she talks sense to colleagues, and she eats and she drinks and she jogs every morning as if nothing has changed. As if everything hadn't changed forever. But inside the darkness is devouring her, cell by cell.

Time passes. Then two weeks after Heidi's funeral, a second child goes missing. Another girl. Older than Heidi but still young. Just eight years old. Heartbreakingly, she had disappeared on her birthday. While her mother was out picking up the cake. She'd begged to be allowed to stay home by herself for the thirty minutes. This time it is a little farther south, but still on the coast, in Aptos, a well-heeled beach community beyond Santa Cruz. The mother is interviewed by the *Moon News.* She pleads. She is already using the past tense. *She was my baby.*

She was mine. Who can fully understand the impact of those words, spoken in the past tense? No one who has not had a child. No one who has not been inflamed by the fever of mother love. No one who has not stroked the silken skin of a tiny hand and thought *she belongs to me.* To hold a small head to your breast and feel the pull of hungry lips. Jane had marveled at her own ability to give sustenance from a place she thought could produce only bile. When her child was born, for the first time in her life Jane felt that she truly belonged on this planet. Did not this child finally make her a member of the human race? And to have this taken away from her! But not right away. The child had lived, was destined to grow and thrive for many years. And each day Jane had with her fed a hunger of Jane's own, one that could not be satisfied. She wished for the child's immortality. For she knew that if anything happened to her child, she would not survive.

The cruelest thing that God wrought is that Jane did.

The FBI finally arrives. Men and women in suits — unusual in Half Moon Bay — descend on the town. Jane gets stopped on the street multiple times. *You're Jane O'Malley, right?* Then a nod and they continue walking. She has been profiled.

The second missing child, Rose, is on everyone's mind. The FBI have established an office in an empty storefront that used to be called Pleasant Things, full of local handicrafts and food. It had lasted about two years before the owner ran out of cash, as with so many of the interchangeable Main Street shops. The strange men and women are everywhere, as well as the T-shirt-and-jeans-wearing journalists who have established camp. All the area hotels, B&Bs, and Airbnbs are full. Bloggers are driving down from accommodations in San Francisco to get a piece of the action. That's how Jane thinks about it. When Angela died, the fuss was on a much smaller scale. Much less drama, although the end was the same: the death of a child. Although Angela was sixteen, nearing the end of childhood. The age of innocence had been over for her for some time, and the manner of her death was much less spectacular. The only mystery about it, the only suspense, was whether the wealthy and well-connected driver who mangled Angela's body would get off. She did. End of story.

Here, search parties are being formed. Volunteers are being directed by police to trawl through the marshes and on top of the cliffs overlooking the sea. They're also putting up signs as far north as Pacifica and as far south as Santa Cruz.

You know, you are free to take part in any of these search parties, Jane's boss at the nursery, Helen, tells her. *If you feel you need to help out in some way, I'd understand. We could get by.*

But it's your busiest time! Jane protests. She realizes that what she's feeling is resentment. She does not want to search for Rose, put up posters, or bring coffee to hardworking cops. No one did that for her. Why the fuss over this one life? What was one life worth?

Jane is careless. She is always losing things. Her comb, her keys, her lipstick. She long ago cultivated the habit of keeping multiple copies of important things. An extra set of keys in the motorbike saddlebag. A second toothbrush in her bathroom cabinet. But Angela was one of a kind. No heir and a spare. Jane had wanted another child, specifically, another daughter. She and Rick had talked about it, had calculated the funds for day care, for medical insurance and braces and broken arms, and college. They had almost agreed to do it. Then Jane was flattened by influenza. It lasted more than four weeks. Thirty-two days before she got out of bed. In the midst of her illness, everything aching, it hurting even to blink, she thought, *I can't do it.* Even though Rick was watching Angela, he couldn't keep her out of the bedroom, couldn't keep her from snuggling up to Jane shivering with chills in the sickbed. *No, I can't do it,* she murmured out loud. On the third day back on her feet, Jane went to her gynecologist and had an IUD fitted. Enough was enough.

With this latest disappearance, the town closes into itself. The mood on the street, in the stores and restaurants, goes past uneasy to unstable. Neighbors pass on the street without saying hello. Arguments break out among the kitchen staffs at restaurants. The air has a burned, bitter smell. Heavy clouds sink to blanket the tops of the hills, turning the entire San Mateo coast into a dank, unwelcoming cave.

Jane takes long walks on the beach at dusk. She drinks in the darkening air. Signs admonish: MIND THE SURF — MANY PEOPLE HAVE DIED IN THESE DANGEROUS WATERS. But the current mood of the sea is not one of anger but grimness. The ocean a gray plate of water reaching out to infinity. Flat. This is what despair looks like. This is hopelessness. The horizon erased, the sea the same color as the sky. Jane remembers that the sea itself is dying, as degree by degree its temperature rises, killing off everything that lives in it. But before it goes, it will have its revenge. Jane imagines the ocean rising up, engulfing the harbor, Route 1, and eventually her cottage. She once clicked on an interactive map on the Internet that showed what different parts of the world would look like in ten, twenty, thirty years as humans continued to ruin the planet. In Angela's would-be lifetime, Half Moon Bay would no longer exist.

Jane is bundled up against the wind, the hood of her jacket over her hair. Still, some strands have escaped and blow behind her like a bright red scarf. Her face is visibly raw from the salt in the brutal breeze. She likes being the only one intrepid enough to be out on the beach in this weather, is resentful to see another figure farther down the beach, walking toward her. Unisex at this distance, but as she gets closer, she sees that it is male — the height and something about the way he carries himself, a superior swing of the leg forward before planting his foot confidently on the sand and the next leg following. A solid straight trunk. She thinks of Neptune, how his torso is always massively developed, his abdomen muscles tight and visible, his shoulders broad. Jane could desire a man like that. The man comes closer. Jane believes she is sexless in her garb and imitates his aggressive walk so as to pass him without notice. She doesn't want to be a woman to this man; that feels dangerous in these conditions. The sea so flat and nonresponsive, an impassive witness. The wind invasive and the sand soft and sinking underfoot with no one in sight for the miles of beach that stretched in either direction. But at the last moment, her hood blows off and her hair streams out behind her in the wind. Still she strides resolutely past the man. She sees him nod. Then he pulls down the scarf covering his mouth and chin. She doesn't look straight at him but has a sense of a naked visage, one that is open to the universe, a lovely face. He shouts through the wind, *Do you*

know how beautiful you are? without stopping or slowing down. Jane keeps going, but
her mind whispers an exhilarated *how
beautiful, how beautiful* as she continues to
walk. An unexpected gift.

Dread paralyzes everyone. Parents hold on
to their daughters' arms, lock their doors at
night. Even Adam at work, usually so sunny,
is subdued. Jane? She's back to her normal
state, barely containing her terror and rage.
At night she can't sleep. Instead, she paces
the cottage, walks to Mavericks Beach at
2:00 a.m., 3:00 a.m., greedily sucking in
the sea air with each step, exhaling noisily.
Breathing, breathing. But instead of calm-
ing her down, it revs her up, increases her
adrenaline, makes her stride faster and
faster to reach the promontory of land that
is Mavericks, in the depth of the night, feeling like the edge of the world where the
earth touches the sea.

A few days after Rose's disappearance, a
headline in the Main Street newspaper
stand jumps out at Jane. SIX CHILDLESS
WEEKS. She pulls her motorbike over, stops,
inserts a quarter in the newspaper dispenser,
and puts the *Moon News* in her saddlebag.
She reads it when she gets to the nursery. It

is a profile of the first victims, the Mc-Creadys, Heidi's parents, on how they are coping. Or rather, how they are not. The mother has quit her job as a systems analyst at a big Silicon Valley software company, the father has taken a leave of absence from his San Francisco law firm. Jane hadn't realized that Heidi was their only child. They are in marriage counseling. They are falling apart.

The woman in the picture looks washed out, vapid. The man, resolute, even smiling a little bit for benefit of the camera. They are not touching each other.

Been there, done that.

The anguish of loss. The agony of betrayal. Bereft twice over. Three times if you count her mother. Four if you count her father (she doesn't). *To lose one parent may be regarded as a misfortune; to lose both looks like carelessness.* What about losing both parents, a husband, and a daughter within nine short months? Catastrophic negligence.

A Sunday morning in mid-September. 8:00 a.m.

Jane is at the D-A-R-L-I-N-G shrine in San Gregorio, patting the earth around a cluster of California asters (*Corethrogyne filaginifo-*

76

lia) — she plants indigenous flowers here, they last longer than exotics, and a lot longer than cut flowers — when she hears a car approaching. Early Sunday mornings, not many vehicles pass on this isolated coastal road, which is why she usually comes at this hour. But the car doesn't drive past. She feels, rather than hears, it stop behind her as she kneels, the heat of the engine warming her back. It's the coast's usual balmy September, but there's still a chill in the air, a promise of rain. The weather here predictable for its unpredictability.

So you're the one. A male voice. An uplift at the end of the sentence so it sounds like a question.

Jane doesn't turn, but continues tamping down the soil around the base of the asters.

One of many, she says finally. She doesn't want to acknowledge the person or persons in the car or encourage them. No one who understands the significance of the shrine, who truly *gets it,* would approach in such a way.

You make quite a startling picture. A deep voice. He would sing bass in a choir. *O freunde, nicht diese Töne! Sondern lasst uns angenehmere anstimmen.* Beethoven. Beethoven understood what was what.

77

Jane doesn't look or answer, and so the reverberations from the idling car are the only sounds for a few moments. She knows what's coming. And, yes, here it is: *Can I take your photo?*

This happens a lot. Don't assume anything, Jane isn't any great beauty, especially not now. It's the hair. A shade of red that makes people stare, makes them ask — sometimes quite rudely — if it's real. Jane wears it straight and long, past her shoulders, and today it's loose, down her back, and, she knows, dramatic. Only a few wisps of gray that, if anything, make the red stand out more. Recent DNA studies in Ireland have determined that all red-haired people are descended from one person. Another exclusive society to which Jane belongs. She likes that, *belonging* has been a lifelong struggle. Although she's not enamored with the fuss people make about her hair. Whether she's at work in the greenhouse or walking on the beach, people surreptitiously lift up their cell phones, snap pictures. Annoying. Intrusive.

Jane sighs and answers without turning around. *I'm going to continue doing what I'm doing, and I'd rather you just left.*

He doesn't depart even though she hears nothing but silence after she speaks. The car continues to idle. She imagines him pulling out his phone, centering it, trying to frame her against the memorial and the pale yellow pampas grass (*Cortaderia selloana*) that encroaches wild everywhere up and down the coast, displacing the precious native flora.

Finally, the man's voice again.

Okay, I'm leaving, O Ammut. Then, with a hint of laughter, *Greeter of death, eater of hearts, I do you homage.*

This finally makes Jane look. A silver late-model Mercedes sedan, with the big hood and long trunk. A man is the only occupant. He is leaning out the passenger's window, the side closer to Jane. She nearly forgets to breathe. He has a face that would heal wounds. Dark-complexioned, high cheekbones. Very black coarse wavy hair. Deep brown-black eyes. A hint of sadness, the way the lines around his eyes crease downward. A dark archangel. He looks vaguely familiar. She remembers the walk on the beach. *How beautiful.* It's he.

Don't mind me. It's just that you make for quite a startling image, against the grave there.

It's not a grave, it's a memorial, Jane says, and turns back to the flowers. She is afraid of what might show in her face. She hears a faint *Keep up the good work* as the car moves on.

Something has begun.

Later that day, Jane can't settle. She keeps thinking of the encounter at the shrine. She's wound up. Agitated. What will she do with the rest of her day? Sundays are very quiet in Half Moon Bay. Read a library book? She is finally making her way through the twentieth-century French writers Rick had loved so much: Maurice Druon, Boris Vian, Sartre, Camus. Jane had always thought it an affectation — Rick read them in the original French — but she now finds herself attracted and, in an odd way, comforted, by the bleakness and absurdity of the worlds portrayed. They make her world tolerable.

One excerpt from *The Stranger* has been her companion for several weeks now:

> I said that people never change their lives, that in any case one life was as good as another and that I wasn't dissatisfied with mine here at all.

That's what Jane tells herself these days. *One life was as good as another.* But she is perturbed after meeting the stranger at the shrine. Stirred up. Something in the universe has been disturbed. If she believed in past lives (she doesn't), she would think she knew him from one. There was some familiarity, recognition, between them. She wonders if he is the new man in town. If so, she understands the town women's barely suppressed excitement. She is excited too. Darkly thrilled.

Jane's mother used to tell her that doubting others led to wisdom but doubting yourself led to madness. When Jane was small, she thought she was mad. She *was* mad, by her mother's standards. Jane doubted everything she said, felt, or did. At dinner she'd watch her parents and sisters eat the same food as she did, but with more apparent enjoyment. She wondered what they were tasting. Was it as salty, as sweet, as savory as her meal? When they drank water, was it as clear and cold and good as *she* thought? Was their milk richer than hers? She ached with questions over such things.

When they watched television, she knew for certain that her experiences differed from the rest of her family's because they would nod and laugh at spectacles that had Jane close to tears. Videos of a toddler getting gobsmacked by a snowball in the face, a man wearing Plexiglas wings jumping off a roof and plummeting to the ground, all sorts of extravagant accidents and, presumably, injuries, and Jane's family roared. This was the most popular show on TV at the time.

Jane was considered odd for that, and for other reasons. Her sisters could talk her into doing anything. *Don't you have any sense?* her mother would ask after finding her plastered in mud from being instructed to roll in a large puddle after a thunderstorm. *Or moral compass?* she'd ask after Jane was caught stealing various items — chewing gum and, later, lipstick and mascara — for her sisters. Jane had no answer to these questions. On one particularly shame-making occasion when she was eleven, this odd tendency to be cajoled into doing things she knew were not quite right made her the laughingstock of the neighborhood. Jane had been babysitting for a mischievous six-year-old neighbor. One of her duties was to supervise her bath, and somehow as she rinsed the conditioner out of her charge's hair, the little girl managed to convince Jane that she too was meant to remove her clothes and take a bath. It was expected. And so the mother came home to find Jane naked in the bathtub. The six-year-old, by now in a towel and sitting on the toilet observing, laughed uproariously, as did the mother, after a nonplussed silence. The news was all over the neighborhood within twenty-four hours, and Jane's sisters had a field day. *Time for a bath, Janey,* they'd taunt.

Eventually Jane escaped, and came west, where having her own thoughts seemed less dangerous. She was wrong. It wasn't having her own thoughts, but having her own life, that was the risk. After giving her too, too much, the God Jane only half believed in couldn't resist. He took it all back.

When Jane quit her job at the Botanical Gardens in Berkeley — or, rather, when it quit her, since she woke up one morning simply unable to go on — her supervisor got her the position at Smithson's Nursery. He was a close personal friend of Helen Smithson, the owner, although Jane knew her by reputation only. Smithson's Nursery about as far away from Berkeley as you could get and still be in the Bay Area. *At least you'll be tangentially in your field,* Dr. Blackman, Jane's supervisor, had said. *Helen's doing interesting work with Zone 15 and 16 indigenous plants.* He'd taken his glasses off, massaged the indentations on either side of his nose, and looked at Jane before putting them back on again and continuing to type out his email to Helen. He was, is, a kind man. He knew Jane was in trouble, understood many of the reasons, but, unlike other people, didn't probe. *When you're ready to come back, call,* he'd said.

Jane didn't intend to do anything of the kind. That life was gone forever. If there was another life for her, it lay elsewhere. Perhaps on the coast. Jane loved the sea. She looked on a map, located Half Moon Bay. Yes. She thought she'd leave her ghosts behind in Berkeley. She thought she'd feel free. But no. *Wherever you go, there you are.* Jane remembers that adage from her father's many attempts to get sober. Yes, here she is.

The second missing little girl, Rose, is found on Pebble Beach, just south of Pescadero. Exactly eight days after her disappearance. Where children go to collect the multicolored stones washed smooth by the rough surf on that stretch of beach. Technically it's against the law to take any stones from the beach, a directive no one with kids pays any attention to.

Like Heidi, Rose has been carefully made up and posed, this time propped up against a rock next to a half-finished sand castle.

Like Heidi, she has not been violated in any way. Nothing has been taken from her. *Except my life, except my life, except my life,* Jane thinks when she hears the news from Adam, who passed by the crime scene on his way to work on Route 1 from Santa Cruz that morning. He'd gotten the scoop straight from an officer guarding the scene. *There's a monster out there,* the cop had said.

Rose had been found by a man walking his dog — or rather, by the dog — at dawn. Given the tidal schedule, authorities were able to calculate that Rose had been placed on the beach after 3:00 a.m. on Tuesday morning. Another two hours, and she would have been washed away by the waves. So it was someone who knew the locals' habits, or they wouldn't have taken that chance. The horror of it seeps into everything in town. People look at neighbors with suspicion, at strangers in the streets with something akin to terror.

The *Moon News* publishes guest articles written by experts. An FBI agent writes that a serial killer is someone *who commits a series of two or more murders as separate events.* Usually, but not always, such murders are committed by one person acting alone. *It is typically in service of some abnormal psychological gratification.*

The agent writes in a stilted, pedantic voice. *Although it is true that most serial killings involve sexual contact with the victim, the motives of serial killers can include anger, thrill seeking, financial gain, and attention seeking.* The murders may be executed in a similar way, or the victims may have something in common: age group, appearance, gender, or race, for example, he lectures. Women serial killers are rare. *The fact that the majority of serial killers are men leads researchers to believe this abnormality is associated with the male chromosome set.*

Jane thinks of all the people she has known whom she distrusts. No. She has no reason to believe that such madness is confined to the male sex.

Helen Smithson is Jane's hero. Mid-fifties with iron-gray hair, she runs Smithson's Nursery efficiently yet with kindness and humanity. The lines starting to appear on her face are all laugh lines; she will be a remarkable-looking old woman. She has taken Jane in with kindness. She is the only person who knows Jane's full story, and Jane trusts her to keep it that way. She is married to her second husband, Hugh, and her two children from her first marriage are grown. They all seem to coexist amicably together. Holiday meals at their house are confusing. Once, when Jane was there for Sunday dinner, Helen's ex-husband introduced himself as Hugh's husband-in-law.

How are you coping with all this? Helen asks Jane to her office, invites her to sit down. She takes two bottles of water out of the mini-fridge next to her desk, hands one to Jane.

This being . . . ? although Jane knows well what Helen is talking about.

Helen gives her a look.

I'm fine, Jane says. The plastic bottle is cool. She longs to place it against her cheek, which she fears is burning. *Just fine.*

Good, says Helen, but she doesn't move or smile, and Jane knows she isn't done yet.

I've noticed that you're spending less time on the retail floor.

Perhaps. Jane gives in and brings the water bottle up against her forehead. Ahh, lovely coolness. *My plants have needed some extra attention. I had to dig up the batch of* Ceanothus *and repot them due to some mold.*

Your plants are fine. If anything, they are way past expectations. You have the proverbial green thumb. Here Helen smiles.

But, she continues, *I do need you on the*

floor. *You're my native plant expert. I know we discussed how you're not a salesperson, but your knowledge is essential for making some of the tougher sales.*

Jane studies Helen's coffee mug. Emblazoned on it was a smiling sunflower with a bubble coming out of its mouth. *Everybody digs me!*

The thing is, Jane begins, and stops. She puts both hands on the seat of her chair and pushes herself straight. *The thing is, people want to talk. They want the local gossip. They want to talk about the girls. And I can't. I can't do it.*

Helen nods. *I thought as much,* she says. And then, *Are you still seeing Dr. Blanes?* Dr. Blanes is Jane's shrink.

When Jane shakes her head, Helen says, *It's time to go back to her. You need to be in touch with and talking to someone smarter than me.*

Helen left it at that, but Jane went back to her *Ceanothuses* knowing she has been given a warning.

It is the last week in September. The weather has changed for the better. Some of the coast's most beautiful days come in autumn. In summer, the heat from the peninsula meets the bitter cold of the sea, creating fog so thick that the summers are often the coldest days of the year. On the rare day in summer when the fog bank hangs just offshore, Route 92, which connects the coast with Silicon Valley, turns into a virtual parking lot. Everyone from Redwood City to Sunnyvale eager to get to a sunny beach.

Of course, the water is still too cold, even in July and August, to swim. But out come the volleyball nets and the beach barbecues and the coolers and umbrellas, and for a day or maybe, miraculously, two, people in Northern California get a taste of what it's like on an East Coast beach. Then the fog rolls in and shrouds the landscape again, turning it into a painting by Schoenhausen. Gray shapes in the mist rather than houses, cars that suddenly appear out of the dense fog, startling you when you cross the street. That's summer in Half Moon Bay.

But autumn and winter belong to its inhabitants. Thus, September 23 dawns a glorious morning, the bluest of blue skies and the ocean a deep aqua to match.

Jane gets a call on her cell. No one ever calls her, so at first she stares at her buzzing phone. It's a 202 number. Washington, D.C. Who does she know in Washington, D.C.? No one. So she ignores it. In a moment her phone pings to tell her she has a message.

She listens. It is a woman's voice. She identifies herself as FBI. She wants Jane at temporary headquarters today at 11:45 a.m. *Please be punctual. You can find us at 854 Main Street.* Jane knew the place. Everyone did. They'd papered over the windows of the storefront with old *Moon News* copies so you couldn't see in. The address alone is displayed on the door, no other identifier. Nothing gives it away except the suited men and women coming and going.

The unmarked door is locked, but when Jane identifies herself over an intercom, she is buzzed in. Inside, the space is surprisingly vast, filled with desks and four men and two women working on laptops and talking on phones. A hive of activity. Papers are pinned to walls, photographs of the two girls, both alive and dead, are everywhere. Jane averts her eyes. The woman who greets her and leads her to a chair is brisk. Blond hair, cut in a neat bob. Not unkind. But not wasting any time either. She clicks her phone on *record* and places it on the desk in front of Jane.

Where were you Saturday, August 17, at midday?

Jane has to think to remember. This would have been a day or so before Heidi's body had been found. Was Jane reading at home?

At the beach? One thing is for sure: she was alone. She tells the FBI agent this.

And the night of September 23 and early morning of September 24? From, say, 2:00 a.m. to 6:00 a.m.?

Alone again.

In bed? Asleep?

That I couldn't say, Jane says. She had decided to answer their questions precisely, no more or less information than the question required.

But you were at Mavericks the evening the McCready girl disappeared.

Yes.

We're not happy that you were at that location at that particular time, the woman says. She had introduced herself to Jane when first greeting her, but Jane has forgotten her name already. Agent . . . Brady? Haden? Something unmemorable.

Jane shrugs. *I can't help that.* She is indifferent to the woman's questions. Of all the crimes Jane has committed, this is not one that can be pinned on her.

The woman leans back. *Frankly, if it weren't for the fact that you don't have a car, you could be in a lot of trouble right now.*

Well, I don't. Have a car. Jane finds her right hand straying to her mouth. She deliberately moves her hand away, fiddles with the button on her jacket instead.

No, you don't, the agent agreed. Silence for a moment.

It's just that we find certain . . . coincidences in dates and time that make us unhappy.

You keep using that word unhappy, *as if it's an emotional thing for you,* Jane says.

Does that surprise you? the agent asks. She holds Jane's eyes for longer than Jane is comfortable with. Jane looks away first. *Two little girls have been murdered. Isn't that something to be emotional about?*

I suppose.

You suppose?

I mean yes. Of course. Jane remembers whom she is talking to. She must pretend normalcy. *One doesn't think of the FBI as acting on emotions.*

The agent allows herself a smile. *Call them professional instincts, then.*

The agent pauses before continuing. *There are certain facts that we are . . . pursuing . . . that make you a person of interest.*

She holds up one finger. *First, you yourself lost a daughter last year.*

Jane is startled, although she knows she shouldn't be. She knows certain facts are a matter of public record. Yet she has flown under the radar here in Half Moon Bay for so long. She should know, in this age of free-flowing information, that she would be caught. Busted.

Then there's the fact of your erratic behavior at that time. Allowances were made. But still. Evidence suggests you are not always in control of yourself, that you are capable of unpredictable, not to say illegal, activities.

Jane nods. She has nothing to say on this point.

Then there's the fact that this all started about eight months after you moved here. She holds up another finger. Three. Then she hesitates.

Jane speaks up. *And you think it's a woman.*

The agent's face is impassive. A pause. Then she makes a decision, and nods. She is watching Jane closely as she speaks. *Yes, we do. There's the makeup. The tenderness with which the girls are posed. The tableaux suggest a woman rather than a man.*

A bell sounds. The front door buzzes, and the door to the storefront opens. Both Jane and the woman stop and turn. In walks the man whom Jane had last glimpsed in his Mercedes at San Gregorio. She would know him anywhere. The dark broodiness. Out of his car, he is tall. Loose-limbed with broad shoulders. Casually dressed. Wearing jeans and a T-shirt. He doesn't look in their direc-

tion but is greeted by a man in a suit —
another agent, Jane assumes — and led
away to a far corner of the room.

The woman agent's eyes have followed
Jane's.

Know him? she asks.

Seen him around, Jane says. *Another sus-
pect?*

You know I'm not going to tell you that.

Jane likes this woman. She's straight-
forward and blunt. She's efficient. She's doing her job — all qualities Jane admires.

The woman plunges in again to the ques-
tioning. *So we know your history.*

Jane says nothing.

*We know that you have been what many
would call unstable. That you are, as they say,
capable of going off the rails.*

Jane pushes back. *These . . . abductions . . .
are the work of a planner, not someone impul-
sive,* she says.

*We know you're that too. A scientist. A care-
ful and precise thinker. Someone who is
patient enough to allow things to grow naturally.*

So I'm being investigated, Jane says. The
agent nods.

Jane's attention drifts. She has her eyes on
the man at the other end of the room. He
seems cheerful. He is smiling as he answers

94

the agent's questions. His shoulders show that he is relaxed; he leans against the back of the chair, stretches out his legs. Now he is laughing at something the agent has said. She sees why the women were smiling in the grocery store as they talked about him. Even from here, she feels his energy, the pull.

The agent clears her throat to recall Jane's attention.

Don't leave town without telling us. We may have more questions.

Jane nods meekly and gets up to go. But she has no intention of obeying this woman.

Jane is accustomed to inquisitions. She is nearly always deemed the guilty party. When growing up, her father would call all eight of the sisters into the television room, where he sat in his reclining chair, the judge and jury for their crimes. *Who borrowed my razor? Who opened the box of cookies? Who left their bicycle in the driveway?* Jane was punished most frequently. Oh, was she punished! She refused to cry, would hold out until she couldn't bear it any longer. Then she'd given in, finally. This delighted the father.

Other things amused her father. When bored, he'd summon the daughters. He'd bark out orders. *Age!* he'd say, and they'd line up, oldest to youngest. *Height!* And they'd rearrange themselves accordingly. But often he challenged them. *Beauty!* he'd call. *Intelligence!* There'd be squabbles and jostling as they fought for positions. There'd be animosity. Hitting, pinching, even biting on occasion. For this game was important to them. It was a competition. They took it seriously. Sister raised hand against sister. The father laughed. *That's entertainment!* he'd say.

But these games also hurt the sisters deeply. Because in other ways, they were all so close. Each could say the names of all the sisters quickly, in birth order, to the amazement of friends and neighbors, none of whom could keep the daughters all straight:

Bridgetmeganjanereginalucycarolinebarbaraagnes.

They knew each other's secret names too. *Vain One. Hairy Breasts. Smelly Butt. Pimple Back.* Ugly names.

Shameful names, especially Jane's. *Black Heart.* Her sisters would taunt her because of a fascination with a Mass card she'd found in her grandmother's underwear drawer, of Jesus opening his chest to reveal a glowing red heart. *Yours is different. We*

96

The Three Sisters Café has been open only a year, since just before Jane moved to the coast, but is already the place in Half Moon Bay to have coffee, power up the laptop, and hear the local gossip. The owners are the twins, Daphne and Chloe — their parents had a sense of humor — and their younger sister, Margaret. Jane now can tell them apart. She knows Daphne is the cook; she has a burn mark on her right wrist from an accident involving a frying pan and hot oil. Chloe is the marketer and businessperson — she orders the supplies, puts the ads and coupons in the *Moon News,* and pays the bills, always before they are due. But it's the twins' younger sister, Margaret, who holds it all together. She knows everyone and everything that is happening in town. But unlike some natural gossips, there's no hint of meanness or pettiness in her reports. When she tells Jane, *They say it's Fred Barnes, they say he has a thing about dolls,* she is withholding judgment and there is no joy in her passing along what is actually quite terrible news. Fred Barnes!

Look at Jane. Look at how she is attempting to calm herself down. See how she takes a small bottle out of her messenger bag and pops a small white pill. See how her fingers gradually unclench. See how her leg stops going up and down. The pill works fast. It helps that Jane hasn't eaten anything yet today.

Why should Jane care? She hardly knows Fred Barnes. Just to say hi to, just from the photos in the newspaper as the football team loses again and again. Fred Barnes has a broad, open face, a triple chin, and a beer gut so massive, it is said, he has to custom-order his belts online. She thinks of him as a genuine, yet crude, sort of man. The killings would seem to require someone with a more delicate touch.

What's the evidence? Jane asks next time Margaret comes around with the coffeepot.

They found a weird collection of dolls in his basement. He'd painted them too. Just like those poor girls.

Is he in custody?

He's at the FBI offices now. But they haven't charged him yet. Margaret moved on.

It doesn't feel right to Jane. As she told the FBI agent, the abductions seem to have a woman's touch. Although she supposes she should be grateful that eyes have moved past her.

Jane, unstable? Capable of acting irrationally, as the FBI agent had said? Oh, yes.

One week after Angela's funeral, Jane tracked down her daughter's murderer. It was all so easy, what with Facebook and LinkedIn. The woman had a large modern house in Oakland Hills. Surrounded by other new houses in the area where the massive Oakland fire of two decades before had burned down all the charming turn-of-the-century wooden craftsman homes. This house was like all the other glass McMansions that had been built with insurance money. Treeless and exposed to the glaring sunlight, large windows glinting in the sun, many-gabled roofs. Jane parked outside the house. No one was visible.

The woman had been charged and found guilty of vehicular manslaughter. But she had connections. Her husband was a special prosecutor high up in the court system. The woman was put on misdemeanor probation. She was told to pay $1,000 in fines. She strutted out of the courtroom in red high heels without a glance at Jane or Rick.

One thousand dollars would barely pay the monthly gardener's fee for the embarrassment of rose bushes surrounding the steel-and-glass monstrosity. Jane knew the enormous care and feeding — and the gallons upon gallons of water — it would take to have a rose garden of that kind. There must be two hundred rose bushes there, magnificent specimens of Damask, and Centifolia, and Gallica. Angela had always loved roses.

The woman had wept on the witness stand in court, but the tears had all been for herself.

If you could know what I've gone through.

Yes. If you could know, thought Jane, sitting in the courtroom, her hands clenched, her fingernails biting into her skin. The woman had had her own five-year-old child in the car. Neither had been injured. The car hadn't a scratch or indent. Killing Angela had not made a mark on it.

The woman had not been texting, she insisted. She had not been talking to anyone. Yes, her cell phone was in her lap. Yes, there was a call to her husband of fifteen seconds duration at approximately the time of the accident, but that was a mistake. *A butt call?* the prosecutor asked scornfully. *When your butt was in the seat?* Still, the jury declined to convict her. They accepted her story that Angela had run out suddenly from behind a parked car on the dark street. There were no witnesses. The woman got away with murder.

Jane chose a night when the moon was on

the wane. Some light, but not a lot. Two a.m. She carried her industrial sprayer from the arboretum and a five-gallon vat filled with sodium tetraborate. She sprayed all the roses thoroughly. She didn't miss a single one. She made sure to get the roots as well as the leaves.

One week later, she drove past the house. It was a glorious disaster. Withered stalks and the blackened remains of the once-towering bushes. A grotesque wasteland, the house's ostentatiousness mocked by its surroundings. The woman, Hope was her name, came out the door. She did not look at the devastation around her. She got into her BMW and began backing out of the driveway.

Jane pressed gently on the gas and pulled out of her parking spot so that when Hope finished backing out of her driveway and straightening out her car, her car was face-to-face with Jane's. They were perhaps five feet apart, but there was no room on either side to pass. Hope made a preemptory gesture with her hand. *Get out of my way.* Jane is sure she was not recognized. She stepped on the gas and slowly edged her car forward so that it was nearly touching the BMW. Hope looked enraged. She shook her finger at Jane. Jane smiled. She stepped on the gas so that her car kissed the front fender of the BMW. She kept her foot steady on the gas. The BMW, a heavier car, held firm. Jane put her car in reverse. She backed up two feet. She put the car into first gear and stepped on the gas, hard. This time she felt the fender of the BMW give. Hope opened her mouth and shrieked. Jane saw her put her car in reverse, but by that time, another two cars had pulled up behind her and she had nowhere to go. She honked her horn but was merely answered with more honking behind her. Hope picked up her cell phone and began pushing buttons while Jane backed up her car again, this time farther. Ten feet. Changed gears. Gassed it. This time there was a distinct crunch. Jane backed up, and again accelerated, harder and faster this time. Again. Until the front of the BMW was crumpled metal and the windshield cracked, smashed. Broken glass was strewn all over the road. Hope opened her car door and made for the house, talking on her cell phone as she ran.

Jane calmly turned her car and drove home.

One of the policemen who came to the house later that day had delivered the news about Angela. He was sympathetic but firm. Charges were being pressed. Jane had to come into the station. Jane had to be booked. In her mug shot, she looked mad, her hair awry, an elated expression on her face. Truly insane.

They found the sodium tetraborate in her garage. Rick had been spending more and more time away — business travel, he'd said — so he couldn't confirm her presence at home the night the roses had been destroyed. Ultimately all the evidence was circumstantial. Still, that was enough. Jane was fined the exact same amount as the woman who killed her daughter for willfully damaging property — $1,000 — and had to pay a $6,500 car repair bill on top of that. She handed over the check with hands shaking in rage. *Next time,* she thought. *Next time she'll lose more than a car and some roses.* She gloried in having an enemy. A face. A body. Bodies can be broken. They can feel pain.

The court is very sympathetic to your situation, the judge had said. *Nevertheless, this is not behavior that can be tolerated.*

Her shrink told her to get away.

Her boss found her a new job.

The woman, Hope, got a new cell phone number. She took down her Facebook and

LinkedIn pages. Later, a sold sign went up on the lawn, scraped bare of the desecrated rose bushes.

Jane's friends took turns staying with her. *Babysitting time,* Jane heard one whisper to her phone from the spare bedroom.

Jane moved to Half Moon Bay. To keep herself safe. To keep herself out of jail. To go where no one knew her or her history. But nothing could rid Jane of the rage and shame. It was merely tamped down. Waiting to be ignited.

Every Saturday morning, no matter the weather, the flower growers show up at the parking lot of the First Methodist Church in Half Moon Bay a little after dawn and begin setting up their stalls. Jane never misses the market. She's not there in a professional capacity, since Smithson's doesn't sell cut flowers. It's known instead throughout California for its indigenous plants, some of them impossible to get elsewhere. But the Ferrochinis, Garibaldis, and small organic farms from Bonny Doon and Santa Cruz come with their vans full of blossoms, which they sell to tourists and locals alike. Jane likes the vibe. The *busyness.* The canvas tents, as much to protect against wet wind and fog as sun, as the weather can turn in minutes. The large plastic white tubs filled with banksia (*Banksia*), bachelor's buttons (*Centaurea cyanus*), and zinnia (*Zinnia elegans*), amid the usual roses and lilies. And of course the people. Only happy people buy flowers at 7:00 a.m. on a foggy Saturday morning. Maybe the sad people come later, Jane didn't know. Perhaps that's why she never buys flowers. She's not emotionally qualified. Her plants at the nursery, they're used to her moods, they even feed on them; her melancholy somehow nourishes the hairy alumroot (*Heuchera villosa*) and threeleaf foamflowers (*Tiarella trifoliata*) that she's growing there. That's what she tells herself, anyway. The other employees, they just say Jane has a green thumb.

Saturday, September 27. The flower market. 7:30 a.m. Poorly attended despite glorious weather. Posters of the two lost girls, Heidi and Rose, still papering the streetlight poles and shop windows. Jane makes her rounds as usual. She has found that conforming to habits, going through the motions, is better than the alternative. Structure, Dr. Blanes had told her, is the key to survival.

She's on her way back to her motorbike when she hears a call. *Hey. Red!*

Naturally Jane looks. You don't grow up an O'Malley in Big Cabin, Oklahoma, without answering to this, among unkinder things. Other people are looking too.

She locates the origin of the voice, a man about ten feet away. Dark complexion and hair and eyes register before she realizes she's looking at the man from the D-A-R-L-I-N-G shrine in San Gregorio. The same one she saw at the FBI office. Closer, he is at first glance less impressive. Tall, but perhaps a bit too thin, his jacket sleeves falling over his wrists. A scarecrow with insufficient stuffing. A narrow leather bag hangs from his shoulder. *A man purse,* Jane thinks scornfully. But then he smiles. She likes his face. *Like* is perhaps not the right word. She understands why the women who had seen him kept something back. Secrets about him, themselves. His smile is so personal it should be an affront, yet somehow it isn't. He is recognizing her, he is promising that he will take her, Jane, seriously.

And then, with the smile, it happens.

Jane feels dizzy. She's worried she will lose her balance.

She slowly approaches the man. She finds she is reluctant to get too close. It's not safe. When she is within easy conversing distance, he smiles again. Another powerful hit. Jane is definitely unsteady on her feet. The man holds out his hand.

We finally meet properly, he says.

She takes his hand. It is a shock to feel its warmth, its solidness. She grasps it tighter than she intended. It feels like a lifeline. It steadies her.

Jane struggles to think of what to say.

What did you call me? Back at the shrine? she finally asks. They are perhaps two feet apart. It feels too close. It feels too far.

He thinks for a moment, then laughs. The lines on his face indicate he does this often. She estimates him to be in his early to mid-forties.

Ammut. An Egyptian goddess. She sat in judgment of the dead. She weighed the hearts of the deceased on the scales of Ma'at. If found wanting, she devoured them.

Jane takes this in.

What is your real name, O Ammut? He takes his hand back — Jane hadn't realized she was still holding it — and hoists his leather bag up further on his shoulder. He bends to one side to let a family pass on the crowded street. He is not a scarecrow, she realized. His body is lithe, agile. The clothes simply a little large for his wiry frame.

Jane. Jane O'Malley. The handshake felt too intimate. Now she finds she can barely look at his face, afraid of what hers might look like. She turned her face toward him, but her eyes focus over his shoulder. She looks directly into the face of a striking dark woman who, like the man, is smiling.

Edward, are you going to make introductions?

It takes several beats. But Jane eventually understands that this woman is in fact talking to the man, that she is his companion. Jane's face grows hot, she can feel the flush traveling from her head down her body. Why should Jane feel ashamed? She's done nothing wrong.

I'm Alma, the woman says. *And this is Edward.*

Jane takes a step back. Out of confusion, she ignores the woman's extended hand. But the woman doesn't appear disconcerted. Her arm goes back to her side, gracefully and naturally, as if she meant to raise and then lower it all along in precisely that way.

The woman is carrying nothing. No purse. Jane can admire that. A woman without a purse is a true revolutionary.

Where can one get a good breakfast here, O Ammut? The man again. This time Jane looks directly in his face. It requires all her willpower. She remembers reading that it takes a hundred muscles to execute a smile, and understands she doesn't have the power to control those muscles at this moment. So she stands straight, unsmiling.

There's the coffee shop down at the other end of Main Street. And the German bakery across the street has good coffee. Jane motions with her hand. She is still looking at the man. He is still looking at her, Jane.

The woman, Alma, moves forward until she is shoulder to shoulder with the man. With any other woman, this would have seemed aggressive, proprietary. *He is mine. Back off.* But somehow that's not the case here. Jane pulls back her gaze to include both the man and the woman. Edward and Alma. Margaret from Three Sisters is right. They are beautiful.

Jane relents and tells them what no one tells strangers in Half Moon Bay. *Go to Three Sisters,* she says. *That's the best place in town. You've already been there, I understand. Keep going. No place else is worth it.*

The woman smiles. Like Edward, when she does, she has your full attention. Despite her dark hair and skin, her eyes are a strange blue-green, very intense. Sometimes flipping through a magazine, Jane gets stopped by the images of beauty served up by the advertising agencies. Fantasies, she knows;

no one looks like that, really. But here she is looking at flesh-and-blood beauty. How can you resist? She notices that other people around are looking at the couple, equally struck as Jane.

Yes, we've been there! she says. *We loved it.*

Come with us, says the man, who is Edward, Jane now knows. *You can help us out. Tell us more about the town.*

Alma nods. *We're new here. Just getting to know our way around.*

To her astonishment, Jane is tempted. They have broken through some barrier. They are offering something. They are the perfect match, her beauty, his . . . what? Empathy? No. Not that. Perhaps perception. As if he can see her soul, if she believed such a thing existed. He is not feeling her pain. No. But he sees it, recognizes it. And he has positive energy — for she sees that underneath the too-big clothes is a body pulsing to move, to get things done.

No, she says hurriedly. It would be too much. Allowing these people into her life would not be wise. This she knows. Yet magic is in the air. Dangerous magic.

Please, says the woman, Alma, and Jane almost relents. Then she shakes her head and breaks the spell.

110

Another time, she says, not meaning it, anything to get out of the situation.

Until later, then, says Edward.

Let's make it soon, says Alma.

Jane makes a noise that could be interpreted as an assent, and escapes. But for how long? She is caught, and she knows it.

Rose's funeral is even larger and more of a circus than Heidi's. Now that the words *serial killer* have been used, every story-hungry reporter, employed or independent, is in town looking for something, anything, that has been overlooked and can be fed to an insatiable public. The local channel even has a Coastal Murder Countdown icon on the television screen that states how long the murders have gone unsolved. More than forty-five days by now since Heidi disappeared.

The people in town don't call them serial killings. That feels too impersonal. These are deep, personal losses. If one has to, one refers to them as *the deaths.*

All families with daughters between three and thirteen years old are warned to keep them close, inside if possible, and to know where they are at all times. Doors and windows are to be locked at all times, especially at night, but also during the day.

Dogs are left free to roam at night in the house or stationed near the door. Alarms are to be set.

We are under siege, the mayor says. *Behave accordingly.*

Across the street from Three Sisters, a storefront left vacant since Millie's Yarns closed six months previously is suddenly occupied. A hand-lettered sign, YOUR BEACHES.ORG, is taped to the front windows. Inside, bustle. A notice for an administrative assistant, minimum wage *but satisfying work* goes into the *Moon News,* and economic times being what they are, a stream of young men and women are seen going in the door, dressed better than your average Half Moon Bay millennials.

Jane is leaving Three Sisters with her morning coffee and heading toward her motorbike when she is accosted. That's how she thinks of it. She doesn't allow herself to think that she may have been lingering in the street, or may have deliberately crossed the street to walk past the YourBeaches front door, that she had tried to see inside past the blinds.

O Ammut, woman of mystery, don't pass me by again!

It is Edward. He has stuck his head out

the door of the YourBeaches office. This time he's wearing jeans that fit more closely and a short-sleeved white T-shirt, appropriate for the day, which is surprisingly warm and sunny for late September.

When are we having our lunch? Alma has been wondering, he says.

Jane is not having a good day. She hasn't showered. Her hair is pulled back in a stern ponytail. She had woken that morning in a rage and could barely restrain herself from driving across the bay to Oakland to track down her daughter's killer, the restraining order notwithstanding.

Edward takes his phone out of his pocket, taps some keys. He looks up. *Today okay? It works for us.* Jane can't keep her eyes off his hair, so dark and full, with thick waves in it. James Dean hair. Any woman would kill for it.

No, Jane says, but she doesn't move. She is, she realizes, desperate to agree but is waiting to be convinced. She wants to be wooed.

Edward seems to know that he must proceed carefully. He comes closer to her. He leans in.

Please come, he says. *You're on the short list of people we'd like to know better.*

I don't see why, says Jane. She waits for

his response, hoping for something that will flatter her, make her feel that she is truly wanted. But Edward does something audacious. He reaches around and pulls the end of her ponytail.

We're not asking you to marry us, he says, and Jane flushes as if that is exactly what he has been doing. Being near him makes her think of sex in a way she hasn't since she was in her twenties. Images are teasing, exciting her.

See you at the Sisters at 1:00 p.m., he says, and then puts his hand on her shoulder. Jane, the untouchable, has been touched for the second time by this mesmerizing near-stranger. Her skin burns under her shirt. She shrugs but the sensation remains. Edward doesn't seem to notice.

Catch you then, he says.

The word is that the FBI has let Fred Barnes go without arresting him. That they have no one else in their sights.

Everyone is on edge. They know more is coming. Terrible things are coming. Parents of small girls buy dog leashes at the Feed and Grain, hook their children to them just to walk down Main Street. Strangers are everywhere, distinguished from the usual tourists by their laconic attitudes. They are waiting. They are ready. They are predators as much as the murderer. When he or she is caught, they will descend and destroy. In the meantime, they are bored. They interview and reinterview the same people. They learn about Margaret, at Three Sisters, and camp out there, drinking cup after cup of coffee and peppering her with questions. They wait. Everyone is waiting.

Jane is early for her lunch with Edward and Alma. She is always early. This is her curse. When invited to a party, she inevitably is forced to walk around the block twice or stop by a café for a cup of coffee so as to not show up embarrassingly early for the event. Once in Berkeley she'd gotten the time absurdly wrong. She came two hours early. The hostess, a woman she worked with at the arboretum, was still in her shorts and sports bra. Jane was given a glass of water and waited miserably in the living room, her offers of help refused. Now she checked invitations twice, three times, to make sure she understood the time right. And still she was early.

She didn't want to be seen alone at a table obviously waiting — even though she was frequently alone at tables in the Three Sisters. But this was different. She should have brought a book. She studied the time line on the back wall. The sisters had created a huge wall collage of their lives' paths to the café, which encompassed high school, college, law school for Margaret, MFA programs in creative writing for the twins, and countless rejection letters for stories, poems, jobs, and, later, bank loans for when they opened the café. *The Trail of Tears,* the twins said. Everyone else had been invited to post their rejection letters — from prospective employers, colleges, former girlfriends, boyfriends, and other failed endeavors. *The Bong Wall,* it was called. Margaret explained to Jane that it was the sisters' stand against the shame and silence that typically accompanies failure. *It's so depressing to always hear about people's successes,* she says. *What we needed were some good failure stories.*

Jane longed to post her own failures up there. *Bad mother. Doctoral program dropout. Failed wife. Stalker and harasser. Destroyer of property.* She certainly had the documentation to show it. One day she would post it all.

Edward and Alma finally arrive. Jane has chosen a table that is too small for the three of them, so when they sit down, Jane's knees momentarily touch Alma's. She pulls them back, hurriedly.

We've done some googling. Edward is speaking in a low voice so no one but the three of them can hear. Not that anyone is paying any attention, everyone absorbed in their own business. *We know,* Edward says.

Alma places her hand on Jane's. Jane's first instinct is to pull away. But she doesn't. A sense of calm is somehow transmitted. A drug. Jane has a cache of Xanax and clonazepam large enough to make any college student jealous. But this is more powerful than any drug. Alma's hand is firm and holds Jane's tight.

It's okay, Edward says; his voice is low.

Margaret comes for their salad selections and Alma orders a bottle of wine, red, for the table. *I think we need this,* she says.

Why talk about needing? This is a celebration! says Edward. *We've captured the elusive Ammut. Let's see if she finds our hearts wanting or not.* It's said as a joke, but Jane is pricked awake by the words. *Their hearts.* Isn't that what she wants to know about? What is in their hearts? What their intentions are? Jane is suspicious. What do they want from her?

What's happened to these girls must be traumatizing you, says Alma. Her dark eyes are sympathetic, her hand still firm as it cov-

117

ers Jane's.

Yes, says Jane cautiously. *It has been deeply . . . unsettling.*

A loss of the kind you endured does not go away, says Alma. *It's a wound that won't heal.*

Jane says nothing.

You must experience a certain amount of . . . satisfaction . . . ? And then there's the inevitable shame that accompanies this satisfaction. It's complex. All on top of an open wound.

There was a moment of silence, Edward turned his chair slightly away from Alma, as if giving her space to expand.

Jane is stunned to be named so precisely.

How do you know this? How could you possibly understand?

Alma doesn't answer at first. Then she says, *It's possible I've suffered similarly.*

The way she says it forbids questions. But that, plus the drug being transmitted through her hand, touches something deep inside Jane. She nods. She will wait to learn more.

The wine comes. Jane drinks hers, too fast. Edward immediately pours her another glass. She has not looked at him directly since he arrived. She does so now. She finds his eyes on her. The dark features. The strong thick hair. Again she feels that pulse

118

in her neck, her chest. What a beautiful, beautiful man. She drags her eyes away and drinks her wine. The effect of the wine combined with the touch of Alma's hand makes Jane feel that she is not quite in the world. It's not an unpleasant feeling.

I have to get back to work, she finds herself saying.

But we haven't eaten yet. Look, here are our salads. Relax and eat.

To Jane's surprise she does. Everything has a fresh taste to it. She discovers she is hungry as well as a little tipsy.

I won't be able to drive back to work in this condition, she admits.

I'll give you a ride, says Alma. *You can pick up your motorbike later. Now eat.*

Jane picks up her fork.

Change of subject, says Edward, and his voice is brisk. Jane glances at him. The electricity has been turned off. Here is an efficient man, getting down to business. She feels herself relaxing.

Tell me about Dunes Resort, he says.

Jane pulls herself together and does.

It's being built in a special place, she says. *You drive south of downtown Half Moon Bay for about a mile. You park at Bob's Fruit Stand, on the east side of Route 1, or you risk getting towed. Bob — if there is a Bob, as the* stand is manned by local farmworkers who don't speak much English — *doesn't seem to mind. You cross Route 1 and walk about half a mile due east on a dirty path through the artichoke fields. It's hard to find, but it's there. You climb down the cliff. There are two ways down: a steep and a steeper. And you don't go down at all unless you're quite confident that you can make it back up. Most people come this far and then turn back. But for those who persist . . .*

You have to really want to go there, Jane finishes. *But when you're there — it doesn't matter what the weather is. You're on a long stretch of pure white sand, the cliffs shielding you from the sight of everyone except the occasional fishing boat. Nothing but you and the waves and the sand. But you have to be very careful not to stand under the cliffs. They're eroding. Once I got caught in a rock slide, had to run straight into the ocean. My back and legs got hammered pretty badly, needed stitches.*

And that's where the Dunes Resort will be built, says Edward.

Yes. Right at the top of the cliff. Replacing the artichoke fields. There was a lot of talk against it, but it went through, Jane says. *They're going to build concrete steps down to the beach for the guests,* she adds. She is more bitter about this than she can express. Desecration of a sacred site. Secret Beach, another one of Jane's places. This is where she scattered her daughter's ashes.

Edward reaches into his leather satchel and pulls out a card. He hands it to Jane.

Edward Stanton
Senior Advisor
YourBeaches.org

We're organized, we're funded, and we're ready to go, he says.

But it's too late, Jane says, and hands back the card. *You were needed last year. There were protests, but it didn't do any good.*

It's never too late, says Edward, and picks up his fork. *This I can promise. Now eat.*

That night, Jane dreams of Edward and Alma. *It's all right,* Alma tells Jane in her dream. *You can love him too. There's enough for both of us.*

Jane wakes up, thinking not of Edward but of Alma. She-who-was-oh-so-lovely. She wasn't a competitor. She wasn't a sister — sisters were natural predators in Jane's experience. She was a different kind of woman altogether.

How beautiful Alma was! The skin, patterned into exquisite spider wrinkles emanating upward from the edges of her eyes. *An eye smile,* Angela used to call it. *Give me an eye smile,* she'd say if Jane had been cross with her for some transgression — chocolate on her shirt or evidence that she'd gotten into Jane's things. Alma's cheekbones that would retain their high-sculpted sharpness, growing more angular, more powerful, with age. And that dark hair, turned white! Never would Alma cut it, Jane was sure. She would wear it long and straight, a white mane that would flow over and past her shoulders, contrasting with her velvet dark skin. A muse for all ages.

Jane relaxes and goes back to sleep.

But the next day brings more horror.

A three-year-old girl goes missing while her father is shopping at the Twice as Nice warehouse in Princeton-on-the-Sea. The alarm previously reserved for earthquakes, tsunamis, and other catastrophes wails through the towns of Princeton, Half Moon Bay, and Montara. Jane, at work at Smithson's, chills when she hears it. All the customers in the nursery look to the staff for answers. They have none. People block the exits in their hurry to get out. Jane finds out later that parents froze in the street, grabbed the hands of their children, and crowded into the police station, the *Moon News* offices, and the Three Sisters, anywhere there were others, to get news and comfort.

When the child is later found a block away, behind a warehouse, playing in a mud puddle, the people in town don't relax. They are reminded that they are in a war zone. Jane doesn't sleep that night. Adrenaline pumping through her veins, she washes down the walls of the kitchen, scours the toilet, does anything to avoid her cold bed.

In many ways, Half Moon Bay is a strange place to live. Small but not small enough to be called neighborly. People know each other by sight. They know many names. But they can't necessarily put them together. Instead, they identify each other by their jobs, the clubs they join, unique physical characteristics. The tall sixtyish man who plays sidekicks in the theater group productions. The woman who leads the coastal trail preservation group. A member of the poker club.

There are no jobs on the coast except service and retail. Professionals like scientists or engineers or accountants, even doctors and dentists, commute to San Francisco or Santa Cruz, Stanford, or Silicon Valley.

So the sort of people whom Jane would previously have consorted with are gone from 7:00 a.m. to 7:00 p.m., and tired when they are in town. They-who-work-over-the-hill. That's how they are referred to. Jane is known as the redhead who works at Smithson's Nursery. She is distressed by even this level of familiarity. Anonymity was and is her goal.

When Jane escaped Oklahoma for Berkeley at the age of seventeen, she discovered the amazing fact that things grew, actually flourished, in the soil. In Oklahoma, if they were lucky, tufts of crabgrass might appear in the field surrounding the truck stop before the summer heat parched the dirt into jigsaw puzzle pieces. But in Berkeley, between the cracks in the sidewalks on College Avenue or Shattuck grew gorgeous blue, pink, and yellow flowers. Jane began collecting them, pressing them between waxed paper in the pages of her chemistry textbook. Jane began learning their names. Checkerbloom (*Sidalcea malviflora*). Peppermint candy flower (*Claytonia sibirica*). Hummingbird sage (*salvia spathacea*). Her decrepit student rental house included someone's long-ago garden grown out of control. She began spending her time outside, weeding and taking more specimens for her chemistry book. New delights every day. After her flowers were dry, she'd glue them to small white canvases bought at Utrecht Art on University Avenue and carefully label and frame them. Her own private gallery.

Then one day during class, Jane dropped her book, and out fell the dozen or so flowers she was currently pressing. Her professor noticed. She came down the aisle and helped Jane pick up the treasures. Then the professor said, *You should take Professor Silbert's class on native California plants,* and added, *and of course you've been to the university's Botanical Gardens?* Two sentences that changed Jane's life. She felt like a new person. A new start to a new life. She thought she would feel the same moving to Half Moon Bay. But this time she was too laden with emotional baggage to make it work.

Alma hands Jane an avocado. *This one should work.* She is right. It is firm but gives slightly. When Jane slices it open, the pale green foamy interior smells musty, full of mysteries. She doesn't do anything for a moment except marvel at it. Nothing that has been picked ever ripens for Jane. Yet it is perhaps a sign of her madness that she keeps hoping. She buys hard avocados, firm pears, hard peaches. She places them in a bowl on her kitchen table, where they inevitably go from hard to rotten, brown-spotted, smelling of fermented alcohol, festering with fruit flies. Inedible. Jane cuts off pale soft green slivers onto a plate, which Alma takes and shunts into the greens she has been washing. Two women preparing a meal. A man outside waiting to be fed. As traditional a suburban scene as you could get. Yet it feels like anything but. It isn't *safe.* So why is Jane excited rather than frightened? Unsafe was generally toxic. Hadn't she spent the last seven months attempting to build up a haven of safeness and predictability? A job with opening and closing hours? Limiting her contact to other flawed humans? Growing a thicker skin?

They are at Edward and Alma's rental house in Pescadero. It had surprised Jane. She'd driven past the huge iron gates twice before she saw the *No. 12* on the side of the high wall surrounding the property. She had to push an intercom button and announce herself before a buzzer sounded and the gates swung slowly open. She drove up a long winding paved road to a pink stucco monstrosity. Even then she couldn't believe she was at the right place until she saw the familiar silver Mercedes parked along the side and a nondescript beige foreign import compact car she'd never seen before parked next to it.

What is *this place?* Jane asks when she gets inside. It is furnished like a mausoleum, with heavy, ornate dark red and black furniture and fringed lamp shades. The sofa cushions are blocks of green foam that are stiff and don't give when you sit down on them.

Alma greets her with a kiss on both cheeks, European style. Jane is at first surprised, then charmed. It is friendly but nonintrusive. Alma, dressed in a deep blue sari-like garment that sparkles when she moves, and black leggings and bare feet, laughs.

We had three requirements: clean, private, and no rats, she says. *In other parts of the country, rats are a sign you're doing something terribly wrong. There's a stigma. If you have rats, you don't mention it to anyone. Here everyone complains in the grocery store line about their rat problems.*

Roof rats, Jane explains. *A hazard of living in Northern California. Even the high-end places suffer.*

I can't stand them, Alma says, and shudders. She had called Jane the previous

Thursday and asked her to come to Sunday brunch. Now they are standing in the kitchen of the rental house preparing the meal. Edward is writing a newsletter decrying the Dunes Resort hotel that had broken ground in the summer.

So how long have you been married? Jane says, to start conversation.

Three years, Edward, who has wandered into the kitchen, says. *Six years,* says Alma simultaneously. They turn their heads to look at each other and laugh.

So which is it?

Both. We're each married — but to other people. This was Alma. She seems amused, not at all embarrassed. *It depends what you call* together. *I'm counting from the moment I left my husband. He's counting from the time we first got together.*

What?

Neither of us had the confidence that our soul mate would come along. This was Edward. *So we settled. Too soon. Then we found each other.*

And we both paid the price. Alma.

Gradually the story came out. Alma was married to a prominent lawyer in New Orleans, mother of two small children, girls both, and a professor of physics at Tulane. She met Edward on a school trip she was chaperoning for her older daughter's pre-school to the local swamp. He gave a demonstration of how the acidity in the water was killing the native plants. He was married to a fellow environmental activist. She had left him a year previously, but they had never finalized a divorce.

He made a big impression, says Alma. *On the kids. And on me.*

The feeling was mutual, Edward says. Jane feels slightly embarrassed, but they are being very matter-of-fact. Jane senses, however, that below the matter-of-factness lies great emotion.

But, Jane says, *what happened to your husband?*

It wasn't easy, Alma repeated.

You left him.

Eventually. It was pretty brutal.

But the children! What about them? Jane asks. She's been distracted. How could she forget the children?

It was brutal, repeats Alma.

You left them? Her voice is louder than she intended. Then she stops. She doesn't want to be insensitive, although Alma doesn't seem upset.

It was necessary, says Alma. Her face now looks different to Jane. A face capable of things.

To lose your children . . .

Is something you understand quite well.

But to give them up. Voluntarily . . . I don't get it. Jane's voice comes out hard and flat.

You're not expected to. Alma's voice remains even. *I would have lost them, anyway.*

Jane considers Angela at thirteen, at fourteen. The yelling, the hatred, the vitriol.

Yes, she says. *You would have.*

I mean because of my husband. He was turning them against me. He was poisoning their minds with lies about me.

A moment of silence. Then: *Enough of this!* says Edward. *This is supposed to be a celebration! We've captured Jane for lunch!*

Captured. *What a strange word,* thinks Jane. And yet, she realizes, it's true. Only the word she would use is *captivated.* Yet despite Edward's words, Alma persists in carrying on the conversation.

Haven't you ever done something . . . unacceptable . . . in the eyes of the world?

Jane thinks back. She remembers slapping her father, hard, across the cheek when she was fourteen. They were in the middle of one of their fights. She had been waitressing to save money for college, and every night when she came home, he demanded that she turn over her tips. *I'm paying for your everyday living. You owe me. It's my money.*

Her father's face was close to hers, looking smug. He thought he was in control. He thought he had the power. At that point, he was still taller than she was. Weighed considerably more than she did. Was less inhibited than she was. She slapped him but couldn't bear to do it hard. She could feel the whiskers on his cheek from the day's growth of beard. It was more like a caress, she realized later with shame.

He threw her down the stairs. Nothing was broken. No permanent damage done physically. But something switched in her. She would kill him one day. She would. She actually thought of how she would do it. Put ground glass in his wine. Push him down the stairs when he mounted them, heavily, soused and unstable one night. But she never did anything. She'd never acted. She'd felt that way about Angela on occasion. Only then it was more passive. *I wish she would die.* Then she thought of the woman who had killed Angela. Jane was a murderer, in thought if not in deed.

There are things I'm not proud of, Jane says finally. What an understatement.

But they were things you had to do.

At the time, yes.

And there were things you thought about but didn't act on.

Yes.

Do you wish you had? Acted?

Yes, says Jane. *I wish I'd had the nerve.*

We did. Have the nerve. We did it.

But what about the children? Jane persists. *Does your husband have them?*

He does and he doesn't, Alma says, oddly. *They'll always belong to me.* She says this without any emotion.

But think of what they'll think when they get older. Think of what your husband will tell them?

No. They are mine. Her voice was clear: conversation was over.

It's the last Tuesday in September. At 10:30 p.m., the half-full moon is bright. Although the fog is hovering offshore, it hasn't made landfall yet, so Jane can see the stars as she walks down her street, across Route 1, and toward the beach. Princeton-by-the-Sea is little more than a scattering of small houses and a sort of peninsula that juts out into the ocean, forming a natural harbor. There are a handful of seafood restaurants, a brewery-restaurant, and some industrial buildings. Everything is closed and quiet. The peninsula culminates with a tall hill on which a navy station once stood. A huge structure that looks like a giant golf ball sits on top, surrounded by twelve-foot-high barbed wire fencing. Signs are posted warning people away. You can either skirt the bottom of the hill to walk around and see the now-famous Mavericks Beach, or climb the hill and walk around the barbed wire to the bluffs that tower a hundred feet above the breakers. Jane decides to walk to Mavericks. As usual, she ignores the sign that announces it closed at sundown and makes her way around the base of the cliffs. Although she brought a flashlight, she doesn't need it; the moonlight is enough for now. All is silent except the foghorn that bursts out with its mournful four-syllable song every three minutes exactly. *Be-care-ful-boats. Be-care-ful-boats.* Two enormous raccoons waddle past, their eyes shining as they catch the light of the moon. They ignore Jane, who lets them pass in respectful silence. This is their time, their space. She is here on their tolerance.

She walks around the stone labyrinth that someone started building years ago, and to which everyone who passes contributes. Large rocks spiral out in concentric circles on a ridge of land that juts out over the water. She walks the circular path in the moonlight, the deep silence broken only by the foghorn. She reminds herself what the woman at the New Moon bookstore says of the labyrinth: it is walking meditation, a path of prayer. It has only one path. There are no tricks to it and no dead ends. *Unlike a maze where you lose your way, the labyrinth helps you find one,* the woman had said. New Age nonsense. Still, Jane walks along the stones until she reaches the center, then reverses her steps until she is out of the labyrinth, free. She clicks off her flashlight. It is very dark. She cannot even see her feet on the ground.

Jane takes off her jacket, she is so heated, and moves to the edge of the cliff to let the spray hitting the rocks below refresh her. She then continues her walk. She has done this so often her feet know the way almost by touch.

She finally reaches the breakwater and turns the corner. This is where the water from the bay and ocean meet. At high tide, there's barely enough sand to walk on. Crabs scuttle out of Jane's way. The air always smells fresher here, and the headache that has been hovering all day dissipates. Jane breathes deeply. She has to proceed carefully, not to trip. She doesn't turn on her flashlight, instead embracing the darkness around her. She reaches the end of the beach and sits down on one of the boulders, careful to stay out of the reach of the waves. The breakers aren't that high tonight, perhaps four or five feet, but she's seen the Mavericks superwave — the one that reaches seventy, eighty feet in height. Local surfers used to have this beach to themselves, and Jane liked sitting on the sand watching them navigate the monster breakers and rocks that populate the shallows. But then word got out. Like everything. Everything gets spoiled sooner or later. Now there's the international surfing contest every winter, and fifty thousand people descend on Princeton-by-the-Sea to watch. Last year the police had to set up roadblocks to keep the crowds from the beach, forcing people to watch the contest on huge video screens set up in the local bars and restaurants. Hundreds of pounds of food and thousands of gallons of beverages were consumed. Silly memorabilia were purchased. The people of Half Moon Bay cashing in on the Mavericks craze. You can't blame them. What else did they have? Pumpkins.

Jane picks up her flashlight, but again without turning it on, gets up, and starts to walk back toward the harbor. When she reaches the corner where the beach meets the breakwater, and beyond that the dirt path, she first senses rather than sees movement. About a hundred feet ahead. It's too large to be an animal, at least a safe animal. As she fumbles with the switch of her flashlight, the moon emerges slightly from behind the inevitable fog, and a shape can be distinguished from the darkness. A man, by the figure and gait, approaching slowly but steadily. Jane can't make out the face yet. Friend or foe? By now the man is fifty feet away, heading directly toward her. Jane freaks out, drops her flashlight, bends down, picks it up, now gritty with sand, and finally gets it turned on. She shines it on the face of the man — for it is a man — who is now just ten feet away. Edward. It's Edward. Jane exhales and sits down on a nearby rock, weak with relief.

You scared the shit out of me.

Sorry. Can you turn that off? The flashlight is still trained on his face. His eyes glitter like an animal's.

Jane complies. They are facing each other, but it's so dark now she doubts that he can see her.

What are you doing here? Jane finally thinks to ask.

Looking for you, he says, as if it were the most natural thing in the world. *You weren't at your house, so I took a chance you'd be here.*

Some chance, Jane says. *I could have gone in any number of directions.* Had he been watching her? Followed her here?

How did you know my address? she asks.

Jane, you're listed online, Edward says. *Don't be paranoid. And no, you wouldn't have gone anywhere else but here. For a night walk, Mavericks is clearly the only show in town.*

Why were you looking for me? Jane finally asks. Away from the protection of the cliffs, the wind is chilling. She should have worn a warmer coat. She's afraid to hear what he will say, she realizes. It feels dangerous to have asked.

Edward doesn't answer right away. He walks over to where she's sitting and crouches down next to her. It is way too intimate — Jane, with her knees up from sitting on the low rock, Edward, leaning in, his head slightly higher than hers. She can see his lips clearly in the moonlight and wonders that she'd ever thought them womanly.

Because I wanted to see you, he says. This terrifies Jane. She instinctively moves away from Edward. He slowly rises and, with a deliberate step, closes the narrow gap between them. Then he squats again. His eyes, always dark, look black in the fog-veiled moonlight. Jane finds it impossible to read his expression. Her heart is pounding so hard in her chest she wonders that it doesn't scare the seagulls roosting nearby on the sand. She fears she will lose control of her bladder. All she can think is *Go, go, go,* but she can't move from the rock she's sitting on.

They stay in that position for what seems like a long time. He bends down. His hand moves. He raises it up toward Jane's face, then swerves off at the last minute to the hair. Always the hair. He caresses it with such a light touch that she can barely feel it.

Jane is crying. She can feel prickles of sweat on her neck. She endures his touch until she realizes he isn't going to stop of his own volition. The pressure on her hair intensifies. Jane shakes her head violently, throwing off his fingers.

Jane, Ammut, woman of mystery, Edward says. That does it. Something inside Jane contracts.

Leave me alone, she says.

She struggles to get up from the low rock — awkwardly and with mortification — and turns to go, but realizes she doesn't have her flashlight. She loses whatever dignity she had left by going back to the rock and scrambling about on her hands and knees until she finds it. After heaving herself to her feet again, Jane begins following the path around the hill, the flashlight beam trained on the ground two feet ahead of her.

Don't be silly. Here. Wait. I'll walk with you. Edward from twenty feet behind.

Jane starts to say no and then thinks of the alternative: herself walking ahead, followed at a short distance by Edward, who would naturally be watching her. How discomfited would that make her? So she silently waits for him to join her, then begins the walk back. The path skirts the water of the harbor. At this hour, all the fishing boats are tied up, the docks deserted. A seabird calls from the marsh that adjoins the hamlet and is answered by the foghorn, which, now that the entire area is shrouded in a thick fog, comes out as a muffled melancholy lowing, a mechanical sea cow.

I wasn't mocking you, Janey, says Edward. His voice is so soft she has to lean toward him to hear. *Alma and I are . . . interested . . . in you.*

The mention of Alma calms Jane a little.

I like Alma, Jane says.

You and everybody else, says Edward. Jane

feels, rather than sees, him smile.

Jane is breathing easier. They're walking through the industrial warehouse district of Princeton at this point, with the high chain-link fences and dry boatyards with boats up on blocks to be repaired or painted. Right in the middle of all this, on the edge of the water, sits the so-called yacht club, little more than a glorified bar. True, you had to own a boat to belong, but if an actual yacht had ever moored in Princeton Harbor, Jane had not seen it.

Ever been inside? Edward asks, gesturing toward the yacht club building. Jane shakes her head. She's frequently walked along the beach that borders it and seen all the men — for they are invariably men — sitting on the open wooden porch drinking. They have a wooden raft and a sort of pulley rigged up that ferries them out to a platform in deep enough water to anchor their ragtag boats. They look like little boys with toys as they pull each other out from the shallows to their small vessels.

Let's go, then, Edward says, and walks up to the front door. He takes a key ring from his pocket and carefully inserts two wires into the lock. He jiggers them until Jane hear a click and the door swings open.

What did you just do? Jane asks.

He doesn't answer or wait for her, but enters the dark building. Jane hesitates, then reluctantly follows him in. She finds herself in a large moonlit room with a bar taking up most of the left wall and, directly in front, a wall of windows that look out onto the sun porch that in turn overlooks the sea. The water glints faintly through the fog.

"What will you have?" asks Edward. He is standing behind the bar. Jane can see his teeth flash in one of his smiles. *It's fully stocked. Name your poison.*

Jane thinks, *Why the hell not?* in a rare moment of abandon.

Tequila, straight, she says.

Coming at you, he says, stooping down below the bar counter where Jane can't see him. He stands up again with two limes in his right hand and a knife in his left. *So he's a lefty,* Jane thinks, as if that meant anything, as the knife glints palely in the moonlight. She hears rather than sees the knife saw through the thick skins of the limes, then the murmur of liquid being poured from a bottle, and he is suddenly next to her, holding a tray with six shot glasses filled to their brims with amber liquid, and a small bowl of quartered limes.

Jane lifts her eyebrow. He shrugs.

I didn't want to have to go back after each

141

shot, Edward says.

He carries the tray out the back door to the porch, still without turning on any lights. He pulls two chairs close to a little table and sets the tray down. He motions to the closest chair, but Jane isn't ready. She goes to the railing and looks out over the bay. She can't see far because of the fog, but she can hear the lapping of water against the pier and see the little pulley contraption the clubbers had contrived swaying in the breeze. The wooden boarding platform bobs in the restless sea.

Now, this is the strange part: here is a place Jane truly doesn't belong, with a man, another woman's man, who makes her uncomfortable. And yet a sense of well-being floods over her, related to having her two feet firmly planted on the worn wooden floor, the cool air that blows on her face, the faintly sour bar smell of booze and sweat, and three lovely shots of tequila to ingest. She feels that she has found a place of respite on a difficult planet. She walks over and picks up one of the full shot glasses and a quartered lime. Pouring the liquor back in one motion, she then squeezes the lime into her mouth, wincing at the sourness. Suddenly Edward is beside her. Two of his shot glasses are already empty. He reaches over, takes the lime from between Jane's teeth, throws it over the railing. He is not gentle. Jane feels the pressure on her front teeth where he tugged, hard.

And now Number 2, he says, and holds up another shot glass and another quarter of lime. Jane repeats the drinking, the sucking. The liquor goes down warm. She hadn't eaten enough dinner and is running the risk of getting drunk. *The hell with that.* She picks up the third glass and a third lime, and does it again. She *is* drunk. She puts her hand out to steady herself on Edward's arm. He lets her. Then he reaches out and suddenly pushes her, forcefully. She loses her balance and, for a panicked moment, falls backward into space. Then she lands, hard, on a chair.

Stay put until you get your sea legs, says Edward. *Then come over and look at this.* He gestures to his right, at a wall that is covered with what look like nonsense scribbles. As Jane's vision clears, she sees they are words, written haphazardly on the wall using permanent markers of various colors and widths.

Nothing like a little housebreaking to make one appreciative of the idiosyncrasies of one's fellow humans, Edward says, pointing. Jane gets up and walks unsteadily over to the wall. At the top of it, written in large block letters: YOU CAN'T LIVE WITH THEM. Jane attempts to look more closely at the scrawlings. They swim in and out of focus. They are words, all about women, and many are accompanied by crudely drawn pictures. They range from quotes that Jane believes are Shakespearean (*she makes hungry where most she satisfies*) to lyrics from punk rock songs (*you suck at love / get your heart on*) to obscene (*today I ate pussy twice*) and plain insulting (*a pessimist is a man who thinks all women are whores. An optimist is one who hopes they are*).

Hell is empty and all the devils are here, says Edward. He has come up behind her. She feels his hands reach out and touch her from behind. He places them on her waist. Then they gently lift up her cotton T-shirt, slip inside, and slide up her back. Fingers against skin. He holds them there, flat against her back. She can feel his breath on her neck, the warmth of his hands under her shirt. She is intensely aroused. She waits.

But he pulls away, withdraws his hands, pats down her shirt.

Jane turns. Her back, robbed of the warmth of Edward's hands, feels suddenly cold. Edward has moved to the window. He

144

is not looking at the wall of indictments and praise of women. He is staring out at the shrouded sea.

Do you include yourself when you say that all the devils are here? Jane asks, trying to recover. Her voice is somewhat breathless.

Especially myself, he says, and smiles, but it is a humorless smile, more of a grimace. *And then, of course, there's you.*

Jane doesn't ask what he means. She knows. Black Heart.

Tell me, Edward says, and leans toward her. *What do you most fear?* Jane is thinking of his hands withdrawn, the warmth denied, but she says the next thing that comes to mind.

The dead.

Edward raises his eyebrows. *That's a bit abstract,* he says. *Can you be more specific?*

Okay, she says. *My dead.*

Ah, but how do you decide which are yours and which belong to other people? he asks. He turns his back on Jane to look out at the sea. He asks no more questions, but something has shifted. There is a stiffness in his stance, in how he is holding his head. Both hands are now in his pockets.

Jane is uneasy. Yet another transition? To what? The evening has taken too many turns. She is exhausted.

Let's go before someone notices we're here, she says. She is moving unsteadily away form Edward as she speaks, toward the front door. Edward doesn't budge.

After midnight, no one is likely to come by, he says. A beat passes. Then another. Jane feels a flutter in her stomach and her hands feel cold. She is suddenly aware of the blocks and blocks of industrial waterfront warehouses and work spaces that are completely uninhabited between here and her safe cozy cottage. Edward is not smiling. But neither is he frowning. He has turned and is looking at Jane. He is evaluating her, the situation. Jane thinks of the knife in his left hand as he cut the limes, the adept way he wielded it. She can see the handle sticking out of his front pocket of his jeans. He follows her eyes down and smiles. It is his usual captivating smile. But who is it for?

I thought I might need this again, he says, and reaches down and pulls it out. It flashes in the dim light. He then pulls a whole lime out of his other pocket and places it on the table before swiftly quartering it. He hands one of the sections to Jane. *Suck on this,* he says. *It'll sober you up.* Jane finds she can breathe again.

They walk back to Jane's cottage in silence. She does not invite him in. He doesn't appear to expect her to. After a perfunctory good night, he leaves.

And Jane goes into her solitary bed, where she doesn't sleep until dawn.

Jane meets Alma for a promised excursion to the beach at Three Sisters Café the following Saturday. She doesn't mention the yacht club evening. Alma makes no sign that she knows about Edward's visit to Jane.

They'd agreed to meet at 5:00 p.m. Daylight saving time was still on, so it would stay light until 7:30 or 8:00. The light isn't exactly fading, but has softened, festooning everything with a muted glow. A tranquil time.

Jane is naturally first. Alma arrives at five minutes past the hour, motions to Jane to keep sitting, and goes to the counter. *I need caffeine,* she says, coming to the table. *And we have plenty of time.*

She sits down opposite Jane, who is still nursing her own black coffee. *The first thing we are going to do,* Alma says, leaning forward and speaking deliberately, *is talk about the lost children. Not Heidi and Rose. But our own lost children.*

Jane panics. *No.*

Yes.

I can't, Jane says. She reaches into her jeans' front pocket, feeling around for enough change to pay for her coffee and leave a tip. She is more agitated than she can express. She feels that she has been ambushed. Brought here under false pretenses.

Why not? Alma stirs sugar into her coffee, tastes it, puts in another spoonful.

It's not possible. Now Jane is standing up, putting her jacket on. Alma stands up too and puts a hand on Jane's shoulder.

Yes it is, says Alma. Although she is speaking softly, people from surrounding tables are listening with interest, scenting drama. *It's been — When was your daughter born? Seventeen years ago now?*

Jane nods.

Then it's been sixteen years since you lost your baby. It's time to face up to all the real losses you have suffered. Only then can you put last year's loss in perspective.

Jane stops agitating She takes deep breaths. In. Out. In. Out. She is thinking that Alma mirrors something she, Jane, often felt herself as she watched Angela grow up.

Alma pulls out Jane's chair and indicates she should sit again. Alma sits down herself, continues speaking in the same low voice.

148

Raising a child is a series of little deaths. The death of the infant. The passing away of the toddler. The end of the preteen.

Jane doesn't say anything. Images of Angela crowd into her mind. Angela in her ridiculously furry one-piece snowsuit at one year old when they were in the mountains skiing. Angela at three tearing off her clothes as she ran down the beach toward the waves. Angela slamming her door at fourteen.

Think of it another way. Alma has taken Jane's hands and is holding them tightly. *By losing Angela when you did, you missed out on more deaths, more grief. With children, you lose, and you lose and you lose again. And it doesn't end when they've grown and leave the house. If anything, it gets worse.*

And what do you know about all this? Jane asks, her voice deliberately monotone, expressionless. She is feeling much and doesn't want to give anything away.

I remember when I lost my first baby, Alma says. It's as if she hadn't heard Jane's bitter words, instead concentrating on what she has to say.

Jane and Alma are now sitting very still, facing each other. They are still holding hands. *My baby was perhaps eight months old. She was crawling. She could say* mama *and could point to the rain and say* agua, *which she'd learned from her Mexican baby-sitter. I wasn't with her. I was in my office at Tulane, meeting with students, and making the final edits on my latest research paper. That's when I realized it. I hadn't thought of Emily for three hours. I hadn't been a mother for three hours. We were no longer conjoined. Where was my baby? She was no longer. She was gone.*

Tell me about leaving your daughters for Edward, Jane says. *Tell me how you could possibly do that.* She wanted to hurt Alma for her beauty, for her apparent serenity when telling of such horrors.

I weaned my youngest. Susan. It was difficult. Susan was about fourteen months old. It was time. People were starting to stare when I nursed in a restaurant or looked at each other when I took a nursing break at a party. My body rebelled. I got a breast infection and had to bind my breasts. They ached so badly I was eating aspirin by the handfuls.

The day was coming. So I killed my daughter, that daughter, the one I'd been nursing. And then I knew it was time to leave before I got attached to the next version of her. Before I'd experience even more grief.

What about your older daughter? You left her too?

That was even harder, Alma says. *She was four years old. I was deeply attached to her, and she to me.*

Why didn't you take them with you? Would Edward have been so opposed to that?

Bring them with me? Alma gives a half laugh and shakes her head. *No.*

Why not? Jane persists. *I could never have left Angela. Never. Not even when she was being so horrible at thirteen and fourteen.*

Alma's answer startles Jane.

I needed to be pure. I was tainted as a mother. Tainted by love. Exhausted by love. Exhausted by the constant loss that was motherhood.

Most women think of it as additive — they get new joys every day, says Jane. The words sound false even as she says them.

Did you think of it that way? asks Alma. *Be honest.*

Jane doesn't know if it is because of the tenor of the conversation, but the memories that are being aroused are not of the tender kind. She remembers thinking, many times, *I didn't have to do this after all,* meaning, have a child. She'd always felt, before getting pregnant, that her life would not be complete without a child. But having done it, she frequently thought, *I could have done fine on my own.* Without Rick. Without Angela. With Angela's birth had come great love. But also great fear.

Jane has a revelation: she wishes Angela had never been born. That would solve the problem of the always-on pain. It sounded like the name of a church, Our Lady of Perpetual Pain. It was physical, hitting her right below her rib cage, making it hard for her to breathe, causing her shoulders to cave inward and her body to refuse the commands she was giving it. Walk. Talk. Smile.

Let's get out of here, says Alma abruptly. She takes her hands away from Jane's. Jane suddenly feels cold, unsupported. Alma stands up, pushes her chair back. *Let's do this beach walk.*

Where did you park? Jane asks when they exit the café. Her own motorbike is right next to the door.

I didn't. Edward dropped me off. I thought I could catch a ride with you back.

It doesn't matter. Jane gestures toward her bike. *This will get us there. It's only two miles to the beach.*

Can we both ride on that? Alma asks. She looks doubtful, but not nervous, Jane is glad to see. A nervous rider on a small motorbike is always problematic.

No problem. We aren't going far.

Jane straddles the motorbike, then, still standing, gestures to Alma. *Okay, get on.* Alma swings her leg over the back and sits down.

You settled? Jane calls over her right shoulder.

All ready!

Jane sits down. She can feel Alma's hands around her waist, her knees touching the outside of Jane's thighs. Jane hasn't been this physically close to another human being for more than a year. When was the last time? When her sister Dolores had tried to hug her, at the airport in Tulsa, after their mother died. The touch then had been so poisonous that people had stared at the violence with which she'd thrown off Dolores's arms. But now, no revulsion. Instead, warmth. And what was that? Comfort? Jane is being held, her whole body in the protection of another's.

Let's go, Alma says. The words tickle, so close is Alma's mouth to Jane's ear. Alma's cheek must be almost touching Jane's hair.

Jane turns the key. The motorbike hums to life, and they take off. At first Jane drives slowly, conscious of the need to balance with this new, foreign weight on back. But as she gains confidence, she speeds up. They leave town, merge onto Route 1 going south. Gas stations and Mexican restaurants flash by. Jane turns right on Hawkins, on the access road that leads to a small beach, protected by high cliffs, one that only the locals know about.

Jane stops at the end of the road, right at the top of the cliffs. Sixty feet below, waves crash. There isn't a cloud in the sky, but the wind is strong, blowing easterly from the ocean to the land. The sun is edging toward the horizon in the west — in this case, the blue line where the sea meets the sky. Jane notices this. She notices the gulls circling overhead, their raucous calls that echo across the expanse of water and sand below. Alma's arms are still around her waist. *So this is what it's like to feel normal,* Jane thinks. *This is what other people experience every day.*

Cut across here! Alma shouts against the wind. She gestures to a footpath that meanders alongside the sea, along the top of the cliffs. A sign proclaims: NO MOTORIZED VEHICLES. DOGS MUST BE KEPT ON LEASHES.

Jane points to the sign. *I don't want to get in trouble,* she calls back.

No one is here!

I'm not good at breaking rules, Jane shouts over the wind and motor. By which she

154

means that when she transgresses, she gets caught, always, and is punished accordingly. Angela being taken away from her was such a punishment. Jane had wondered why for nearly a year now. What had she done to deserve that? But today she knows. She had had the audacity to be happy. Not all the time. Not even most of the time. But she had experienced happiness in her life. And that was against God's plan.

Jane turns the motorbike off.

So what if it's against the rules? Alma asks. The words come out too loud in the sudden silence.

The air is fresh and salty. The sky a dark blue. The sun is closer to the horizon, a big orange ball. Jane's face and neck are cold from the breeze, but she is still warmed by Alma's body.

Come on, girl! shouts Alma suddenly. She presses her arms tighter around Jane's waist. Jane turns the motorbike back on, lets out the clutch and steps on the gas, noses the front tire onto the paved path. First slowly, then faster. It is spectacular. They are so close to the edge of the sea that one missed curve would send them shooting out and down into the water, which is frigid this time of year. Jane feels the excitement deep in her belly.

Faster!

Jane obeys. She wishes she had her goggles on, her eyes are tearing up from the chill wind. But she doesn't want to stop. She navigates around a rock, comes close to the edge of the cliff, then steers her way back to the pathway. Her heart is beating too fast, her breath is jagged.

Then, trouble ahead. A lone pedestrian, accompanied by a small dog. Off leash, of course. No one obeys that rule. An elderly man, bundled up against the wind, shakes his finger at them as they race past, and they both laugh. Jane is laughing! She astonishes herself. The dog barks as they whoosh by.

They cross a bridge over a ravine only to find the paved path ends. A bumpy dirt trail continues along the cliff tops. Jane slows to a stop, idles the engine. A grove of eucalyptus trees is bending almost double in the wind. A bench sits at the very edge of the cliff. It must have once been a safe distance back, but the cliffs have eroded, and a huge chunk of ground almost directly under the bench has recently fallen. The earth is still red and raw from where it shuddered off. Spidery cracks stretch out in the dirt from where the cement base of the bench was once solidly in the ground. One foot of the bench hovers over empty air, sixty feet above the water.

A yellow tape printed with CAUTION DO NOT CROSS has been wound around the trees, blocking access to the bench. A small hand-lettered laminated sign says DANGER — ERODING CLIFFS.

Come on, says Alma, and Jane doesn't hesitate to obey her this time. They dismount from the bike. Alma leads the way to the edge of the cliff. She steps over the yellow tape and slowly, carefully, sidles over to the bench. Jane follows behind her, step by cautious step. Waves dash into rocks below. A child playing on a finger of beach gets angry at something, throws a handful of sand at another child, and runs away. Her voice as indistinguishable as the cry of the gulls.

Jane hates Ferris wheels, roller coasters, anything that dangles her above empty space. Yet here she is. They climb onto the bench from the right side, from where it is still solidly planted in the earth. The back left foot is cemented into rock, giving Jane confidence. But the front left foot of the bench rests on nothing. Their feet hang unsupported in space. Jane can feel the updraft from the water sixty feet below cooling her ankles. Alma has her hand again.

Just breathe, Alma says, and Jane obeys

again. In. Out. In. Out. She realizes she is doing this in sync with the breaking of the waves below. They are too high for the spray to reach them, but the noise is deafening.

That's good! says Alma. *Keep it up.* She reaches her left arm up and around Jane's shoulder. Jane feels herself leaning forward, drawn toward the hypnotic whitecaps below.

The reason Jane hates heights is that they rob her of her free will. She is strangely drawn to edges. She knows she would throw herself off bridges, jump off cliffs, step off narrow paths on steep mountains if she let herself get too close. It would be irresistible. So she usually stays away. More than that, she grows dizzy with fear when near a precipice. Too much temptation. She feels that now. The inexorable draw. The tingle in her fingers and toes. She moves an inch forward on the bench. Now her knees are over the abyss. Alma removes her arm from Jane's shoulders. She places her hand flat against Jane's neck. It is slight, but it is pressure. It would be so easy. So easy. Another half-inch forward. Jane wiggles her toes. Her right shoe, always a little loose, comes away at the heel. She wiggles her foot some more. Now the only things holding her shoe on are her toes. She gives a little kick and the shoe falls. She counts *one two three four five six* before she sees it bounce off a rock into the foamy water below. The kick has some-how unbalanced her, and the pressure against her neck continues. She is on the edge. She is wavering. What should she do? Her now-naked foot is cold, sending shivers up her leg. She feels something like arousal. This is foreplay. This is nothing compared to what the real thing will feel like.

Hey!

Both Jane and Alma turn their heads. A man is standing by the scooter. He is wear-ing a uniform. A badge on his chest. He has a pad in one hand and a pencil in the other. A ticket. Jane is getting a ticket. *Busted again.*

Get down from there this instant! Don't you know how dangerous these cliffs are? We lost a kid last month who went too near the edge. It collapsed under him.

Alma edges off the bench first, then, when she is on solid ground, holds out a hand to Jane, who gingerly slides over. She feels like she has woken from a trance. What had she been thinking? She looks back at the bench, at its front left foot hovering in air, and shudders. She walks, unsteadily because of her missing shoe, over to the ranger.

He is silent as they approach. Jane imag-ines they must appear a strange couple, their hair in disarray from the wind and the ride. She knows her face must show how high she is, how pumped up on adrenaline, almost beyond endurance. She needs to scream, to let something out, but somehow holds it in.

Officer, we're sorry, Jane says finally, not because she is, but to break the silence. She is vaguely conscious that there is going to be a scene, a script to be followed. She must get a grip.

"Have you been drinking?" the ranger asks. He is young, younger than either of them. He is extremely serious. He is not acting as if he caught them with an off-leash dog. Jane herself isn't sure what just transpired. The ranger steps forward and looks straight into her eyes. He is sniffing, for some trace of alcohol or pot, she supposes.

We're sober, she says, although she knows her eyes tell a different story. The ranger looks at her for a moment, hesitating.

I should take you in for a sobriety test, he says finally.

For being crazy? Alma speaks up. She is composed, even smiling.

The ranger looks at Alma, at her glowing face, and his official face relaxes a little. He reluctantly smiles back. *I should,* he says. But the moment for punishment has somehow passed. They're going to get away with it. He puts his pen and pad back in his pocket.

Still, I'm interested, he says. *Why?*

My friend here was trying to satisfy her curiosity about something, says Alma, and takes Jane's arm. Jane feels warm at the words *my friend.* Then, secondarily, a sense of relief. So that's what she'd been doing! Nothing that bad. Just satisfying her curiosity. It sounded wholesome, even, like something you could earn a Girl Scout badge for.

So she sits on the edge of an eroding cliff? the ranger asks. *Right. That makes perfect sense.*

Sometimes it's necessary to force a decision, says Alma.

Do you agree? asks the ranger, turning to Jane.

Jane thinks back. The wind on her naked foot. The tingle of arousal. Alma's hand pressuring her neck forward.

You came at an opportune time, Jane says finally.

And if I hadn't come?

A decision would have been made, Jane says.

The ranger looks at her.

As you can see, I'm not going to write a

ticket, he says. *But I'm going to recommend very strongly that you get some help.*

Jane links arms even more tightly with Alma, drawing strength from the other woman's solidity and the feel of warm flesh on her own.

Thank you for your concern, she says. *But I think I have all the help I need.*

We know what we are, but not what we might be. Jane's favorite quote from *Hamlet* when she was an undergraduate, because she found it so apropos of her life. She'd be going off in one direction, then suddenly shift due to nothing more than chance or whim. Jane frequently never knew *what she might be* from day to day. Her relationship with Rick before he left, a case in point. Her relationship with Angela, another. Was she a good wife? A good mother? A bad one? Yes, and yes, and no. Depending on the hour, even the minute, the category she fell into changed. And now Alma and Edward. What lay ahead? Who would she be? Jane didn't know.

■ ■ ■ ■

PART II
TRESPASSES

■ ■ ■ ■

Adam drinks his caffeine-free tea like the connoisseur he is. He buys it in a specialty vegan store down in Santa Cruz. No animals have been harmed in the making of this tea. No humans have been exploited. He keeps it in a special tin in the break room. It looks like a child's tiny treasure chest: dark blue with rockets and spaceships and planets on it in glorious reds and yellows and greens. The tea itself comes in individually wrapped cloth bags, like those in jewelry shops. He always pours the hot water into his cup first, then dips the tea into it. He wouldn't despoil it with milk or sugar. He sips at it all morning, it must be stone cold by noon when he takes in the last dregs, but the expression on his face as he swallows the last of it is as ecstatic as with the first taste.

Adam's been trying to get Jane's attention all day. He's been walking by her station in the back greenhouse, offering her, in sequence, some of his foul tea, a banana, a handful of raisins, and the last wild bluebell of the season. The flowers apparently blanket the ground to the rear of the warehouse every summer, under the live oaks, he says. He paces back and forth in front of her station in the greenhouse. He's like a dog spoiling for a walk. *What is it?* Jane finally asks. He's silent for a moment, standing in the doorway of the greenhouse, his blond hair sparkling in the filtered sunlight. He looks like a holy innocent. *Nothing, man, really,* he says. *You look nice today.*

Adam is in superb shape, his hair is thick and bleached by the sun, and he wears it down to his shoulders, typically in a ponytail but sometimes loose. He uses tons of sunscreen so he doesn't have any lines on his face.

Madonna and Jesus, Helen liked to call them, and indeed, Jane felt toward Adam matronly in a safe way. He was male, and he was younger and not particularly vulnerable so he didn't suck her in, he triggered no emotions except a mild distant fondness. He was very safe.

Come here, he says. *Smell this.* And she sniffs at the leaves of the flower he is holding. Delight! Calmness!

Aromatherapy, Adam says. *It's very real.*

■ ■ ■ ■

Jane had sought all the details of what exactly had happened to Angela that day last July. She had to know. Because Angela was her baby. There had been a time when Angela couldn't poop without Jane's awareness. No rash appeared on that tender flesh that Jane didn't rush to apply lotion to or call the doctor about, even.

Angela used to get what Jane figured were medium-bad headaches and would lie in her bed with a cold towel over her forehead, moaning. *Don't be a drama queen,* Jane would tell her. Jane wondered how Angela had handled real pain when it arrived. She had to wonder because she would never know.

Jane's shrink, Dr. Blanes — one of a long line of shrinks, Jane was crunching them up as if they were candy — told her to get out of her head, to go through the motions, that the mental would follow the physical. Jane had to stand in front of the mirror every morning and smile. Stretch her lips upward and crinkle her eyes and smile warmly in the mirror. She was forced to watch a YouTube video on the power of smiling, in which a twentysomething who had absolutely nothing on his mind except the millions of dollars his start-up was going to make threw stats at the audience. Smiling boosts your immune system. You work harder to frown than to smile. Jane gets up this morning and tries smiling in the mirror. She looks hideous. She does not feel happier.

Jane has ways of coping. Xanax. Clonazepam. Other substances she gets through a Canadian online pharmacy. They have the desired effect — they dull her senses, dull the pain — anything to not feel.

It was nothing, really. Just an old garden trowel. *Old* being the operative word. Jane had had it since she was an undergraduate intern at the Berkeley Botanical Gardens. Slightly larger than a standard hand trowel, with a wooden handle that had worn away to fit Jane's right hand precisely over the years. It had an edge to it that plunged into the earth at exactly the right angle. She kept it sharp, taking it to the local hardware store for sharpening at least once a season. Originally green, the metal had faded and chipped and scratched and rusted so that it was now an indeterminate color. Jane kept it in her cubbyhole at work, along with her gloves and hand lotion and other miscellaneous items.

Then one day it is gone. Jane of course thinks she must have left it somewhere in the nursery, although she's a rather rigid everything-in-its-place kind of person. But she can't find it anywhere. No one understands why she can't go into the back room and pick from virtually every type of garden implement that existed. Jane tries, she really does.

She goes around asking everyone if they'd seen it. She even attempts to draw a picture of it and pins it to the employee bulletin board. She remembers a book Angela had loved when she was small, when a baby duck wandered around asking various objects *Are you my mother?* Angela loved it when the duck asked a power shovel the question. *No, I am not your mother, I'm a SNORT,* it said.

Have you seen my trowel? Jane feels like an infant, but she is lost without it. No one has.

Her anxiety grows. She goes to the Feed and Grain to look for another and finds one that is somewhat similar, but it isn't old and it doesn't fit her hand well. A trowel is an intimate tool. She imagines that doctors might feel the same way about their instruments. You use it to plunge down into earth, soft or hard, to dig out the little holes to contain the tiny plants, to pat over the earth on top or around the stems.

Nothing goes right. She overwaters her California lilac (*Ceanothus*) and they are wilting; she isn't sure if they can be saved. She forgets to fertilize the succulents, and they are refusing to grow. What else can go wrong?

The days that follow grow worse and worse. The nursery becomes a different place. Less safe. Jane starts putting her stuff in her motorbike bag and taking it home at night. She finds herself looking over her shoulder. She feels violated. Panicky. What else will be taken from her? She takes to locking her cottage. Why would the loss of a trowel unsettle her so much? Because of course she is already unsettled. It will take very little to go from unsettled to unhinged.

She goes out for a motorbike ride to clear her head. She rides up to the top of the hill to the cemetery and sits on the promontory that looks down over the coast. You can see the entire coast. When she scattered her daughter's ashes, Angela's best friends had insisted on coming along and helping. Jane gave them the urn and watched them running up and down the beach, throwing handfuls of Angela into the bay. Rick was there of course, in body. He exerted a great deal of effort not meeting Jane's eyes. His new girlfriend, Clara, was also there, looking defiant. Jane would have liked a hand to hold, even one so ambivalent as Rick's. But she had no one.

Coming back, she parks next to Adam's Volvo. She can see his wet suit and his towel and the surf board through the back window. Then Jane does a double take: next to his wet suit is her trowel. No doubt about it. Lying there, still with some earth on it, on its side. Not even hidden from view.

Jane opens the rear hatchback — Adam never locks it — and steals it back. She is so angry!

What was this about? She confronts Adam in the back room.

He flushes a deep red that contrasts sharply with his blond hair.

Jane. Jane. I'm so sorry.

I asked you if you'd seen it! You said no!

I know, I know.

Again, Adam: What was this about? He can't meet her eyes. This is not the Adam she knows.

I wanted something of yours.

Something of mine?

Something you'd touched. Something that

had your vibe on it.

This should have softened her, but instead it makes her angrier. She is tired of things being taken from her. Things she values. Things she loves.

Something shifts between them. Something that can't be undone. Trust? Had she trusted him? She had, and she hadn't realized it.

She turns and leaves without a word. Two things had been taken from her, one she hadn't known she'd valued. And that was something she could never get back, unlike her trowel. Something lovely has been smashed.

The Pumpkin Festival opens. Jane wakes up early on Saturday, is at work by 6:00 a.m. By 8:00 a.m. — they opened early for the three days — Smithson's is swamped. At noon she is given a short break and takes a quick ride on her motorbike into town. She is curious.

Goats! Lambs! Rabbits! Elephants! Yes, elephants. Kids are being taken for rides on them. Straw and elephant dung cover Main Street. The wine stands are doing a brisk business, and soon plastic cups will be strewn everywhere.

The police are out in force. Walking

around with their guns in full view, carefully examining the crowds, singling out the older men, the solitary males, especially the ones dressed on the shabby side.

This is Jane's first Pumpkin Festival. These sorts of festivities were becoming the norm in Northern California, each town claiming a vegetable or fruit to build a revenue-generating carnival out of. Garlic Festival. Artichoke Festival. But the Pumpkin Festival has been going on for nearly a hundred years, when the farmers would gather together, pool their resources, and attract people to Half Moon Bay to witness the contest for the largest pumpkin grown that year. The spectacle of a giant pumpkin — larger than the average horse and buggy — was enough to justify the half-day's journey over the hill at that time.

Wine is drunk. Pumpkins are picked up, examined, either rejected and put back on the ground or placed in a red wagon. The pumpkins can be quite large — forty-pounders, some of them; they can't be easily moved, need two men to hoist them into the wagons. Artichoke soup is consumed by the gallon. Pumpkin bread, pumpkin pie, pumpkin ice cream, even pumpkin perfume are all available. Most of the decorations are for Halloween, but some are for Thanksgiving. Some of the stores even have Christmas lights. Lines are out the door of all the restaurants. Farmers cut paths through their cornfields to create mazes for people to get lost in, charging five dollars to enter. The weather cooperates: it is warm, no wind, clear skies, the ocean as blue as Jane has ever seen it.

The winner of the pumpkin contest is an organic farmer from Bonny Doon. An orange monstrosity that weighs more than twelve hundred pounds. Bigger than a Volkswagen Beetle, it sits in the middle of Main Street on a pile of straw. People gawk.

Except for that brief half-hour on the first day, Jane is needed in the greenhouse every opening minute of the three-day festival. She advises couples from Palo Alto and Menlo Park that, no, the seaside daisies (*Erigeron glaucus*) that bloom so profusely in Carmel and Monterey will not thrive in the sunnier and drier midpeninsula. She tells people from San Francisco to forget the *Celosia spicata,* that they need dry soil and full sun. The nursery staff doesn't even have a chance to eat lunch, they are so busy. Helen orders pizzas and leaves them in the break room for the staff to grab slices when they can. Adam has brought a bag lunch: dolphin-free tuna with sprouts on brown bread, but Jane gladly devours three pieces of pepperoni pizza.

To everyone's surprise, the Pumpkin Festival is a success. Cars are parked illegally all over the place, backed up Route 84 to the top of the hill by the cemetery. All the stores are doing a smashing business, Smithson's Nursery included. The parking lot overflows into a neighboring field. People are buying *alstromerias, phloxes.* Anything with fall colors — reds, oranges, bronzes — is being snapped up. Leashes sell out at the Feed and Grain, and little girls being held by them are spotted all over town.

As it turns out, at least part of the success is due to the tragedies of the dead girls. The visitors are insatiable for news. *What about those two girls?* they ask, after pretending interest in a bush or flowering shrub. Or: *Who do you think did it?*

Girls up to ten years old are on leashes or are being held firmly by the hand. Boys are allowed to run wild.

Jane watches one rebellious girl — a redhead, like Jane, who was probably five years old — repeatedly slip her leash. *Why? Why? Why?* the girl keeps yelling. *Why not him?* pointing to her younger brother who is running free. Jane is curious to see what the parents will say, so she leans close.

Because I love you better than him, she hears the mother say, pulling the little girl close, and whispering. *Because you are my heart.*

At the close of the Pumpkin Festival, everyone from town gathers at the VFW Hall on the south side of town to celebrate. Let the festivities begin!

Jane hates parties. She has not been in a room with this many people since Angela's memorial service at St. Mary Magdalene's in Berkeley last September. Rick's choice, even though neither had attended Mass for decades and certainly hadn't brought Angela up in the church. A mockery. The empty words of the priest, who hadn't known Angela from any other teenager on the street. *We shall miss our sister in Christ.* The saccharine pop-like songs the organist chose with lyrics that could easily be crooned in a nightclub:

You are my desire
No one else will do

What's wrong with Bach? Purcell? Jane bows her head so others can't read her face, so they'll think she is praying with the rest

176

of them. They can't guess her thoughts. How could they? She isn't sure of them herself. She is in a daze. She has been going through the motions. There is no viewing, no casket. Angela has been cremated. Rick was against it, but Jane was firm. Her daughter's mangled body would be purified by the flames. That's how Jane wants her to leave life, not buried in the earth and eaten by worms. Ashes to ashes.

Tonight at the Pumpkin Festival party, the room is hot and pulsing with some ethno-rock music, very loud. People are talking loud, almost screaming, to be heard over it. People are dancing or, because of the crush, simply moving their bodies or swaying to the music. People are almost certainly tipsy, or drunk, even. Someone spills red wine on Jane's shirt. Someone else steps on her toes. This is purgatory. No, it's hell. No redemption possible in a place like this, no matter how much suffering one endures.

What'll you have? asks Adam, who is buzzing around Jane as if she's his prom date. Somewhere, back in a Berkeley storage unit, is Jane's vintage prom dress from the nineties, which she had been saving for Angela. Who was she kidding? Even if she had made it to senior year, Angela wouldn't have worn it. It would have been too traditional for her. She would have gone in a tuxedo or bathing suit or otherwise flouted convention. That was Angela.

Just soda water, please. Even half a glass of chardonnay would put her under. Adam nods and slips easily through the bodies. Jane starts calculating whom she has to talk to, and how long she has to stay, to keep Helen happy, which is important to her. She bumps into Janet Holcomb, the mayor, and shakes her hand.

A success, Jane says, and manages to conjure up a smile. *Against all odds.*

Who would have thought? Our most successful ever. Almost a third more visitors than last year. Some shops sold out of merchandise. I heard that Brinson's took in more than $30,000 with their corn maze alone. Then, lowering her voice, *Maybe we're past it. You know. Maybe* he *has moved on.*

Yes, but the police certainly haven't, Jane says, nodding toward the bar. A group of uniformed policemen and sheriff's deputies are crowded around it. They seem to be off duty, downing beers and laughing. Jane feels a stab of anger. *How dare they?*

Jane sees that Adam has gotten snagged by Julie, the owner of the New Age shop on Clifford that sells crystals and fairies and dream catchers. Julie's color is high and she

178

is holding on to Adam's elbow while she chatters on. His face doesn't portray anything but his usual good nature as he smiles down at the young woman, who is patently drunk and a known bore with her dream interpretations and astrology predictions. Jane is surprised to see such patient restraint. Perhaps it's not empty-headedness after all that makes Adam Adam but genuine kindness. He gently detaches himself and, after negotiating his way through the crowd, reaches Jane with her drink. She gets only one sip before it's knocked out of her hand, soaking her jeans. Adam looks stricken.

Hold on, he says, and turns and starts pushing his way back to the bar.

She deliberates whether she's going to wait for him to come back. The crush is suffocating. The heat is causing Jane to sweat; she can feel the water trickling down the back of her neck. Her jeans are damp, and so is her shirt. As is usual on a working day, she's pulled her hair back in a bun, but she can feel strands escaping, sticking damply to her forehead and neck and down her collar. This is truly intolerable. Jane makes up her mind. She heads for the door.

Jane realizes she is searching for Edward as she maneuvers through the crowd. She hadn't been alone with him since the evening at the yacht club, although she'd seen him about town, absorbed in YourBeaches business. She'd assumed he'd come to the party, with or without Alma, since he had thrown himself into the festivities with such fervor. He'd even volunteered to take charge of the raffle for the romantic weekend at the Shorebird Inn. Although she notices that it certainly served his purpose, as he had a stack of YourBeaches.org brochures in his bag, and was cajoling people to write down their names and email addresses as he sold them raffle tickets.

Jane is disinclined to think about the episode at the yacht club. She puts it out of her mind, frequently.

Jane finds herself stymied ten feet from the door. Too many people coming in, it's impossible to push against them. The room is getting hotter as even more people crowd into the space. But the mood is jovial. The town seems to have shaken off its grim mood. A voice at her ear startles her.

They forget quickly, don't they? Edward, wearing a black shirt and jeans and holding a beer.

Although Jane agrees, she decides she doesn't want to align herself with him too easily. She worries where that might lead.

The two girls were from over-the-hill families,

not locals, she says. *It'd be a different matter if they were truly our girls.*

Our girls? So you consider yourself a full-fledged member of the community now? He is smiling that smile that is so difficult to resist, so warm and full of concern. Jane had looked up the definition of the word *compassion* after her last encounter with Edward: *a feeling of deep sympathy and sorrow for another who is stricken by misfortune, accompanied by a strong desire to alleviate the suffering.* Is she really so obviously *stricken by misfortune?*

Edward is standing uncomfortably close, but then everyone is uncomfortably close. Jane can feel his breath on her forehead, is aware of his hands at the ends of his arms, which are attached to his shoulders. Jane has always had a thing about men's shoulders. His dark eyes unfathomable. That smile. Other women are looking, noticing. It's that kind of town.

Where's Alma?

He doesn't back off.

Faculty meeting. She can't get out of them even though she's only adjunct.

Adam finally finds her, holding up a roll of paper towels to indicate his successful foraging. He hands it to her from the rear, over her shoulder, as he can't get any closer, with Edward dominating. She is virtually sandwiched between the two men. The crowd presses them even closer together. Edward doesn't seem to be fighting it. He puts his left hand, the one not holding the beer, on Jane's right shoulder, as if to steady himself against the crowd. Adam, however, is managing to keep three inches of air between himself and Jane. Again, Jane thinks, *He is kind.*

Jane is not comfortable with this. She finds her anxiety level rising, the same kind of anxiety that she used to feel about Angela. What is happening? What is expected of her?

Edward leans even closer. His grip on Jane's shoulder tightens. His lips against her ear, he breathes, *I've been thinking about you.*

Jane can feel the flush start in her chest and move up through her neck and face. She knows her cheeks are almost as red as her hair. But a wild excitement has also taken hold, replacing the anxiety and making her feel reckless. She is not thinking about what others think. For once, she is not thinking of Angela. She looks up, forces herself to look directly in Edward's eyes. The pulsing music is making her head ache. She sees only the same understanding and acceptance that she's always seen, which belies the kind of restless energy that permeates the rest of his body.

Let's get out of here.

She's sure that's what he says. But the crush is suffocating. The heat is causing her armpits to sweat; she can feel the water trickling down her face. She has forgotten about Adam, she has forgotten about anything except this sense of fierce angry longing. Why anger? *Why not?* she thinks.

Then a voice from behind her.

Are you cool to leave, Jane? I think we've put in our appearance. No one will notice if we scram. Adam. It's like a splash of cold water. Edward lifts his hand from her shoulder as she twists around to face Adam. His face is as inscrutably good-natured, even goofy, as ever, but something in the set of his jaw makes Jane take him very seriously at this moment. *You seem a little on edge,* Adam continues. *Let me push a path out of here for you.*

Jane doesn't know whether to laugh or cry. She decides to cry. Or rather, it is decided for her. She puts her hands on Adam's shoulders as he pushes through the crowd, making a way for her to escape out the door as the tears stream down her face.

Then suddenly it's all over. Business at the

nursery falls off a cliff on the Monday after the Pumpkin Festival ends. The beginning of the nursery's fallow period, until after Christmas. Schedules become more normalized. Restless, Jane earns extra money by working for Tucci's to clean up after the excesses of the Pumpkin Festival. They have one of the largest pumpkin crops in the area. Everyone takes the Pumpkin Festival seriously because it's serious money. But Tucci's brings in large blow-up bouncing castles and ponies for rides and a cider-and-hot-dog stand. Rather than simply picking the pumpkins and leaving them in a great pile the way the other farms did, Tucci's harvests the pumpkins, mows the field, and replaces the pumpkins in the field, as if they were still growing there. Now the remains have to be gathered up and sent in trucks to the Central Valley, where they will be distributed to the local stores to sell for Halloween.

It is near the end of a long day. Jane helps pick up the remains of the ten- and twelve-pound pumpkins, placing them in the truck that moves slowly down the field. It is like a scene from a Flemish painting — harvesters in the waning sunlight, the orange and brown colors warmed by the setting sun.

Jane sees Edward before he sees her. He's

parked the silver Mercedes at the top of the drive and walked into the field, carefully scanning all the pumpkin pickers. Then he sees her, and something changes in his face, although Jane couldn't have said what. Something changes in her too, she sees from his expression. Satisfaction. It all seems foretold. Like it already happened centuries ago — the rich orange against the brown fields, the deep blue sky, and the bright colors of the harvesters' clothes, even the truck idling in the field seems inevitable. Painted and hanging in a museum. Jane finds herself blushing. She bends over to wrestle another giant pumpkin and hoist it into the truck. Her hands are dirty; she wipes them on her jeans and stands there awkwardly as Edward approaches. She foolishly holds out her right hand. He's also wearing jeans and the inevitable T-shirt. By the time he reaches his hand out to touch hers, it's a done deal.

Jane.

Edward.

They simply look at each other for a moment. Then, *Hard work,* he says, pointing to the pile of pumpkins in the truck.

I would have thought red and orange would clash, but in fact it's lovely, he says, pointing to Jane's hair, which is tightly braided into a bun at the back of her neck. *But you should wear it loose,* he says.

In this weather? I'd die of heat.

Then let's go someplace cool, he says. They both know what he's saying.

I'm working, Jane says.

Doing penance.

Of course he's right. Jane has been counting the pumpkins, picking them up in sets of ten and stopping after each set to pause and drink in the scene. The colors, the mild breeze, the softening light — all rewards for her hard work.

On impulse, Jane tells Edward that.

A pumpkin rosary, he says, and takes Jane's dirty hand in his again, this time to lead her out of the field and into the silver Mercedes parked off the side of 92. Jane doesn't care who sees, who knows. She leaves her motorbike parked in the field next to the outhouses. It'll still be there when she returns.

There is a sweetness to making love to a man who belongs to another. Taking a bite of someone else's food while they're not looking, finding it delicious. For delicious it is. Jane is still under the spell of the pumpkins and dazzled again by the colors, now muted in the shadows of her darkened bedroom. Shades of brown so slightly differentiated, brown of hair, of eyes, tawny shoulders, the black chest hair, always hidden from Jane before and therefore much more dear. Everything precious, a gift. And what has Jane to offer? Her visibly altered mental state. *It must be gratifying,* she thinks, *to have this effect on someone else.*

Afterward, at dusk, they walk down to Mavericks Beach. Jane points out the soap plants, half of them already in bloom. The leaves of the soap plant don't get far above the ground, so when the plant begins to produce its six-foot stalk, it is a dramatic announcement of things to come. When the flowers appear, they are worth the wait.

The show begins at the time when dusk disappears into night. The flower buds are elongated striped ovals like small beans. From a distance, they look like feathers in the soft evening light. Up close, the curve of the petals, the shape of the flower parts, and the color of the stamens are sinuous, alluring. There's no point picking them. The flowers fade by morning.

Edward and Jane stand and watch as a flower opens up in front of their eyes. It takes four minutes. Jane thinks this memory will give her pleasure for years to come.

How can Jane describe her attachment to the native flora of California? The state flower of Oklahoma is mistletoe (*Phoraden-*

dron serotinum), the oldest of Oklahoma's symbols. The dark green leaves and white berries show up brightly during the fall and winter in trees that have shed their own leaves.

Jane doesn't like mistletoe. She doesn't like the prickly leaves, the waxy berries, the tradition. For it was always used cruelly in Jane's house. Mistletoe held above a special-needs boy who had a crush on her, so Jane was forced to endure a sloppy kiss. Worse, mistletoe held above the head of the boy she really liked, being forced to watch what he felt while kissing her. Why make mistletoe the state flower? Oklahoma had a bitter but beautiful weed, broomweed, and black-eyed Susans enough to carpet the world. Yet mistletoe it is.

Oklahoma to Jane was flat, surrounded by nothingness, broken by spindly trees, the weak springs that slurred into the stifling summers. In California, Jane could look into the distance and see things: land eruptions and abruptions, the sea in its scale and majesty.

Jane had never witnessed majestic, small or large, in her childhood, certainly nothing like what she experiences tonight watching the soap plants bloom with Edward.

Then they go back to her house, shed their

clothing, and make love again until dawn.

How Jane longs for Edward once he is gone! She sits naked on the kitchen floor, stunned with what has transpired. The cold of the linoleum shocks her bare thighs but not enough. No shock could mitigate what has just happened. She lets only a little piece into her mind at a time, lest she be over-whelmed. His hand stroking her thigh. Her arms roped to his chest. Hurried breathing. Jane doesn't let herself think of how she stroked his face and lips. The betrayal was in that. All else could be blamed on lust. But the kissing committed the ultimate treachery. They didn't speak throughout. How could they?

Jane now gets up to prepare something to eat. She realizes she hasn't eaten all day. She shells peas, noting this time how she automatically counts out ten pods, releasing the green globules from each one into a bowl. And then pausing before gathering the next handful of ten pods. She realizes what she lost when Rick left. How the act of love is so addictive that we crave touch to the point of desperation. It's a human need. She had needed to feel human again. That's what Rick's betrayal and Angela's death had taken from her, and that's what she lost until Edward gave it back.

The next morning begins a day of accounting and self-loathing. She calls a cab and takes it to the pumpkin field where she left her motorbike. At first it won't start. Then, with a cloud of smoke, it fires. It buckles and snorts as she rides it to Smithson's. Dogs bark, cats screech, plants wither, the sun darkens as she passes. By the time she gets to the nursery, fatigued and bleary-eyed, customers are already lining up in her native-plants room seeking guidance on what to purchase. *What to kill,* Jane thinks, hatefully. Adam is trying to fake it, but he is telling one couple that yes, they could plant *Fremontodendron* under their pine trees. Helen does not look pleased.

Jane makes herself a cup of Adam's foul tea and drinks it down, fast. She spends the next hour explaining to various loathsome people why flowers that require partial shade will not flourish in their sunny front yard and that bushes that need sun will not blossom when overshadowed half the day by a large eucalyptus tree. She scorns every asker of every question and hates her own need to ridicule. *Let me forget with generosity those who cannot love me,* Pablo Neruda's poem, her closest thing to a serenity prayer, but it isn't working today.

What is Jane's problem? Simple. She desires something that isn't hers: Edward. She does not want to compete with Alma. She'd had enough of that with her sisters. Now she shrinks from competition with other women as if from poison. It is toxic to her system.

She makes and drinks another cup of tea and busies herself in her work. The soft soil is warm as she presses the shoots into their new pots.

Hey, what's up? Adam, of course.

Jane straightens up and brushes her hands on her pants. She manages a weak smile.

Nothing.

Ah, man, come on. You can tell me. Adam perches on a trestle near the table where Jane has put her now-cold tea. He flashes his engaging smile.

And, surprisingly, Jane finds she can. Not the details, of course. But the broader outlines.

I have this thing going, she tells him.

Thing?

You know. With a guy.

Adam's expression doesn't noticeably change. Yet something has.

Serious? he asks. Jane gets the impression her answer is important.

It depends on what you mean by serious, she says. She is careful to pat the damp earth around the delicate green wisps just right.

Does it have a good prognosis?

Jane considers. Prognosis means future. A future? No. There is no way to think of this except in the present. It is what it is. There's no looking forward. There's no looking back.

No, she says. *There is no prognosis.*

Adam looks a little puzzled, but with a slightly brighter look, he continues.

I haven't heard of a problem yet.

Yes. Well. This person . . . is not exactly unattached.

Adam nods. *It happens, man. It happens.*

And I feel . . . Jane pauses.

Guilty? Adam supplies.

No. Of this Jane is certain. So what is it?

It excites me, she says. *And I'm ashamed of that.*

The thrill of the chase.

No, Jane says again. She shakes her head. *Taking something away from another woman. I want to do it. Like I said, it excites me. Yet it's like pulling out my own heart. And eating it.*

Adam has to think about this. *I'm no shrink,* he begins.

But you're going to give me some advice anyway, Jane says, and smiles for the first time this morning. The thought of Adam in a chair, in an enclosed space, sitting for hours listening to people parade out their paltry woes. Now *that* was funny.

Yeah. I am. He's silent for a moment.

I was in this relationship. She was an amazing person. I mean that. Yet it turned out that she was only in it because her best friend was sweet on me. We all got high one night, and it came out. And at first I was appalled. Because, you know, what kind of person would deliberately hurt someone they said they loved? Then I saw it differently. Maybe it was the weed. But I saw that my girlfriend was really to be pitied. She wasn't trying to take something away from her friend; she was trying to be her friend. If imitation is the highest form of flattery, then she was flattering her friend to the skies. I think she longed to feel something herself, like what her friend was feeling. Liking someone else. Adam blushed a little. *Loving someone. So she faked it with me, hoping it would become real. But her real issue was with her friend.*

Jane has busied herself in her work while he talks. She finds she doesn't want to think about what he has said.

I don't think that's the case here, Jane says.

193

She stands up. Silly her. To think Adam would have answers. She thinks of Edward's head on her pillow, the crook of his arm. She had bent over and kissed it in the early morning, before he woke up. An object of beauty, that arm.

Do you know the other person involved?

Yes, Jane says. She is impatient for this conversation to be over. She does not want to discuss Alma. There is nothing to discuss. She doesn't want to be Alma, adulteress, abandoner of children. No matter how beautiful or accomplished, nothing will change those facts.

Jane. Jane had been so lost in her own thoughts that she hadn't noticed that Adam had moved, was now standing right beside her.

I just want to say, whatever you need, I'm here.

His look is not vapid. It is not trivial. Jane cannot scorn this away, no matter the clichéd words. Adam is a real human being, offering her a lifeline.

Jane feels like crying. Ever present, Angela's ghost hovers at the periphery. *See what happens when you forget,* Jane thinks. *See what happens when you try to snatch some happiness for yourself. You can't even do that without bringing pain to someone else.*

■ ■ ■ ■

Days pass. When Jane's doorbell rings at night, it is Edward. Jane takes his jacket, pours him a glass of wine. He winces when he sips — Jane doesn't have the funds for the more expensive labels to which he is apparently accustomed — and stretches out his legs. He has been busy. The Pumpkin Festival was as good for him as everyone else, attracting people into his storefront. He plied hot, thirsty visitors with free bottles of water and foisted on them materials about coastal protection. He has signed up dozens of volunteers, taken in thousands in donations.

So, Jane says one night.

So, he repeats, and smiles. His legs nearly touch the other wall, so small is Jane's living room. He looks around.

How you can live in such a tiny place is beyond me.

It's like living on board a ship, Jane says. *Everything has a place.* The owners had ingeniously fitted up cabinets and closets everywhere for stowing things, and it was in fact like being in a cabin on a luxury cruise. Jane had to be careful, though, or her stuff easily got out of hand.

Everything has its place, Edward agrees. He seems disposed to linger, to talk. The physical urgency is not there tonight, or rather, it's being held at bay, not unpleasantly. *It's nice,* Jane thinks. It makes the affair seem less seedy. Although she doesn't allow herself to linger on the words *affair* or *seedy.* That's not what this is. This is a self-rescue mission. To keep going down and down until the wreckage has been retrieved and can be reconstructed on safe land. Jane is salvage. She turns on the Bach cello suites. Yo-Yo Ma. Bach is as late as she goes in musical time, is as complex and dissonant as she can stand.

Where's Alma tonight?

Over the hill. A seminar by a guest lecturer. Someone she admires, although I couldn't tell you his name. And then a reception.

I hope she's careful coming back over the hill. It can be treacherous, especially on weekends when people have been drinking. Just last weekend, a Half Moon Bay kid — a teenager — was killed after going to a party in Belmont and racing home to make curfew. The couple in the other car, tourists, seriously injured, were helicoptered to Stanford. It seems odd, expressing concern for someone who, technically, is Jane's rival. But Jane somehow doesn't see it that way.

Alma is extremely careful, says Edward. He is not inclined to join Jane in expressing any concern for Alma. Jane takes pleasure in that. He is somehow hers tonight more than other nights, as if Alma is not on the other side of the hill but on the other side of the moon.

I have something for you, Edward says. He pulls a wrapped package out of his pants pocket and tosses, rather than gives, it to Jane. Casual.

Jane opens it and sees it is the bracelet of Alma's that she had admired more than once — green and blue stones set in ceramic patterns that appear vaguely Arabian.

You can't give me this.

Sure I can.

Does Alma know?

It was her idea.

Who is this from, really, then? Is it from you? Or Alma?

Why not say it's from both of us? Would that satisfy you? He doesn't seem perturbed by Jane's response, although he could hardly have expected a different one. As he talks, he is fastening the bracelet on Jane's left arm. It is gorgeous. As she brings it up to her eyes to examine it more closely, she sees that small clear stones are also embedded in it, creating the overall sparkling effect.

What are these stones, these transparent ones? Jane asks. *Are they glass?*

Diamonds, he says. *And the green ones are emeralds.* At Jane's look, Edward laughs. *Yes, it was expensive, but that's not the point. The point is that you admired it, and you're a very difficult person to buy for. So happy birthday.*

Jane is speechless.

How did you know?

That was easy — I looked at your driver's license. I took your wallet from your saddlebag when you were in the kitchen last week, he says. *I had to know. Happy fortieth, Jane.*

For some reason, Jane is made incredibly happy by this. Her phone has been ringing all day, but she has not answered a single call.

I can't accept this, she says. *It's too much. Besides, it's one of Alma's favorite pieces. She told me so herself.*

All the more reason she would want you to have it, Edward says.

Would *want? You mean she doesn't know?* Jane asks. Edward doesn't answer. He simply laughs. *Relax,* he says. *Enjoy it. Enjoy your birthday.* Which leaves them looking at each other.

Then Edward gets up, holds out his hand, and leads Jane into the bedroom just as her phone begins to ring again.

Jane is riding in the silver Mercedes with Edward. It is 9:00 p.m. on Wednesday, so few cars are on Route 1. They are over-heated. They are excited. Tremendously excited. Or — it occurs to Jane — perhaps she should speak only for herself. She is certainly all those things. Edward never shows much. Yet how could Jane tell where he started and she ended? She is in love.

So they're roaring down Route 1. Alma is teaching her night class at Stanford. She won't be back until 11:00 p.m. at the earli-est. So they do the time-honored thing of il-licit lovers: they sneak out. Because people would talk if they saw them together without Alma after the very public scene in the pumpkin field. Jane is trying to be more circumspect. They drive to Pomponio Beach. It is technically closed, but they park in the lot anyway, behind a dumpster. From Route 1 nothing of the car can be seen. Edward is careful about that.

So there are some rules, Jane thinks.

Edward and Jane have sex under cover of the cliffs. Or make love. Or they *do it.* Whatever euphemism serves best. Jane is beyond caring about words. She has brought blankets, one to place on the sand and one to provide cover on top. Although in the end they throw off that top blanket to let the cool sea wind massage their bodies. The waves gleam as they break on the sand. Except for the muffled crash of the surf and the occasional motorist going north or south on Route 1, it is blessedly silent.

On the way back, Edward kills something. An animal. *An entity,* Jane thinks. Not large, but not small either. Edward swerves but doesn't brake. Jane turns around to look at the black lump in the dark road.

Consider it a sacrifice to the gods, Edward says.

Why do they need a sacrifice?

To atone for our transgressions.

I didn't realize that's what we were doing.

Edward reaches out and strokes Jane's hair — always the hair! — and says, *But of course we are. Why do you think it's so good?*

Jane cannot speak for a moment. *Black Heart.* She rolls down the window to feel the sea air on her face, breathe in deeply.

Of course there's a way to find out, he says.

Find out what?

If it's a transgression or something else that makes this so exciting. You seem to think it's something else, that the clandestine nature isn't the stimulating factor.

The fact that it has to be kept secret has

nothing to do with how I feel.

Edward doesn't speak for a few moments. Then he says, in the most reasonable and grown-up of voices: *There's certainly a way to test out that theory.* His tone is cool, almost scientific.

Jane's elation is dissipating so fast that she is dizzy. What is happening?

What's that? Jane is afraid to know.

We can tell Alma.

Tell Alma? Jane can't control her voice, it comes out in a shriek.

Yes.

Tell her what?

That we've been sleeping together. Jane notes his euphemism of choice. It's the most benign one of all. As if they had been cuddling in flannel pajamas. *We can see if she minds.* Edward is not avoiding looking at Jane. The opposite, in fact. But there is an appraisal in his glance, as if he's not looking at a human but a thing. Jane sees desire in his eyes. No, she sees something else. He wants her, she can tell. But what does that mean?

Any rational response Jane could have had dries up.

If she minds, she says.

Yes.

You bastard, she says, but to her astonish-

201

ment a flicker of . . . what? Is it hope? Ignites within her. She realizes she can't see the end of this. She realizes she is only at the beginning. She sees she is caught. The physicality of her desire for Edward stuns Jane. His face is perfect, as are his neck, his shoulders, his abdomen, his thighs, his feet. She would kiss those feet and everything else. She adores.

Why would you do that? Jane manages to say.

As a sort of probing of limits. Alma and I do have an . . . understanding.

You mean this has happened before? Jane holds her breath.

No. But we discussed the possibility of it happening — to her or to me. We decided it would be all right. Not that we would have to confess or provide details.

She knows, I'm sure. It's really a question. But Edward remains silent. Jane tries again.

You've discussed me.

Of course we have. But not in that context. As a dear person who is becoming a friend.

Cold words. They chill Jane. On the one hand. But on the other, she doesn't care. She is ready to run this affair into the ground, and if the results are ugly or messy, so be it.

■ ■ ■ ■

That night, alone in her house, Jane has one of what she calls her "heart attacks," a deep pain in her chest, a pounding of her heart that endures for three to four long minutes. She lies on her couch, waiting for it to pass. She tries not to panic. She had a series of these episodes after Angela's death, and at first had thought they were real heart attacks. Her doctor told her no, but also cautioned her about taking care of herself when she had one.

A lot of people, after an emotionally stressful episode, are left with heart pain or palpitations, the doctor had said. *It even has a name: broken heart syndrome. And it's real, and can be dangerous. The heart muscle suddenly becomes weakened and one of the heart's chambers changes shape. It's been suggested that it might actually be a mechanism for protecting the heart from the surge of adrenaline that often accompanies shock and grief.*

Shock or grief. That is what she's feeling tonight. After the tenderness on the dunes, the shock of a proposed betrayal. Or was she the betrayed or the betrayer? Jane is confused. She lies on the sofa and holds on to her chest.

Angela, like Jane, had been a loser. Literally. She lost everything. It had been this way since she was small. She lost her special bear — given to her by Rick's mother, Angela's grandmother, when she was born — so many times that Jane wrote to the factory that manufactured it and ordered a dozen identical specimens that she kept hidden in the garage. Each time Barry the Bear disappeared, *voilà!* another one, decidedly less scruffy, would magically appear. Jane liked doing this. She liked being such a devoted mother. It made her feel good. Later, she felt less good when Angela lost her lunch, her book bag, her school ID, her lunch money, her driver's license. Jane got in the habit of copying important documents. Of purchasing multiple versions of things if they were cheap enough (earphones, watches) or insurance when they were expensive (cell phone, bike). She tried to teach Angela how to place everything in one purse or backpack, to always check that she had everything before leaving a friend's house or a restaurant. To no avail. Angela lost her keys so many times that Jane went to the locksmith and had ten keys made of the back door lock to the house, and ten duplicate car keys. She hid five of those key sets in various places around the yard — under this rock, in the roots of this tree — and put five in a drawer. That way Angela was never locked out, and if she lost one set, Jane would simply give her another.

Because of all this, Jane was organized against losing things. She had her purse. Her wallet fit in one compartment, her keys in another, her cell phone in yet another. She never deviated from her pattern. So one night, when it is her turn to close up the nursery after everyone else has gone home, she is astounded that her keys are not in their proper place. She thinks she must have made a mistake when she can't put her hands on them immediately. But fishing down again into the special key compartment, her hand still comes up empty. She empties her purse onto the front counter. Wallet — check. Phone — check. Brush, comb, sunscreen, lipstick (rarely used). No keys. She hunts through the greenhouses, everywhere she'd been that day. Nothing. Nada. What is she going to do? She can't leave the nursery gates and doors unlocked — too much valuable stock. Chances are it would be safe, but she isn't one to take chances. She calls Helen and sheepishly explains the situation.

For circumstances like these, Jane keeps an extra key for her motorbike and a spare house key in her saddlebag. After Helen drives up with a spare key to the greenhouse, she locks up and drives home.

That night, Jane can't sleep. She double-bolts both the front and the back door to the cottage — although the cottage is so small it is ludicrous that it even has two doors — and closes and bars her windows for the first time since she's moved into the cottage. At her landlord's house — next door, but separated by a thick eucalyptus tree grove — the dog is barking at something. Cars drive by, throwing grotesque shadows across her walls and ceilings. The cottage, approximately a hundred years old, creaks and groans in the wind. Jane gets out of bed and places chairs across both inward-opening doors. She balances a glass on each chair to make even more noise if someone attempts to come in.

The cottage is stifling, airless. Desperate for air, Jane inches open the window next to her bed. Immediately the sound of the ocean comes through. A refreshing breeze blows in. But Jane can feel things. The world is unsafe tonight. The darkness hides many dangers. The pressure in her chest is building up again, a full-scale attack is in store.

Jane takes two Xanax and waits for the calm to overtake her. It doesn't happen. She tries reading. No dice. She finally paces, from the living room through the tiny kitchen, looks out the back door window onto the garbage cans and a small white picket fence that anyone could climb over. Anyone. And with her keys in hand, they could enter while she is asleep . . . and do what? What is Jane afraid of? Rape? Murder? Such things hold no terrors for her. What can they take from her? Nothing that she wants or needs. And yet she is afraid. She is protecting something inside herself, something that still deserves to be protected. What is that? Her soul? She has to laugh. She never thinks of that anymore, although she had been fixated on the cleanliness of her soul as a child. Before she lapsed. Over the years she has forgotten about it. But now, at 3:00 a.m. on a windy moonless night in late September, she is deeply concerned about losing it.

About 3:30 a.m., as Jane paces, slowly and silently, back and forth through the rooms, she notices that one car doesn't pass the house but is paused, its headlights shining directly into her living room through the curtains. The sound of an engine idling. Then the lights and engine switch off with one motion. Silence and darkness again. A neighbor coming home late from the bars? The crackle of footsteps on the eucalyptus leaves. Slowly. Trying not to make noise. Coming closer. A shadow against the curtains at her front door. Jane can't help it. She tries to scream, the terror overwhelming her, but all that comes out is a faint croak. She is paralyzed. Then the shadow recedes. She hears the footsteps moving away, not quite so quietly. She tiptoes to the door and pulls aside the curtains. She can only glimpse the person from the rear, but the blond ponytail, the height and slimness, means it can only be one individual. She unlocks and pulls open the door.

Adam. She speaks quietly. He hears her and turns. Now she can see his face. Definitely Adam, wearing a Santa Cruz sweatshirt and jeans. He turns and comes back. Jane retreats into her doorway.

What do you want? Her voice comes out louder than she'd intended.

Your keys.

What?

He points. On Jane's front stoop are her keys.

I found them in my bag. I don't know how they got there. Either I picked them up by accident or you dropped them there. I thought you might need them. When I saw your motorbike here, I knew you must have had a spare set.

Why didn't you call?

I was out with some buddies. I didn't get home until after 2:00 a.m. I didn't want to wake you up.

Jane's broken heart starts beating again. *This isn't like the trowel, is it?*

Even in the moonlight she can see him blush. *Of course not.*

Well, come in and have some tea.

He hesitates. *Decaffeinated?* he asks.

Or a glass of water. Noncarbonated. That's one of his things too, she remembers, says the bubbles are artificially injected in the lower-priced carbonated waters for sale at the Safeway. *Whatever. Come on.*

But he hesitates.

Are you sure? he asks, but there is something in his face and his voice that seems to be saying something else. His eyes seem to be taking in her from her head to her toes. There is something about the way his gaze travels down her body, from her face to her bare feet. Not sexual. Reverent? Jane realizes what a sight she must be, her long red hair loose and disheveled, in her nightshirt, an old football shirt of Rick's that reaches halfway down her thighs.

What?

You look so lovely.

Jane has to laugh.

Okay, have it your way. I'm going back to bed. The heaviness in her chest, the anxiety that has fueled her all evening, has vanished. She feels light-headed. With her keys in hand, she is suddenly safer. The chairs can come away from the doors, the glasses back in the cabinet. The windows open, the sea air moving through the cottage as usual.

The world is safe. Her guardian angel has blessed the house.

The next morning, Jane gets to the nursery early, before seven, but Adam has beaten her. His Volvo is already parked out front, and the doors are unlocked.

Man, I hope I didn't startle you last night, he says when she tracks him down, drinking tea in the break room. He looks fully rested — odd, given that he lives in Santa Cruz, a good hour down Route 1 from Jane's cottage, and it'd been well after three when he'd left.

No, Jane says. She realizes she has forgiven him for the trowel, and any other transgressions. Who could hold a grudge against that sunny face? Together, they go to their separate corners to work until the official opening at 10:00 a.m.

But Jane, farther to the front of the nursery, hears a car crunch into the gravel parking lot well before then, around 8:45. She wipes her hands on her smock and goes to warn whomever it is away. To her astonishment, it's Alma, whom she hasn't seen since their ride on the beach cliff. Now under very different circumstances.

Her prepared speech of *I'm sorry, but we're not open yet . . .* dies on her lips.

Hello? she says. It comes out like a question.

Jane! Alma reaches her and again kisses her twice, once on each cheek, her usual style. Alma is dressed professionally, in a white blouse and black silk pants. She smells faintly of hydrangeas. One of Jane's favorite flowers.

It's been so long since our . . . adventure! Alma says. She walks farther into the nursery, past Jane, turns right to go into the orchid room. Jane, unsure what to do, mutely follows.

I was on my way to campus and thought I'd stop. So you take care of all this? she asks with a sweep of her hand.

Jane finds her voice. *Not these. I work in the native plant section. It's primarily what we're known for.*

Apt, says Alma.

Jane is puzzled. *In what way apt?* Her voice comes out more hostile than she'd intended. But really, how is one supposed to deal with one's lover's lover? It was too much for Jane.

I think of you as a native plant, says Alma.

You couldn't be further from the mark, Jane says.

Your Oklahoma roots? says Alma, startling Jane. Very few people know about those. Most think she originated from Berkeley. Edward. Edward knows. They'd discussed her, then.

Incidental, Alma says. *Totally incidental. We choose our places, or rather, our places choose us. You were born for Half Moon Bay. Admit it.* She fingers a warty hammer orchid (*Drakaea livida*). *How ugly these things are. Show me* your *plants. They must be more attractive than these.*

Jane leads the way to her room, where she's been planting *Fremontodendron californicum* (California flannelbush). *These will grow to about five feet tall, and are covered with gorgeous yellow flowers, like soft gold trumpets,* she says. Then, warming to her subject. *They're very popular down in Monterey and Carmel. Go down there around Easter, and you'll see these bursting out everywhere.*

And what are these? Alma points to some seedlings on the back table. Jane smiles. These are her favorites. *These will actually grow into vines,* she says. *They flaunt the strangest flowers in the fall.* Aristolochia californica *(Dutchman's pipe). Here, I'll show you.* Jane heaves open a large dog-eared book and points to a delicate purple-and-white-striped flower that could be construed as a high-heeled boot or a pipe. *We almost lost these,* says Jane. *They were being crowded out by invasive species.*

Yes, says Alma, and she seems to be choosing her words carefully. *To be supplanted is not a particularly fun position to be in.*

Is this for me? Jane thinks. Her whole body heats up, she can feel the creeping warmth from her torso to her neck, up to her face. The greenhouse is hot and moist. Jane is used to it. She should be used to it.

Of course, Alma continues, *there is such a thing as coexistence.* She fingers the tiny green shoots. She isn't looking at anything in particular.

Yes, says Jane, after a pause. She doesn't know what else to say or do.

An agreement of sorts, says Alma.

A truce, says Jane, but here Alma shakes

her head.

No, too adversarial. It doesn't have to be like that. The resources — Alma points down at the dirt in the pot, then the sun through the window — *should be sufficient for all.*

That night, after dinner, and then after three hours in which Edward didn't come, Jane decides she needs to get out of Half Moon Bay, even if only briefly. She realizes with a shock that she has not left the coast in more than four months. Her last trip was down to the Bonny Doon Nursery to pick up some seeds for Helen. But even that didn't count, Bonny Doon being high in the Santa Cruz Mountains. Jane hasn't been anywhere near what might be called civilization in months and months. No movie theaters or cinema multiplexes. No shopping malls. No Macy's, Kmart, Toys R Us. The San Mateo coast has escaped all that.

She stops by the Shell on Ocean Drive to gas up, then hits the road. She's put on extra layers, knowing that although the weather is mild down here, it could be frigid in San Francisco. Despite being bundled up, she's still chilled as she rides up Route 1 past Montara, El Grenada, Princeton-by-the-Sea, Pacifica, and Daly City.

She's not taken Route 1 between Half

Moon Bay and San Francisco in years — since before they closed Devil's Slide and drilled the tunnel. So she no longer has to circumvent the dizzying cliff that was constantly eroding, causing frequent road closures. It was said that drivers used to unwisely close their eyes as they drove around the hairpin curves of Devil's Slide. Now people on foot and on bicycles enjoy the new park that was built on the remains of Route 1 that hugs the cliff. She'd driven Angela across Devil's Slide once when she was six, and to Angela, the trip had taken on mythic proportions. *Remember when we went across Devil's Slide?* Angela would ask, as if they'd crossed the Arctic tundra to reach the North Pole.

The tunnel turns a former journey of excited dread into a humdrum affair. You turned inland well before reaching the cliffs, past the parking lot for the park, and into the tunnel. And that is that. Jane finds that she is both relieved and disappointed.

Jane follows Route 1 until it reaches the 280 highway, and takes it north to 101, after some thought getting off at Cesar Chavez Street. She chooses her neighborhood deliberately. She doesn't want Pacific Heights or North Beach or Noe Valley. She wants something different tonight, something she can't get in Half Moon Bay.

Even in the year and a half since she'd been down Mission Street, to her and Rick's favorite Mexican taqueria on Fifteenth Street, there have been massive changes. The Mexican restaurant is gone, replaced by a futuristic tapas bar, all steel and glass. Formerly graying decrepit Victorians have been refurbished and painted splendidly with all colors of the rainbow. Fewer people are begging outside the Walgreens on Twentieth. It is all very pretty. As she idles at a light on the corner of Eighteenth and Valencia, a massive bus with shaded windows pulls up next to her and disgorges an army of young — very young — men with a few women, all wearing jeans and T-shirts, carrying laptop cases and wearing backpacks. The McDonald's on Nineteenth Street, previously notorious for the used needles in the restrooms, now sports a big banner advertising free Wi-Fi, and serious-looking men — again, young, young, young — are tapping away at laptops. The Good Vibrations sex toy shop is still there, she is glad to see, where she and her Berkeley friends spent many a bachelorette party evening.

She parks the motorbike on Guerrero and, on impulse, buys a bottle of tequila in a small liquor shop — that too has been sanitized with less beer and more exotic wines and liquors on the shelves. Jane asks for a bag to put the bottle in. She loosens the top and walks down the Mission occasionally taking a gulp. Before too long, she is feeling the effect. It has been too long since she cut loose.

She finds a movie house that is playing an old John Waters film starring Divine. Instead of regular movie seats, people are sitting on mismatched couches with broken springs. If she had been sober, she would have worried about what exactly she was sitting on. Instead she settles herself next to a woman with a red wig on that is almost the same color of her own hair, only made up in a fifties flip hairdo. It is stiff, like cardboard. The woman is slurping thirstily from a large sweating plastic cup and eating Doritos from a bag at her feet, despite a large sign on the wall behind her that reads NO OUT-SIDE FOOD OR DRINK.

Hey, honey, if you don't tell on me, I won't tell on you.

The voice is deep and the Adam's apple a dead giveaway. The southern accent a hammy fake. Jane instantly feels safer. Another imposter. A sister in implausibility.

No problem, Jane says, and offers her the bag with the tequila bottle in it.

Don't mind if I do. The woman pours a liberal portion into her cup. Jane takes a few Doritos. They munch in companionable silence as Divine belts out a song, something about cowboys longing for home.

Jane is only half watching the movie. She's drunk too much, and the room is starting to spin. Suddenly the urge to sleep is too much. She closes her eyes.

Hey. HEY!

Someone is shaking Jane awake. It is her neighbor with the red hair. The lights are on, so bright they hurt Jane's eyes.

Closing time, darling.

Jane stumbles to her feet. She notices that the bottle of tequila is about three-quarters gone. She is wondering if she drank it all herself when she sees her companion is also stumbling. The red-haired woman sways before falling back on the sofa. A rubber breast, complete with realistic-looking nipple, falls out of her shirt.

I hate it when that happens.

Come on, missy — you and your friend have to find another place to hang. This from a man who is obviously in charge. He is pushing a broom between the couches.

I know a place. The woman puts a finger to her lips, sticks the breast back into place, and heaves herself to her feet. She is large

— well over six feet tall, Jane estimates, and probably a good 250 pounds. Her fashion sense is impressive considering her size. She manages to look elegant in a black dress that fits her shape admirably. When her eyes are open, her lashes nearly touch her eyebrows. Jane marvels that she can close her eyes or blink with such things glued on.

What's your name, honey?

Jane.

Janey, I'm Sheree. I have just the spot for us to continue this little party.

Before Jane understands what's happening, they are in the street, Jane's arm held tightly by Sheree. Both are having trouble walking.

Don't worry, it's not far.

They stumble maybe two blocks until they get to a small park with swings and slides and a spiderweb-like climbing tower. Jane notices that the black surface under her feet is soft, spongy. If you fell in her playground as a child in Big Cabin, Oklahoma, you fell on hard dirt. Here, even in what used to be the dubious part of town, they don't let their children scrape their knees.

Sheree sits on one swing. The entire structure creaks. She puts her stockinged feet out and begins to pump so she is swinging back and forth.

Come on!

Jane sits cautiously on the other swing. The whole structure is shaking as Sheree goes up and down. She'd hated the playground when Angela was small. She considered it the dullest, most useless, and infuriating place to waste time. The other mothers seemed content to sit there and watch their offspring run around screaming and playing, and to comfort them when they came crying due to a spill or some other minor hurt. Jane couldn't stand it. The tedium, the boredom. Neither could she stand the small talk of the other mothers — talk of where to buy the best organic produce and the safest toys. Jane knew she was judging them too harshly, that she was critical simply because she didn't fit in, being only a visitor at the playground on weekends, as Angela was in day care during the week. Another strike against Jane.

Now she'd give anything to have those interminable minutes back again. To look up and see small Angela clambering up the slide or falling down in the sand.

You seem a bit melancholy. Somehow Sheree's voice has changed. It's less campy, less southern. Deeper.

I lost someone.

Recently?

A year ago.

Oh, sweetie, that's like yesterday.

It's like last hour.

Have you noticed how much grief is like fear?

Yes! Jane tries to sit up straight, but the swing doesn't let her. The metal is cold against her hands.

I didn't think that one up. I forget where I got it from.

I'm very afraid.

So am I, my dear, so am I.

Who did you lose?

Who haven't I lost?

Does the fear ever go away?

You're asking the wrong person. Sheree slows down her swinging. *Any more of that tequila left?*

Jane passes over the bottle, but not before taking a swig herself.

Let's take a little ride, Sheree says.

You've got a car?

I guess you could call it that.

Then what are we waiting for?

Absolutely nothing.

They somehow manage to locate an old Ford station wagon, patches of rust and indentations covering its body, parked up on the curb on Eighteenth and Valencia. Sheree takes the ticket on the windshield and throws it in the backseat.

Where are we going? Jane thinks to ask.

Fort Point. Ever been?

No.

Right under the Golden Gate Bridge. You're in for a treat.

At this hour, 1:00 a.m., no traffic is left on the road. Sheree manages, with a few heart-stopping lurches, to keep the car steady. Somehow Jane isn't thinking of her companion as Sheree anymore. She deserves a name with more dignity. More gravitas.

I'm going to call you Victoria, she says.

Call me anything but late for dinner. Victoria executes a rather wide right turn.

Jane of course had heard of Fort Point, but had never gotten around to actually visiting it. It predated the Golden Gate Bridge, having been built in the mid-1800s to defend San Francisco Bay. It was positioned at the immediate entrance to the bay. The Golden Gate Bridge loomed high directly over it, so the fort was always in shadow. It wasn't a cheerful place and there wasn't much to see, Jane had always heard.

Rain is sprinkling down when they turn into the parking lot of the dark brick fort. The Golden Gate Bridge soars directly above the car. Even at this late hour, cars and heavy trucks are roaring across it. The wind has picked up, and the swell from the ocean side of the bridge is causing great waves to crash over the cement bulwarks protecting the fort.

Sheree/Victoria gets out of the car, stretches, then walks to the edge of the parking lot, facing the water. She stands with her face to the spray, holding her hands up as if welcoming the waves.

You gotta embrace the elements, she calls. Jane can barely make out her words over the sound of the surf and the wind. It is a good place, she thinks, for her to be on this night of escape. The majesty of the bridge above their heads, the roar of the wind and the waves. The salt spray from the water mixing with the rain. Jane realizes she's imitating Sheree/Victoria's stance. They stand there in silence for perhaps half a minute. It feels splendid, like they are conjuring up the storm rather than being battered by it.

Then, without warning, a large splash sounds about ten feet off the pier. As if a large fish had jumped up and fallen back down again. Or something heavy has plunged into the water.

Jane opens her eyes. She can't see much in the dark. *What was that?* she asks.

Perhaps another lost soul, Sheree/Victoria

says calmly. She hasn't changed her stance, is still welcoming the rain and spray to her ample bosom. *More than two thousand have jumped since the bridge opened.*

Are you serious?

Never more so.

Do they die instantly?

Most do, but those that don't suffer horribly. It's not a nice way to go. But don't worry, honey, that was probably just a fish. If it had been a person, we'd been hearing sirens by now. They keep a close eye on this bridge.

How do you know?

Sheree/Victoria is calmly wiping rainwater from her eyes. *I work on a suicide hotline,* she says. *The one thing they all say is* I'm gonna take the bridge.

That's terrible!

Oh yes. In fact, I have to get to work in — she checks her watch — *less than two hours. I gotta get dolled up and go out to the movies to take my mind off of what I hear, day in and day out.*

A rogue wave arches up at least five feet above the cement and crashes down, soaking both of them.

It'll be dawn soon.

Time for bed for you, and work for me.

Yes, says Jane, reluctantly. For some reason, she feels a little better. Less like terror. More like plain fear. The weight in her chest is still there. But then it will always be there.

Did that remind you of your loss? Sheree asks, pointing to where the splash had occurred.

I don't need to be reminded.

Oh. That bad, huh?

Then, *Where's your wheels? I'll drop you off.*

Jane is tired and cold and hungry by the time she is left at her motorbike, but when she thinks of the alternative, which would have been sitting in her cottage alone, thinking of the strange early-morning visit from Alma, she is glad she got away. Off Nineteenth Avenue, she pulls into an all-night McDonald's and devours a chicken sandwich and some limp fries that had clearly been sitting around for some time. Then she heads home.

She sees the headlights in her mirror just south of the tunnel. She hadn't met any traffic going either way for at least twenty minutes and was beginning to feel like the last person on the planet. Here she is, all the way on the left side of the country, with only the highway separating her from the rocks and beaches, the luminous waves coming in and out of focus as the fog thins and thickens again. She could be at the end of the world.

The car is coming up fast. It has its brights on — Jane can see the four lights, two stacks of two. She moves deliberately over to the center of the lane — it sounds counterintuitive, but Jane always operates on the premise that being in the middle of the road made her more likely to be seen, less likely to be hit. The car keeps coming. Because of the brightness of the lights, Jane can't see into the car. She doesn't know if she's been seen.

A small motorbike wouldn't be expected driving the Pacific Coast Highway at three in the morning. The car is now ten yards behind Jane and isn't slowing down. Jane unconsciously presses on the gas and speeds up. Fifty, sixty, sixty-five miles an hour, and the car is still gaining, Jane sees that the driver is wavering a little, sometimes going over the yellow line in the middle into the opposite lane. Five yards, then four. Jane pulls over to the right to let the car pass, but realizes if the driver doesn't see her, that won't do any good.

Jane doesn't want to go onto the soft shoulder, so she swings into the opposite lane, seeing, as she does so, a car clear the crest of the hill in front of her. Jane is directly in its oncoming path. Frustratingly, the car behind now seems to have slowed down, even as Jane wills it to pass. *Come on, come on,* Jane mutters as she keeps an eye on the oncoming car, which also has its brights on. The fog clears momentarily, and Jane is nearly blinded. The driver of the oncoming car finally sees her and lets out a loud, prolonged blast of its horn. Jane slows down to twenty-five miles an hour, brakes, and waits until the car behind her — a red Range Rover, as it turns out — finally whooshes by. She pulls over back into the right-hand lane behind it, just in time, just before the other car passes, its horn blaring. Jane slows down and pulls over, stops. She doesn't trust herself to drive. So she simply sits there for five minutes. The alcohol still in her bloodstream makes the whole experience seem surreal. She wonders if she imagined the whole thing: Sheree, Fort Point, the splash in the water, this near-death on the Pacific Highway. Then she turns the motorbike on again and heads home.

Jane wakes to pounding on her door.

She looks at her clock. Eleven a.m. How did she sleep so long?

She stumbles to the door, peeks through the curtains. Two men in suits stand there.

Their faces are grim. One of the men points to the door and gestures for her to open it.

Jane unlocks the door, and the men push it open, come in without asking. One casually flashes his badge. FBI.

Where were you last night?

Jane is still half asleep. She has to think before she answers.

In the city, she concludes.

Until when?

Jane tries to concentrate. She remembers Fort Point, vaguely. She remembers the splash in the ocean. She remembers Sheree. The rest is blank. She doesn't know how she got home. She thanks God she got here safely.

Late, she says. She sees her overcoat lying on the floor. It is still wet.

The detective notices that too.

Out in the rain?

I suppose. What is this about?

Instead of answering, the detective says, *Where were you between midnight and six a.m.?*

I told you. Up in the city. Then home.

Anyone can verify this?

Of course not, Jane says, but then thinks of Sheree/Victoria. But she didn't even know her real name, much less her address. They'd been in that dark movie theater.

Would anyone remember Jane? Her hair, her most distinctive characteristic, had been tied into a tight ponytail and hidden beneath the hood of her jacket and her scarf. You probably couldn't have told if she were male or female.

No, she says again. *No one.*

Then you need to come down to the station with us.

A third girl has disappeared. From Half Moon Bay itself. Stolen from her house sometime in the night. The mother had looked in on her at midnight. Her daughter was there, neatly tucked in under the blankets and sheets. Then the mother had gone back to the room to wake her up for school at 6:30. Empty.

It was one of the ranch houses, all rooms on the ground floor. The window had been forced, but it hadn't been difficult, the wood rotted from the salty sea air and continuous dampness from fog. The bushes below the window trampled. Because of the rain the night before, no clear footprints. The house was the last one on the block, the window facing a wild field directly fronting the sea.

No witnesses. Jane, among other people, gets questioned, then released. Once again, the fact that she has no car seems to save her.

We're not unsympathetic to your situation, one of the FBI agents told her. *We know about what happened in Berkeley.*

Do you? Jane thinks, but doesn't say anything except *No one here knows about . . . what happened . . . except Helen Smithson. And I'd prefer it stayed that way.*

We'll try, ma'am. This was the second FBI officer. Bad cop. *But as you know, this is a small town. Word gets around.*

My daughter had a different last name. Most people wouldn't put the two of us together.

Yes, but your own name is in the public record as the mother of the victim. And a perp herself. A quick search and it's all there.

Whatever. Jane knows she sounds rude, but she's upset. Her cover has been blown?

It raises a lot of questions, ma'am. You lost a daughter yourself. You move here, and shortly thereafter other people's daughters go missing.

What's the logic? That I'm acting out some kind of revenge fantasy?

It has occurred to us.

But they did nothing, after all. They let her go with the usual warning not to leave town.

■ ■ ■ ■

More posters. More headlines. Everyone dreading the eighth or ninth or tenth day when this third missing child, Amy Cross, would show up. Only four years old. Checkpoints materialize on the roads at night where men and women in dark clothes and with badges intermittently stop cars, shine their flashlights inside them. On occasion, they asked for trunks to be opened. The ACLU published a letter in the *Moon News* notifying the citizens of their right to "reasonable" searches, but most people are happy with the roadblocks, feel the intrusion is worth it. Since the first two children had been found north of Pescadero and west of Route 1, the bulk of the FBI and police activity takes place in that area.

The FBI spokesperson is quoted in the *Moon News: We have a limited window of time if the perpetrator follows his usual M.O.* More search parties are organized.

Jane studies the picture of Amy on the Three Sisters community board. She is, finally, a poster child for missing children. Blond and blue-eyed, with shoulder-length curly hair and a wide smile, looking straight into the camera. *At whom?* Jane wonders. It is someone the child loves and trusts, that is for sure. Jane remembers what Alma had said. Even if Amy had not been taken, that look would not last. It would be gone as certainly as if Amy were dead.

Jane is not stopped as she rides her motorbike along Route 1 between Half Moon Bay and Princeton after work. It is growing dark as the sun sinks below the horizon of the ocean, and the unmarked sedans are starting to congregate and form checkpoints. There are two, three, no four of them in the three miles between where Route 92 intersects with Route 1 and where Jane turns off to get to her cottage. No one would get anything — or anyone — past. She notices a tripod with a black box set up near each of the checkpoints. The FBI is photographing each vehicle as it passes, Jane's motorbike included.

Jane thinks about what Alma has said, about losing your children. She thinks there is truth there. Jane first lost Angela when Angela was thirteen. The shock was brutal. The shrinking away from physical contact. The slammed doors. The hostility soaking through every word in every conversation.

Did you eat your breakfast?

No.

Did you do your homework?
Duh.
You're so stupid.
I hate you. So much.
I can't believe you said that. You're a moron.
Don't speak to your mother like that. That would be Rick, spared the hostility himself, but ineffectual in protecting Jane from it.

Silences. When not abuse, silence.

Jane hated in return. There was no other word for it. She went to bed earlier and earlier to escape the ugly battleground her house had become. This was before Angela had her driver's license. That was a completely different story. Then she stayed up later and later.

You know your curfew is midnight.
Everyone else can stay out until 2:00 a.m.
That's too late.
Everything that's fun happens after midnight.
Everything that can hurt you happens then.
As it turned out, Jane was wrong. Bad things happened before midnight too.

Edward comes to her the night after her San Francisco adventure. She doesn't know if he tried to find her the night she was out. It doesn't matter. Sinking. She is sinking into something, and it's not unpleasant. She is being asked to let go of her inhibitions, her

233

cynicism, the irony that had permeated even the nursery. *I suppose you're going to lie there while I do all the work,* she's saying to Angela as a baby lying on her changing table. She is being anesthetized cell by cell, getting to a feeling of glorious numbness.

Sleep is important. If you can't sleep, do something productive. Jane remembers this advice from her mother, who also suffered from chronic insomnia. Their toilets were never so clean, their school lunches never so elaborately prepared, as when Jane's mother was struggling with her sleep issues.

Two evenings after her trip to San Francisco, Jane tries to go to sleep. Goodness knows she's tired enough. When that doesn't work, she takes a page from her mother's book and cleans, gets down on her knees and clears out the kitchen cabinets, washing the pots and pans and putting them back in exquisite order. By then it's 2:30 a.m., and her body seemingly has no intention of slowing down.

She gets on her motorbike and rides down Route 1 in the opposite direction of San Francisco, to Santa Cruz. It is damp and foggy, but she doesn't feel cold at all. If anything, she wants to strip down further to feel the wind against her bare skin, to have the wind cool down what Edward's hands had touched earlier that afternoon. *In love.* What does that mean? *I'm in love with you* is different from *I love you.* The latter implies rights, societal approval, conventional relations. Marriage. Family. The former has no such niceties. Wilder. More possibilities.

She is *in love* with Edward. Which didn't mean she likes him or trusts him. His face above her, his hands stroking her, his scent. She is intoxicated. She can barely drive straight. The sun is beginning to rise when she reaches the outskirts of Santa Cruz. She stops at an all-night café on Seabright, orders a full breakfast, and finds she is unable to eat any of it. Eating is beyond her abilities right now. Her throat is constricted; there's a tingling in her chest that extends out to her arms, as if an electric current were emanating from her heart out to her extremities. She reaches out and touches her fork, half expecting a shock on contact.

She's not yet thinking rationally, not yet sure what this all means. She is simply besotted, and the universe feels like a more exciting and dangerous place than it did the morning when she walked onto the pumpkin fields the day after the Pumpkin Festival. She watches an elderly couple eating their breakfast. They are taking it very seriously, carefully buttering their toast, salting their eggs, pouring cream and sugar into their coffee. Every movement deliberate. Was this from old age, or the early morning, or simply habit? The sun shines on the face of the woman. She is . . . what? Seventy? Seventy-five? Jane can't tell ages very well. The woman's hair is not yet completely gray, and in true Santa Cruz former hippie style, she wears it long and loose, over her shoulders, much like Jane's is right now. Streaks of black among the gray. The lines carved into her face are beautiful; in the early-morning sun, she is glowing. Now she smiles at something the man — her husband? partner? — has said, puts down her coffee, and reaches out and strokes his face. A gesture of tenderness. He says something else, and she laughs, and you can see how lovely she once was, still is.

It is nearly 7:00 a.m. when Jane stands up, pays her bill, and walks out into the early-morning sun. Her phone chirps, and she looks down to see that she has a text. It is from Edward. It merely says, *When next?* Words that make her shiver with joy.

They're in the Three Sisters and have already drunk too much wine, but aren't ready to stop. There's Helen, and Jane, and there's Adam, although of course he isn't drinking alcohol, his body being a temple, etc. So there are two empty bottles of wine on the table in front of them, and one of those designer teapots, red-plated with an enameled handle. Adam has asked one of the twins, with his captivating smile, for the hot water to be refilled five times. She's enamored, you can tell. Jane pulls her chair slightly away from Adam's and pours some more wine. She will not enter into any ridiculous female competition. She has no need to. She has Edward, and there is no competition there. Alma is seemingly part of the package.

Adam leans closer, and Jane catches a wisp of body odor. *Not unpleasant, the scent of youth,* Jane thinks. The sun hasn't damaged his skin, but kissed it into a sort of glow that seems fed from within. He's a good soul. You know that by looking at him. Jane is nicer to Adam these days. She is warmer. She can afford to be. He is nothing to her. She cannot see past the flames that have ignited in her life.

Amy has not yet been found. The mood in the city has darkened even further, if that were possible. It feels like a city under siege. Some families with young girls even leave town. Alibis are checked. Even Edward and Alma are questioned, although they arrived after little Heidi had been stolen, Edward tells Jane. *Otherwise, no doubt we'd be in the suspicious pool along with everyone else.*

People are drinking too much, Margaret from the Three Sisters confides. They've sold twice as many alcoholic beverages since the disappearances as in previous months. At the time of year when business should be getting slower, it is getting busier. They've even hired a local high school girl to help Margaret wait on tables. Poor thing, she is shy, and doesn't know how to serve the men, some of whom openly ogle her, all of whom flirt and tease.

Angela's budding sexuality. So painful to Jane. First the men, then the older boys, then the boys her age eyeing her in her too-short shorts and midriff-baring top. Only fourteen years old when she started giving boys blow jobs. Jane figured it out the first time because of a white stain on Angela's cheek and the fact that she immediately brushed her teeth after coming in from a "date." Which consisted of hanging out at the 7-Eleven with a group of other high schoolers, not necessarily bad kids; still, Jane, who had always been so studious, could not understand it. But then she remembered her own early teenage years, how everything shimmered in the heat of her budding but ignorant desires. Cars figured prominently in seductions in Big Cabin. The open plain offered little protection or privacy, and the parents mostly stayed in at night. In Berkeley, few of Angela's friends had cars, but they all had houses patrolled ineptly by busy parents. The kids seemed to have an instinct where the unsupervised rooms were. It was a traveling party.

The day Angela was killed, they'd had another fight, not a bad one. Normal. Just after Angela got home from summer school.

Where are you going?

Just over to Sally's to hang out.

Keep your phone on.

Oh Mom! (roll of eyes).

In fact, Jane had surreptitiously installed a phone-tracker app on Angela's phone, so she knew exactly where she was at any time. That didn't tell her what Angela was doing or whom she was doing it with, but Jane's guess was that it wasn't too dangerous, as no cars were involved. She had purchased a big box of condoms and taken Angela to Planned Parenthood to have birth control implanted in her arm. It would be good for two years, until Angela was eighteen and about to graduate from high school. She never made it that far, of course. After the death, Jane found the box of condoms in Angela's desk, unopened. Sometimes she had smelled liquor on Angela's breath and sometimes pot on her clothes, but that wasn't what worried her. No. What did, then?

This is what it was: all the people Angela was trusting who didn't love her the way Jane loved her. Couldn't Angela see that Jane was trying to keep her safe? But people without her best interests were giving her advice. Feeding her attitudes. She was smashing the bonds capable of keeping her secure, leaving her vulnerable, leaving Jane bleeding inside.

Jane's shrink at the time was not particularly helpful.

How rebellious was she when she was two years old? Three?

Not at all. No terrible twos. She remained affectionate and cheerful.

Then this is perfectly normal. They need to establish themselves, their boundaries. If they don't do it young, they do it all the more later.

But the sex! She's growing up so fast!

Yes, they do, today.

Jane sometimes cried taking Angela to school. She cried picking her up. She dreamed about Angela servicing boys, on her knees. Mortifying! Oh, Angela!

It's not something your generation understands.

I sure don't. Jane doesn't know where her rage comes from. Her disgust. Her feeling that her darling has been despoiled. Wasn't she the same Angela who could turn sweet and loving, and bring her coffee and her favorite muffin on Mother's Day, who could peer at her face when she got home from work and say, *You look tired, Mom,* and take her side against Rick's in one of their rare fights?

Rick was no help. He aged considerably the last two difficult years with Angela. Not that this showed on the outside of the family. *What a lovely girl!* they would say, seeing her playing her flute in the school orchestra or helping tutor disadvantaged youths in math.

What a lovely girl you've raised, Jane! And Jane would nod. Sometimes she and Angela, after one of their fights, would collapse, exhausted onto the bed and just hold each other.

I don't want to hurt you, Mom, Angela would say, and Jane would pat her on the back and say, *I know, sweetheart.*

Jane tried grounding her, but Angela

turned sullen and hostile and wouldn't talk. She wouldn't do her homework and just stayed in her room and talked and texted with her phone. Then the minute she was free, she would be up to her old tricks, which were God knows what.

What was Jane's complaint? She supposed it was the sex. She supposed it was the lack of any one special boy, although one's name came up more often than those of others. Stephen. Stephen this, Stephen that. Jane didn't believe in *easy* girls. She didn't believe in what they called it now, *slut shaming.* But she had to admit: her daughter, the straight-A student, was abysmally promiscuous. Jane took her to the doctor to test for disease. She could not get pregnant, but there were so many other bad things! Jane had her inoculated against HPV. She took Angela to a shrink of her own, an adolescent specialist, but the two closed ranks against her, and so she ended up writing large monthly checks to someone she felt was encouraging Angela to rebel against her, Jane.

Jane tried putting herself in Angela's shoes. After all, her virginity had been a mere technicality by the time she went away to college, having done nearly everything possible with her high school boyfriend except the ultimate act. But that seemed so innocent compared to what she convinced herself to think of as Angela's *explorations.* Having the incomplete evidence of course made it worse. It didn't seem to change Angela's standing at school. She had the same friends she'd had from elementary and middle school. And there were times when the girls were all in Jane's living room watching *The Music Man,* eating popcorn, and laughing at the dancing scenes, when she thought she was mistaken, when she thought she was overreacting.

But then would come a night when Angela would come home drunk at 3:00 a.m., her clothes disheveled, her underpants crushed into a ball in her coat pocket, her socks missing, and Jane would despair.

Angela was a beautiful girl, with her red curly hair — she got the color from Jane, the curls from Rick — and her big dark eyes, and the cheekbones, also from Rick. Striking. A striking girl. Tall and willowy, she was a *heartbreaker,* Jane's friends would say from when she was very small. A heartbreaker. That Angela's heart was never broken — at least that Jane could see — was both a relief and a worry. Sometimes Jane felt that she had given birth to a different species altogether, a tall, Amazon-like creature with the sensibility and intelligence of a Renaissance woman and the language of a sailor.

Fuck that. Isn't that the most acrimonious shit you've ever heard?

It was the most motherfucking exquisite rendition of St. Matthew's Passion *ever, Mom. Fucking out of this world.*

And what was there to say about Rick? Jane had met him while in graduate school, he, pursuing a doctorate in music. Now he made an extraordinarily good living writing mini soundtracks for video games. Snippets of suspense. Buildups of excitement. He had his own company, but had handed management over to someone else so he could concentrate on the creative. Always the creative. They had run out of things to say to each other before what Jane characterized as "the troubles" with Angela had started. Spending more time apart, Rick with his music — so Jane supposed — and Jane at the Berkeley Botanical Gardens, where the drought had created a lot of her attention for her native plants' environments. There were obviously native plants that were naturally drought-resistant, that flourished in the Central Valley, but others that were from coastal or wetlands regions that required more water than the university could spare. It took a careful balancing of resources to keep these things alive. Jane was often there on weekends, from dawn until the sun went down. She knew she was in hiding. But she didn't think of it that way at the time, not until she lost it all.

Six a.m. The sun barely risen. Adam and Jane are the only ones in the greenhouse. The doors don't open to the public until 10:00 a.m. Adam is there because he'd originally intended to go surfing, but a shark sighting by one of his surfer buddies scared everyone out of the water.

I'm bummed, he'd said when he saw Jane. *It's the warming water. We're seeing more of the bastards.* Last summer, a surfer had lost a leg below the knee to a shark a little farther down the coast, at Secret Beach. Adam had been sitting on his board nearby when the victim got pulled under. Adam had beaten off the shark with his fist. If the other surfers hadn't witnessed it and told the *Moon News,* Adam wouldn't have mentioned it. An unsung hero.

A bloody sport for a pacifist, Jane says, meaning to tease him, but he takes it seriously.

We're all in this world together, man, he says, and goes to brew some of his foul tea.

Jane's tending to the hummingbird garden. Helen's idea. Today Jane is moving in the western redbud shrubs she's been nurturing in the west greenhouse. When fully grown they will be twenty feet high and fifteen feet across. A magical flowering bush with dangling winter seed pods that look like small embryonic sacs. Fairies might well come out of them.

They've already attracted a fair number of hummingbirds, so much so that the brawls between the tiny winged creatures have been written up in the *Moon News.* Since hummingbirds have to eat twice their body weight in nectar and insects each day, they're protective of their good food sources in the garden and will fight aggressively to defend them. They like red flowers — not for any aesthetic reason, but because bees avoid red flowers and the lack of bees means that there is usually better nectar quantity and quality. Jane had done a lot of research on them when she first moved to Berkeley, there being no hummingbirds in Oklahoma. She was enchanted to find out they got their name from the humming sound created by their beating wings, flapping at high frequencies audible to humans, around fifty times per second.

At their house in Berkeley, they had a

small backyard full of red monkey flowers. A hummingbird's garden of delights. Angela was six before she stopped believing that the garden was full of fairies, and at the age of fifteen she swore that an exquisite iridescent redheaded Anna's hummingbird came back year after year. It was possible, Jane had conceded. Hummingbirds can live for more than a decade. They can fly forty miles per hour for five hundred miles without rest. The day after Angela died, Jane and Rick sat in the garden. The Anna's hummingbird — which Angela had imaginatively named "Anna," although it was male — pulled a strand of Jane's red hair, hard. She knew it did. She knew it was a sign.

Hummingbirds visit between a thousand and two thousand flowers every day. They drink from each flower two to three times per day. So a yard needs between four hundred and a thousand flowers to support one bird. Adam, with Jane's help, had planted enough flowering bushes to attract at least fifty birds to the back of the nursery, where the garden was situated. Standing in the middle of it was like being in the middle of a beehive. Adam planted *Penstemon rattanii, Arctostaphylos* species, manzanita *Diplacus* species, and monkey flowers of all colors. Jane planted dudleyas in Angela's honor. The name means *live forever.*

For the sake of little Amy Cross, for the first time, Jane agrees to join a party to search for a missing girl. She feels that her abstaining from them has set her apart. People at Three Sisters are beginning to look at her questioningly, she feels.

So she puts on thick pants, heavy hiking boots, and a sweatshirt. She gets to the meeting place at the coastal path by 9:45. A sizable crowd has already assembled. She sees many familiar faces. The day is beautiful, clear, and cold. Jane is assigned to a team of six — four women and two men — none of whom she knows. Out-of-towners, drawn by . . . the drama? A sincere desire to help? Jane isn't sure. They introduce themselves, but she promptly forgets their names. They are assigned to search the fields directly south of the Birch Street parking area, the ones that overlook the ocean from the top of the eroding cliffs, on which is perched a forest of live oak trees. Other teams will search the beach itself, fifty feet below, and the fields to the north of the parking lot.

One way or another, we'll find her, says the leader, grimly.

Jane's group starts in a line at the top of

the parking lot, spread six feet apart, and slowly walks to the cliff's edge. They move south and repeat it, carefully moving over every inch of terrain. Nothing escapes their gazes: candy wrappers, bits of discarded plastic, even, surprisingly, any number of pennies. As they walk, they pick up this trash and put it in plastic bags that someone has thoughtfully brought along. They go fairly quickly at first, as the terrain is flat here, with mostly short dried grasses and knee-high nettles. But then they hit a steep ravine into which the ocean extends a finger of water.

What's that? asks one of the guys, a large man with a handlebar mustache. He points. He has a competent air about him. Jane wonders why he's free on a weekday morning. Unemployed? He seems too self-assured for that. Retired? Too young, although you never know today with all the Silicon Valley stock options. A seasonal worker? Self-employed? California was strange that way. In Oklahoma, everyone had a profession and an easily defined place, even if it was simply *loser.* But here he could be a trust-fund baby, for all that his looks would give away. He is pointing to a red object at the bottom of the ravine, half in the creek. It takes one of the women, a fit-looking blonde in her early thirties, to climb down and pick it up. She stands looking at it, then looks back at us. She shakes her head and shouts something.

What did she say? asks another woman, who has somehow been designated the leader by mutual agreement. She is in her forties, Jane estimates, with dark hair that is starting to gray gracefully. She has a natural air of command that made the group bow to her when she assigned them to segments of the field. It was a nice kind of authority; no one minded, not even the men.

A shoe, says the large man.

He cups his hands around his mouth and shouts back down. *What size?*

Faint words, *Too big* and *high heels* come back.

Jane exhales noisily. She hadn't realized she's been holding her breath. The group starts moving again, skirting the edge of the ravine and moving into the next field, which is thick with live oak and eucalyptus trees. They slow down. Some of the branches of the oaks are large enough for a full-grown man to sleep on.

I'd have loved this for a fort growing up, the mustached man observes to no one in particular, pointing to the massive trunks and limbs of the trees, any one of which would have supported a substantial fort or tree house.

Jane falls behind the rest of the seekers. She has decided to let them be the finders of the horror she somehow knows is ahead. She walks slowly on the soft ground carpeted with leaves. She has a brief flash of well-being. The silent woods. The majestic trees. A Jane before Angela enjoyed such things. Could not a post-Angela Jane enjoy them too? She closes her eyes briefly, listens to the sound of the waves beating the rocks below.

The hand. That's what she sees first. It appears to be disembodied, hanging in midair from one of the large oak trees. Small and pink. Jane moves closer. She sees that it is attached to an arm clothed in a green sleeve that blends into the leaves of the tree. The arm is attached to a tiny torso wearing a green sweatshirt imprinted with a line of ducks. The head is turned to the side, cheek against the branch, you can only see the edge of an ear and blond hair. Little Amy is lying on one of the limbs of a gracious oak, positioned cleverly in the cleft of two branches. She looks like she is sleeping. Her eyes are closed. At first, Jane thinks she *is* sleeping. A cute kid.

She will never get to that age of *I hate you*

and *Leave me alone* and *Drop dead.* She will never climb out of her window after midnight with a bottle of her parents' Scotch and a baggie full of weed to meet the local boys and girls from Berkeley High. She won't lose her virginity against the back wall of a 7-Eleven.

She is an innocent. She has been spared.

Jane had been possessive, Jane had been controlling, Jane had punished when she should have encouraged. She had restrained when she should have set free. No wonder they butted heads. No wonder Jane was despised.

It had gone too fast. Jane wasn't ready. She wasn't that different at forty than twenty-three, whereas Angela had transformed from a zygote to a woman. Not really. Jane hadn't grown with Angela. She hadn't gotten herself used to certain ideas.

Jane opens her mouth and tries to call, but all that comes out is a soft croak. She attempts it again, and this time is a little more successful at making a noise. But no one comes. The team must be farther ahead than she'd realized. She finds herself retching in the bushes. She must get help. But she can't leave Amy. She knows how mad her thoughts are, but *if something happens to her, it will be my fault.*

■ ■ ■ ■

She doesn't know why the police must question her over and over. Jane happened to see the body first. She didn't see anything else, didn't touch anything. Yet a man and a woman have brought Jane to a room in the FBI headquarters with a mirror covering an entire wall, behind which more people are undoubtedly watching and listening. Jane has watched enough crime dramas on television.

Are you sure you didn't touch anything? asks the man. He is one of the suited gang who moved into the Days Inn on Route 1. She's seen him there and at the Three Sisters.

Yes, says Jane. She let others do that, especially as the other, nonmustached man in the search group turned out to be an ER nurse. He easily ascertains that little Amy was indeed dead.

And you didn't see anything or anyone? asks the other detective, a thin woman with short blondish hair.

No one but the people on my search team, Jane says.

How do you suppose they missed it? The body, I mean?

It was pretty well camouflaged by the leaves and what she was wearing, Jane says.

Then how did you happen to see her? This from the man.

They'd been over this at least three times already. Jane tells them again the steps she'd taken up to the discovery of the body. She doesn't say what she'd been thinking at the time. She realizes she looks as though she is hiding something. She tries to make a mask of her face.

Did you feel that anyone in your search party was deliberately . . . steering you . . . toward that tree, toward that discovery?

No. It was the territory we were assigned.

No one in your group specifically asked for that territory?

Not that I heard.

No one joined your group after the territories were given out?

Jane shook her head.

I understand that you lost your daughter last year.

Yes.

This must feel very personal to you.

My daughter was quite a bit older.

Yes. But still. Losing a child. That's a trauma. You might even have PTSD. People do strange things when they've had a trauma like that. Do you do strange things, Jane?

Jane feels almost hypnotized. *Yes,* she says. *I do very strange things.*

Like what, Jane?

Jane considers what to say. That she spits on the earth before inserting a seed to ensure good luck? That she gets up in the middle of the night and calls strangers on the phone and hangs up, just to hear human voices, no matter how cranky or anxious? That when she takes a disliking to a customer, she sells them plants that need full sunlight for their shaded yards and flowers that can't stand too much sun for their sunny places?

I mislead people, she says.

In what way, Jane?

But then there is a disturbance at the door. Voices arguing. Raised tones. The door opens, and Helen storms in, followed by Adam.

Did they read you your rights? Helen asks Jane.

Jane thinks. *I don't think so,* she says, but she is confused. She seems to be waking from a dream.

Of course we did, the man says. *It's all on tape.* He points to a black box mounted in the corner of the room.

She's had a shock, says Helen. *She is in no condition to be questioned. At least not without someone present.*

If she'd wanted a lawyer, she could have had one at any time.

Are you going to charge her? This is Adam, surprisingly authoritative.

No.

Then she's free to go. Come on, Jane.

To Jane's surprise, Adam barks more legalese at the detectives before they leave.

How do you know so much? she asks him when they're in his Volvo.

I finished law school before I went into botany. I never took the bar. I wasn't suited for it. But I know enough to understand that they are taking advantage of you. Never talk to them again unless someone else is present. You may need a lawyer even now.

No, says Jane. She isn't in trouble. How could she be? It's not that she hasn't done wrong. But they are asking all the wrong questions.

Earlier that day, as Jane had stood looking at the child, after the rest of her team had assembled in a horrified circle around her, Jane found herself in a strange removed state. Something familiar about this. The obvious attractiveness of the small child, the tiny hands, the delicate bones, posed against the sturdy trunk. All the trees that Angela

256

had climbed in their Berkeley backyard, at Muir Woods, along the Marin coast. The pink delicate skin against the centuries-old rough bark. The incongruousness of it all. The indecency. Yes, she knew it all.

Of all the aspects of finding the third girl, of seeing her in the flesh, what stuck with Jane was the makeup. It hadn't been obvious at first, so skillfully and naturally had it been applied. But the leader of the search party pointed out the foundation, the blush, and the lip liner. As much as any other thirteen- and fourteen-year-old girl, Angela had plied on the makeup, overdoing it with all of her friends, of course, with their overshadowed eyes and unrealistic lashes and bright red cheeks and lips. Like brightly colored Christmas toys. That stage lasted a year or so, and then they calmed down and started applying makeup more rationally, in a way that enhanced rather than hid their natural beauty. That's what the murderer had done. He — or she — surely had exquisite taste.

Two days pass. All is quiet in town. It's October 30. The eve of Halloween. Not yet time to panic. But it's coming, it will come, Jane knows. Tomorrow night. October 31. The dread will start curdling meat and drink, sour the notes of the Bach she's put on her CD player, seep into her very bones.

One of the Three Terrible Nights. Ever since she was small, Jane had hated them. The three eves. All Hallows Eve (Halloween). Christmas Eve. And New Year's Eve. All the nights when she'd felt most lonely. Even when surrounded by her seven sisters as a child. Even when married with a child of her own. There was something about those three nights that reminded Jane she was utterly by herself on the planet.

Her phone rings. It is Helen.

Jane! So glad I got you! This is not the voice of Helen, the boss. Or Helen the friend. This is Helen the Giver of Charity.

Jane is not glad. She knows what is coming. Prompted by pity.

You left the nursery so quickly this afternoon I didn't have a chance.

Yes. Here it comes.

I'm having a small Halloween party — can you come tomorrow night? Dinner. Very informal. You don't have to wear a costume if you don't feel like it. And Helen went on to list the people who would be there. Hugh (her husband). Anthony (their twenty-six-year-old son who lived in San Francisco). Some neighbors (Jane doesn't catch their names).

There is no way out. Adam would have told Helen of his unsuccessful attempt to lure Jane to Santa Cruz for a party with his household of surfer buddies. And maybe it wouldn't be too bad. Maybe the conversation would be fluid, not stilted. Maybe no one would drink too much.

And, anyway, it wouldn't matter. She would go, and the really bad part, Halloween, the *eve of All Hallows Day,* would be over.

Jane has a trick. For things that are really horrible, really terrifying, threatening to her soul even, she divides time into *before* and *after.* She does the opposite of what the Buddhists do. She refuses to acknowledge the moment. This gets her through many things. One moment, it is *before* and the next, *after.* The moment itself doesn't exist. But this didn't work on Halloween. It didn't work on Christmas Eve or New Year's Eve either. But it was on Halloween, when magic was supposed to be strongest, our connection to our loved ones and to the spiritual world the closest, that Jane felt the most vulnerable.

Okay, Jane concedes, and on her way over to Helen's house, she keeps saying into the unseasonably balmy wind rushing past her: *Okay. Okay. Okay.*

She gets to Helen's Victorian house, located a little south of the center of town, a little before 8:00 p.m. Neat. Not in the least ostentatious, although Helen, affluent businesswoman, could certainly have afforded to be. Discrete Halloween decorations: a line of uncut pumpkins on the porch, a string of orange lights on the border bushes. California holidays. Even after nearly twenty years, Jane isn't used to it, to the mild breeze, the lack of ice and snow and shivering. She rides her motorbike around the block a couple of times to make sure she isn't too early. She remembers how, in her previous life, she would be dismayed if a guest arrived before the expected time. The panic of the first knock on the door before everything was perfect.

At five minutes past eight, she parks the motorbike by the curb, combs her hair back with her fingers, and walks up to the front door. It opens before she can knock, and she is enveloped in a warm embrace by Helen. She smells rum on her breath. The living room is already full — it seems as though there has been a predinner get-together, but that she, Jane, had been invited for the meal only. A boisterous, red-faced man — Jane finds out later he is one of the neighbors, wearing a pirate's outfit —

insists on getting her some punch. A woman who gives off an air of elegance, with smooth white hair in a neat chignon and pearl earrings, makes room on the sofa for Jane. A young man, who looks as if he feels as out of place as Jane does, is on her other side. This is Tony, Helen's son from her first marriage. Hugh, Helen's husband, Jane knows well, of course. She likes him, as she likes Helen. But that doesn't mean she wants to be uncomfortably dressed, making small talk, in their living room on one of the Three Terrible Nights.

She thinks of her last Christmas Eve with her family. That is, *her* family: Rick and Angela. Holidays had decidedly less charm since Angela had entered her sullen teenage years, and the wonder and magic of Santa and presents had faded. How short those years were! And yet, in the middle of them, they seemed to last forever. *I will forever be Mommy and will be thinking at all times what will delight my child. I shall bake and shop and wrap and do everything I can to make this experience truly magical.* That last Christmas, they were in Hawaii, at a rental beach house, they hadn't even eaten together. Angela had opened her presents on Christmas Eve, as she always had, appeared gratified at all the stuff Jane had contrived to pull together from the local stores, from Amazon, from other online venues that would deliver to the islands. Jane had brought an extra suitcase so she could get all the presents home. Angela photographed herself wearing the new sweater and earrings, toyed with the perfume, and then retreated to her room to talk to her friends on her cell phone.

Rick and Jane had spent the evening companionably enough, reading on the porch overlooking the beach, so different from the Northern California one. They ended the evening in bed with some lovemaking that felt somewhat obligatory on Rick's part — he knew how Jane feels on Christmas Eve — but nevertheless was reassuring. All in all, the abyss had been kept at a distance that evening and the next day. And then, of course, everything had changed.

The mood in the room shifts. They are talking about the children. The girls.

It's a sleeper, someone who's been here a while, declares the neighbor man, whose name Jane has already forgotten. *Something's been triggered in him.*

Or her.

No, it's a him. It's gotta be.

A woman could easily do it. And would.

Women are more dangerous. This is, surprisingly, from the petite elegant woman.

Why would anyone do such things? Helen asks. The meal is over, and she is serving coffee now, and her watchful gaze is on Jane, but Jane feels in control. She's had three glasses of champagne and is feeling no pain. She's thinking of Angela, but then she's always thinking of Angela.

She remembers her dream of the night before. The lost girls gather around Jane. Heidi, Rose, and Amy. They play ring around the rosy. Jane is filled with inexplicable happiness. Little Amy grabs her hand, pulls her into the game. *We all fall down.* They do, and suddenly they are all dead. Jane too is no longer alive; she can't feel her limbs, she can't blink her eyes. But she can still see, lying on her back on the grass, the sky and the sun and the tops of the trees. Someone bends over her, checking her heart for a heartbeat. There is none. Jane is not breathing either. The person is satisfied and goes away.

Then they are at the top of the bell tower at Berkeley, and Jane pushes the three girls off the edge, one by one. Others watch. No one interferes. *It had to be done,* Jane explains to the people who have gathered around to watch. At the bottom of the tower, three small broken bodies. Jane has no regrets that she can detect. But she woke up gasping for air.

You okay, Jane? Helen. She looks concerned.

No. Yes, Jane lies. Then she quickly makes her excuses and leaves the party, rides her motorbike home. She can see from an empty wineglass on the table that Edward has been there, from the level of the wine in the bottle that he must have waited some time for her. But for once she's glad she missed him.

When everything you value is gone, when you've been stripped to bare flesh and bone, what then?

You have to laugh.

There have been many incidents. Here is one. One day in the cafeteria, sixteen-year-old Jane had been approached by an older boy, a football player, not one of the stars but a lesser of the gods on Mount Olympus. A benchwarmer, but even that carried considerable cachet in Big Cabin. His nickname was Tree. *Tree! Tree!* The cheerleaders chanted Friday night at the end of the game when he was finally allowed to play for two minutes, when he could do no harm, he was that kind of fuckup for sure.

264

Jane didn't know his real name. He was an envoy, she could tell from the snickers coming from the popular table where he'd been sitting. His intent, malevolent; you could tell from the way his fingers twitched.

Jane was at a table across from the school's only Asian girl, Lisa Lee. Jane didn't exactly like Lisa, but there was always space at her table and Jane hated eating alone. She could have looked around, squeezed in next to one of her sisters, but that was admitting defeat. Lunchtime was a battleground, requiring a tightening of the stomach, hours of anticipatory terror. Once in the cafeteria, Jane always entered a sort of fugue state, the din of voices and the odor of burned tater tots and sour milk barely registering. She simply had to endure. She sometimes tried to find a safe place to sit, on the fringe of a group slightly outside what was considered okay but not so far that they attracted attention. She kept her eyes fixed on the clock, mechanically eating her tuna fish or peanut butter sandwich, her mouth dry.

What was she afraid of? Something like what was happening now.

Tree was, as his name implied, enormous and implacable. A thick trunk, heavy shoulders like trestles. He tromped rather than walked toward Jane. He was also hairless, having shaved his head. A skinhead. Typical Big Cabin. Someone on the cutting edge of the 1970s in the 1990s. He'd even shaved his arms. A skinarm. A new twist on an old, old theme.

Tree reached Jane. He seemed to have trouble stopping his forward momentum. He put his hairless arms out and felt for the edge of the table, steadied himself, and relaxed into a slouch. Jane had to crane her neck to see his face, he was that big and that close to her. *You going to the dance?* he said to the air. He wasn't looking at Jane, but he could hardly have meant Lisa Lee. She was, according to the caste hierarchy of Big Cabin High, an untouchable.

Lisa picked up her tray, loaded her trash and milk carton onto it, and stood up to leave.

Please don't go, Jane managed to say, but Lisa just shrugged and high-tailed it off.

Still without looking at Jane, Tree lowered himself, not so much onto the bench as on top of Jane. It was as if she didn't exist. She saw his massive Levi jeans-clothed bottom descending and quickly moved over, but was still trapped into uncomfortable thigh-to-thigh contact. Jane tried to wiggle away but was prevented by a steel support bar under the table. She was trapped.

Go with me. It was not a question.

He moved closer. He reached one thick-boned arm behind Jane, around her but not touching her. His hand on the seat on the other side. Locking her in.

His breath was foul. Day-old fish.

Jane could hear the continued laughter from the popular table as Tree leaned closer. The lunchroom was emptying fast. The sun no longer shone through the high windows. It was afternoon now. Time for trig, then English, then home. A respite of sorts. Although in the chaos at home she often wished for the classroom, for the lines of desks, the straight rulers, the rows of books lined up on the windowsill. Order.

I gotta go. But Jane can't move. His arm is blocking her. She feels a tightening in her groin, almost sexual. Terror? Excitement? He is so close she can see what an uneven job he'd done shaving. Little tufts of blond hair stuck out amid the shiny scalp. A thin red line sliced across one corner of his mouth. An accident with a razor blade.

DO IT! a male voice boomed from the other table.

Jane felt a hand grab her shirt on her left side, yanking it up so her belly was exposed. Then on her right side, another yank by a second hand, this time so violent that it

267

pulled the shirt over her head, catching her arms in it, the cotton fabric covering her head so she could neither see nor breathe. She struggled to pull it down, but the pressure was relentless. Her shirt was dragged over her head, catching her long hair in its decorative buttons. It hurt. She was sitting in her bra and skirt. Tree tossed her shirt onto a puddle of spilt ketchup on the table, but before Jane could escape, he had her by her bra strap, fumbling with the clasp, grunting with frustration until he finally gave up and with a mighty effort ripped the bra off. All Jane could think of was her mother saying *Always wear clean underwear* as Tree ran off whooping triumphantly, waving Jane's bra above his head like a captured flag.

What size? cried a girl's voice.

This made Tree stop and look.

34B.

What a loser.

Totally.

A roar of derision as Jane, naked from the waist up, covered herself with her arms. She would not cry. She would not. Instead she laughed. She began slowly and softly, but got louder and louder. She laughed and laughed. What a fool. She deserved the ridicule. She laughed at her shame.

Look at the cunt. She doesn't even know she's been humiliated.

That's because she's a natural slut. Invite her to the postgame party, Tree. Bet you get past second base next time.

Bitch. This was Jane calling it out, hardly able to get the words out because she was laughing so hard. *Moron.* Still holding her arms to her chest, she retrieved her shirt from the ketchup pool and put it on, the red stain covering her chest and belly. She ran from the room still laughing.

Why is Jane thinking of this now? She is a grown woman. Much worse things had happened to her, to the world. She had borne, and buried, a child. Wars had been started, and continued, displacing and killing hundreds of thousands of people. She herself is in a safe place now. She is lying naked in her bed, naked by choice, and she is happy. She is. Edward has just left, and she is alone, but it doesn't matter. She pushes all other thoughts away.

People are gossiping. About Jane. Somehow the word has gotten out. About Angela. About the incident with the roses. About the wrecked car, although it's apparently interpreted as *attempted murder with a vehicle but they didn't charge her.*

Now instead of ignoring her and giving her the space she needs at Three Sisters, at the Safeway, at the Rite Aid, Jane finds herself being scrutinized around town. People smile at her and say *hello* and look her up and down as she wheels her cart through the frozen food aisle. She leaves the half-filled cart in the dairy section and goes home to eat cereal out of the box.

How are you today? people ask, so solicitously! Foot traffic at the nursery increases. Jane is barraged with requests to be friends on Facebook, gets texts from numbers she doesn't recognize. She ignores them all, stops logging on to her email, turns her cell phone off. The only people she can bear are Helen, Adam, and the three sisters at the café. They treat her just the same. And, of course, Edward and Alma. Her saviors.

One incident occurs in the Three Sisters. Jane is having her morning cup of coffee, idly flipping through the *Moon News* (*Supervisors say water rationing will start this month. Feed and Grain says prices of puppy chow to go up*) when Fred Barnes, the one who was the subject of gossip after the second disappearance, of the Ames girl, walks in. He was cleared because he had an alibi for the disappearance of the third girl, Amy.

Hi, Jane, he says. *May I?* He points to the

270

empty seat across the table from her. Taken by surprise, she nods. They don't really know each other. Before his wife left him, Jane had paid a visit to their home in Montara as a courtesy consult visit, to see why their garden wasn't thriving. She found they had planted their expensive purchases in the wrong places, in the wrong soil, and were watering them way too much. He hadn't shown much interest at the time, except to upbraid his wife on how much she had spent on the garden.

He sits there in silence for a moment. He orders a beer. At 8:00 a.m. He follows her eyes down to his glass, and laughs.

Don't worry, I'll be sober for my first class at ten, he says. *Just a little pick-me-up.*

I'm not worrying, it's none of my business, says Jane. She waits to hear what he has to say.

He seems loath to start talking. He sips his beer, gazes over at the paper, attempts to read the headlines upside down. *More water troubles ahead, I see,* he says.

Good for my business, says Jane. *People replace the silly things they've planted with drought-resistant native varieties. We do our best business during droughts.*

Guess ill winds do blow some good.

You could say that.

He clears his throat. *Here it comes,* thinks Jane.

So, he says, *how does it feel to be in the hot seat?*

And what seat might that be? Jane keeps her eyes focused on the paper. She reads, *Water rationing will take effect November 15, and people exceeding the levels established by the council will pay fines.*

You know. The goddamned hot seat I was in myself three weeks ago! As if I could do such a thing! I have three daughters of my own.

And a painted doll collection.

Fred's face flushes red. His hand clenches around the handle of his glass. Jane remembers he has a reputation for temper. Once after a bad call during a football game, he picked up the school mascot, an undersize freshman in a fox's outfit, and threw him three feet into a crowd of fans. Luckily, no one was hurt, not even the mascot.

That's nasty gossip. I kept my girls' dolls after they outgrew them. I kept them safe. I thought they'd want them for their own daughters.

And you painted them?

To keep them fresh! They were fading! I went over all of this with the authorities!

Slow down, Fred, I'm not the police. You've

got nothing to worry about, is what I hear.

Yes, but you *do.*

Me? Jane is startled, not at the news, but that someone would state it so bluntly. She wonders if it's his first beer.

I hear you have no alibis for any of the nights in question. I hear that people do mighty strange things when they lose a kid.

I have nothing to say to gossip.

Well, I do, having been the butt of it. I almost lost my job. Which would have meant losing my house. As it is, I'm left with almost nothing. No wife. No kids. Just a stupid job and an empty house.

Fred, I'm sorry, but I don't see what this has to do with me.

If it turns out that it's been you. Or that you had anything to do with it. I swear to God I'll impose the death penalty on you myself.

He has said this last sentence loudly enough for coffee drinkers at tables around them to hear. They are waiting to see what Jane will do, what she will say.

She says nothing. She looks down at her paper again.

Jane has a weight within her chest. She carries it at all times. A tumor, a malignant one, that appeared the minute she got the news about Angela. It impedes her breathing. She has not taken a clear, deep breath in more than a year. According to Sartre, though, she is free:

> He was free, free in every way, free to behave like a fool or a machine, free to accept, free to refuse, free to equivocate; to marry, to give up the game, to drag this death weight about with him for years to come.

Deadweight. That's what it was.

But she wouldn't be entirely truthful if she said it started with Angela's death. It started, in fact, with Angela's birth, with the knowledge that she, Jane, was inextricably tied to someone else for life — or, rather, until death. Her marriage vows of *till death do us part* had been a sham, said in church, in front of a priest and witnesses for the sake of Rick's family and her family. All wacko Catholics, Rick and she agreed. But the words had no weight for Jane and, she suspected, little for Rick either. Did they love each other? They did — up to a point. Either, in retrospect, would have loved anyone kind to them. And Rick was kind. He valued Jane, once. He valued her keen mind, her curiosity, her quirkiness. And Jane valued that Rick valued her. She admired many things about him too: that he was hardworking and as honest as he needed to be, which meant he wasn't above lying when it suited his purpose. To her relief, it rarely did, and only for small things. *Did you take out the garbage? Did you really pay the utility bill?* Such things she could fix. It seemed a small price to pay for security, for good enough sex, for not returning to an empty house after work. Then she got pregnant with Angela. An added bonus, and a burden. A real commitment this time.

Once she caught Rick in one of his lies when his mother was visiting, after his father passed away. They'd had a pleasant enough day, taking Angela to the Oakland Zoo — she was five at the time, and crazy for the monkey house — and then out for some Mexican food. Back in Berkeley, they sat on the front porch of their bungalow, enjoying the parade of students, professors, and hipsters walking by. While they were lazily sipping their wine and chatting about Rick's job, Jane's job, Angela's alternative kindergarten, Jane remembered she had an appointment the next day to look at some native plants that had been discovered in Gilroy. She asked Rick if there was enough gas in the car. This was not as simple-minded a question as it might sound. The gas gauge in their aging Subaru was unreliable, and they had to keep careful track of when they'd filled it up and what the mileage was when they did so. It was one of the basic tenets of their household, as serious as going to Mass on Sunday when Jane was growing up, because so much of their lives was choreographed over who needed the car. Mostly they got around by bicycle, both working in Berkeley. They had an attachment to their bikes that included a seat and wheels for Angela to pedal behind them when they dropped her off and picked her up from day care.

Plenty, Rick had said. *I just filled it up.* On the surface, this lie made no sense, as it was one that was bound to be caught. Rick's lies were like that. They were plausible enough when he told them, but there was no way he was going to get away with them — the situations of the lies themselves ensured he would be busted. *Did you change Angela's diaper? Did you buy milk? Did anyone call me while I was gone?* This put Jane in an odd position. Unsure of whether she could trust his answers, she took to verifying, always, what he said, or find out the electric bill hadn't been paid, or, in this case, run out of gas on the Peninsula, right off the San Mateo Bridge. Rick's mother was with her and calmly took charge of the situation, calling roadside assistance and arranging for gas to be delivered, and getting them out of the car and well away from the cars streaming past on the busy highway. *You can't expect people to change,* she says. *Richard always was an optimist. He would imagine the world was the way he wanted it to be and forgot it might inconvenience other people if it turned out not to be so.*

You're saying he's delusional, Jane had said flatly, and Rick's mother had mildly reproved her. *Wishing things are the way you want them to be is the way to make the world a better place.*

Wishing the car had gas in it didn't do us much good, Jane says, but let it pass. Still, on the whole, she believed it was better than being alone.

You might wonder — Jane did, frequently — why it was worth it for her. Why continue? With the night terrors and the crushing weight on her chest. It was a valid question. Why suffer so miserably? Because Jane feared what was next. She didn't believe she'd see Angela, or her mother, or her father — the latter of which she was glad about. But she did believe she would be punished. More pain awaited. That she knew for sure. That's what kept her alive:

the fear of what was worse.

Later that night, a knock on the door. A strange woman stands there. *Strange* as in both unknown and odd; the woman's hair is disheveled, her eyes wide with madness. Jane recognizes herself. Somehow she knows. *You're Amy's mother,* she says.
And you found her.
Jane nods.
May I come in?
Jane is uncertain about this, but the woman steps forward confidently, so she moves to the side and allows her to pass. She's picking up on something, but she's not sure what it is. It isn't grief, or, rather, it isn't only grief.
The woman sits down on the couch.
What's your name? Jane asks. She can't keep calling her Amy's mother. Besides, she isn't anymore, and that would rub it in. Jane knows this.
Anne.
Anne, how can I help you?
You can't.
Jane understands. She almost reaches out to touch Anne's arm but thinks better of it. Touch can be lethal. She understands that too.
Let me phrase it another way, Jane begins

carefully. *What do you want from me?*

Jane is assuming that Anne wants to hear firsthand how Amy was found, what she looked like. Although all that would have been clear from the crime scene photos. Jane hadn't touched anything except to lightly feel the little hand that had hung down. It had been cold. Jane had withdrawn her own hand quickly. She had told no one about that quick gesture.

I hear you were unaccounted for the night she was taken.

I was in the city.

Alone?

No, Jane says. *With a . . .* she almost says *friend,* then changes to *acquaintance.*

But you can't produce him or her.

No.

The police say you don't even know this person's name.

Not for certain. She called herself Sheree.

Let me get this clear: you were running around San Francisco in the middle of the night — a rainy night — on a motorcycle, with someone you didn't even know the real name of?

Jane has to admit it sounds odd. *Yes,* she says, then adds, *I do odd things sometimes.*

I hear you also lack alibis for the other . . . disappearances.

Look, says Jane. *Is it likely I could be the murderer? I don't even have a car! How would I transport the girls? Keep them hidden after I took them from their houses?*

It's strange. The police think so too. And that you happened to lead everyone to the body — to a place off the track that everyone else had missed.

They can think what they want, Jane says, even though she goes cold inside to hear this. This was where she was supposed to be starting anew, with an unsullied life, with a clean reputation. This was her sanctuary. Would she have to move again? When would it end, the nightmare that is her life?

Anne is looking around Jane's living room. Searching for something. What? Some evidence? What evidence could there be? Her makeup in the bathroom? A supply of woven blankets?

The police have searched, Jane tells her, remembering the feeling she had going back into her house afterward, after strange hands had picked up and touched all her possessions. They'd made themselves coffee, left dirty cups on the sink, a detail that stuck.

Anne nods. She seems distracted. Jane notices her eyes are wet. Jane understands, she truly does. But she doesn't want this hostility and suspicion in her life. It is too much. She feels guilty. She looks Anne in the eyes, she makes sure not to cover her mouth or touch her face. *I didn't kill your daughter,* she says. *Let me get you a tissue.*

She gets up and retrieves the box of tissues from where it lives, by her bedside, always. When she re-enters the room, Anne is standing by the door. At first Jane is relieved. Thank God, she's leaving. Then she notices the gun. It is pointed at Jane's chest.

Anne, Jane says. She says it softly. *You're making a terrible mistake.* She sees Anne's finger moving back and forth on the trigger. Jane recognizes what is in the room in addition to grief. Rage. Jane's intimate friend.

I read about you on the Internet, Anne says. *I know everything. You are a coveter. You are destructive. You are a killer.*

Jane couldn't deny any of those things. She didn't try. *If you only knew,* she thought. She forced herself to stand up straight, her arms by her side. So this is how it ends. So be it. She closes her eyes and waits. The gunshot echoes in the small room. Jane can't believe how loud it is. A hot flash in Jane's head, and then nothing.

Jane opens her eyes. She is on the floor of

her living room. Her head is burning.

She reaches up, and her hand comes away red. But she is alive.

Jane tentatively wiggles her fingers. She sits, then stands, leaning against a chair. Her legs are weak, but they are working. She lifts her right arm, then her left. Everything seems to be working. She has literally dodged a bullet.

The room is empty. The front door is open. Outside, she hears tires squeal as a car pulls away from the curb.

She slowly gets up — she is dizzy — and goes into the tiny bathroom, looks in the mirror. The bullet must have grazed the side of her head. She dampens a washcloth and cleans the wound. A surface scratch. Although it is bleeding profusely, and the hair matted with dark red liquid, it does not appear serious. She has been extraordinarily lucky. It won't need stitches, even.

Back in the living room, she looks for the bullet. She finds it embedded in a book on the bookshelf behind where she'd been standing, in Jane Austen's *Persuasion*. The bullet had reached page 276.

Jane takes the bullet in her hand, and weighs it.

Question: Does she call the police?

On the one hand, if she doesn't, Anne may

try again. Jane isn't eager to encounter the woman after she realizes that she, Jane, is still alive.

On the other hand, hasn't the poor woman suffered enough?

Jane is inclined to leave things be. She goes back into the bathroom. The bleeding has stopped, so Jane is able to soap her hair and rinse off the blood. She combs damp hair over the wound. No one will notice, especially if she wears her hair down.

Jane sets off for a walk on the beach. She will not tell anyone about this incident. She counts it up as her penance, as her mother used to say, *for the poor souls in purgatory.* God knows Jane will need similar help when she gets there.

Jane had few photographs of Angela, but what she really wanted to erase were the memories. Memories had the power to hurt.

Friends and family had to talk her out of it. *You'll feel differently in a few years. You'll want the photos then. Don't do anything rash. Put them in a safe deposit box. Give them to Rick for safekeeping.*

But Jane had destroyed almost all of them, burned them in the fireplace. Rick was furious. So be it. Jane had never been one for photographs anyway. She believed that you lost the real memories when you took photos of something. She knew people who came to the arboretum and spent the whole time behind the lenses of their cameras or phones and missed the whole experience. Rick had photographed himself out of Angela's birth and childhood. He'd stopped taking photos during the bad years because he said he didn't want to remember them. The joke was on him. He'd have those burned into his memory rather than printed onto photo paper.

The evening after the visit from Amy's mother, Jane finds herself in church. At Our Lady of the Pillar, in Half Moon Bay. She hasn't been in a church since Angela's memorial service, and then she could scarcely have considered herself *there*. It's the ugliest church Jane has ever seen, the product of 1970s architectural standards, squat and geometric, with brown and orange colors in the carpets, the patterned chairs, the geometric altar cloth. Nothing inspiring. Nothing grand about it. Jane likes it that way. It reminds her that she hasn't missed anything in the twenty-odd years since she left the church. She sits down on the hard pew.

To her astonishment, she finds herself

praying. She wonders what that means. She finds herself begging. *Please. Please.* What is she asking for? She doesn't want anything from this all-powerful figure who took her daughter away. She doesn't need anything from this deity. She doesn't want money, youth, or beauty, and certainly not things. She simply wants the pain to go away.

Jane wakes up the next day feeling unwell. Feverish. The room spins when she gets out of bed. She fixes her hair so that the wound is covered, gets on her motorbike, and heads to work anyway. It is going to be an especially busy day at the nursery. Members of the Peninsula Garden Club, an important group of customers, are visiting. She is supposed to give them a lecture on native California wildflowers.

The group is due to arrive at 3:00 p.m., but by noon Jane knows she isn't going to make it. All her limbs ache, and she feels cold and hot at the same time. The flu. She hasn't been so afflicted in years. Helen sends her home. Adam is asked to take over Jane's part of the garden club presentation. He was amenable, of course. Always ready to be helpful, Adam.

Then on the way home, going west on 92, Jane gets in an accident. A small one, but a shock because she's never been in one before. One moment she is slowing down to a stop behind a sky blue Cadillac, and the next moment she's hit it with a firm *thump!* Jane can barely get her leg over her motorbike and, shivering with fever, inspects the Cadillac's rear fender. There doesn't seem to be any damage, not even a scratch, but the driver, a woman, rolls down the driver's-side window and gestures at her to come over. The woman, perhaps in her early sixties, is feeling her neck and upper back tentatively with her right hand.

There's no visible damage to the car, Jane says when she gets to the driver's-side window. Her tongue feels thick in her mouth. *But why don't you get out and check for yourself?*

I'm not sure I should, says the woman. She is wearing bright red lipstick and a string of pearls, a tailored suit, but not one that you would wear to a job. What is she doing here in Half Moon Bay? She does not look familiar. Perhaps a hill person Jane hasn't personally met.

Why not? Jane asks. She tries to seem reasonable, but her throat hurts so much it comes out in a loud rasp. She sounds aggressive, ready for a fight. Jane takes a step back from the car in case the woman gets that impression.

I may have hurt my neck and my back. Isn't that what happens when you're rear-ended?

Not necessarily, Jane manages to say. She desperately needs to sit down somewhere.

I think I need to see my doctor.

That is, of course, your prerogative, Jane says. *But in the meantime, there's the matter of the car. If you don't mind, I'll take some photos.* She walks or, rather, staggers back to her motorbike to get her phone.

Are you drunk? calls the woman. Jane ignores her. She unsteadily takes a few pictures of the seemingly pristine back fender of the Cadillac. She writes down her name, her phone number, and her insurance company and insurance policy number. Her writing looks like Angela would have printed it in second grade, crazy stick letters that don't match up. She walks back and gives the paper to the woman. The woman takes the paper and throws it on the seat next to her. Then, as Jane turns to leave, the woman reaches out and grabs Jane's wrist. It hurts.

No, the woman says. *You'll wait here until my husband arrives. Forty-five minutes. An hour, maybe. He's in San Francisco today. He's coming as fast as he can.*

I can't, Jane begins, but the woman interrupts her.

You'll stay. Otherwise, it's a hit-and-run. She's almost gloating. Over what? Her power over her husband? Over Jane?

I can't wait here an hour, Jane tries to say, but all that comes out is *Can't. Hour.* She's losing her sense of time. Cars are slowing down and people are staring, trying to see what is going on. A *gaper's block,* Jane's dad used to call them back in Oklahoma. Everyone needing to see. Jane has never been on the receiving end of the gapes before.

One car swerves suddenly out of traffic and comes to a stop next to Jane's motorbike.

What's the problem? A man's voice. Familiar. Jane opens her eyes. She hasn't realized she'd closed them, or that she is now sitting on the pine needle–covered ground by the side of the road.

It is Edward. His face concerned and frowning. Jane half lifts a hand, then loses her will to do it, or anything else. Her eyes close again. She has the urge to lie down on the pine needles and sleep.

As if through a fog, she hears voices arguing.

Don't be ridiculous. You have her contact information. There have been no injuries. She is free to go.

I may be hurt.

You're not. Edward's voice, decisive. He is standing over Jane. *What's wrong? Are you injured?*

Sick, Jane manages to say. A hand touches her forehead.

Good God, you're burning up. I'm taking you home.

Bike, Jane says.

Forget that piece of crap. It'll be safe enough. You can come back and get it tomorrow. Or the next day. Come on. Get in the car. You're in no condition to be out of bed.

Jane obeys. She has been thinking of Edward. Too much. She has been worried how she would act next time she sees him. But it all feels very natural. She is guided into the car, collapses onto soft leather seats.

You're safe now, Edward says.

Everything in Jane's body hurts, even her eyelashes. She is in Edward's car. She is in her cottage. She is being helped into bed. Her head touches a soft pillow. Ah, relief. A cool blanket is placed over her. She is vaguely aware of some sounds, and then a cold glass is placed against her lips.

Drink.

As she drinks, some of the water drips onto her neck. It is so icy that she gasps.

You've got a high fever.

Some more rustling, then,

Open up. Take these. It's aspirin; it'll get the fever down.

She takes the tablets, accepts some more water, painfully swallows. Then swoons back onto the pillow.

She awakens several hours later. The room is dark, but she senses a presence. Next to her is a form. It turns and places a hand on her forehead.

Better, Edward says, for it is he. She can't see his features, only hears his voice. But she is being cared for. Someone cares. How long has it been since she'd allowed herself to accept generosity from someone? She always felt too obliged, obligated. Now she is merely grateful.

Jane dreams. She is desiring sex, she is excited, she is about to demand it from anyone near her. A man presents himself. He is seedy. Disreputable. Greasy hair and a spindly body. He is not anyone Jane has ever seen before. He is not ideal. He is not sexy. No matter. Hurry up. Rick is on the other side of the bedroom door. No, it is Jane's mother. *Quick. Lie down. Penetrate me. Do it.* But before things can be consummated, the door opens and in comes Edward. He doesn't look disappointed or shocked. Is he pleased? To view her in her degradation? Her desire has not abated. Jane wakes unsatisfied.

The house is dark. She is alone in the bed. Her fever has broken, but she still feels weak. She tries to sit up but falls back on her pillow. Then she senses a presence. A dark form in the armchair near her window.

Come here, she says.

Edward gets up, and sits next to her. She takes his hand and puts it on her breast.

Do you really want this? he asks. *Now?*

Jane doesn't like to be asked. She isn't into rape fantasies, she believes *no means no,* but she hates the idea that she has to be explicit about wanting him. She does want him. But she doesn't like to beg.

No means no, she says. *I have not said no.*

But only yes means yes, he says. *You're not up on the latest thinking.* He has not touched her. He has not made a move toward her. There is nothing sensual in his manner. He has taken his hand off her breast and has crossed his arms over his chest. That means something, that body language, but Jane is still too dazed to figure out what it is.

She is not looking her best. She probably smells bad. This is not an erotic moment.

Yes, she says.

Skin. The parts that are soft and those that

291

are not. Applying pressure of the right kind. The shoulders. The thighs. Skin against skin. Fingers that grasp and stroke. Pressing one cheek against his shoulder blades, her hands meeting on either side of his torso. The pride of possession. Jane has fallen, badly.

■ ■ ■ ■

PART III
LOVE

■ ■ ■ ■

Then it is as if their brief separation has never been. Edward starts coming to Jane every night. Jane has never experienced anything like this. How *physical* it all is! She is still carrying her grief; she still has the heaviness and the chest pains, but along with that is a tingling in her limbs and desire in her loins. She has forgotten . . . no, that is not true. She has never felt this way, not for Rick, not for any of her previous romantic attachments. They seemed trivial, inane compared to this.

Sometimes knowing Edward exists in the world is enough. Then sometimes she has to see him. She walks past his office in the morning, finds excuses to walk down Main Street at lunchtime and after work. She has to see his face, overshadowed by a lock of hair that has fallen in his eyes, his lean body bent over a desk, his fingers touching the keyboard. She has to be sure of the *physical-*

ity of him.

She never knows when he will come. Each night an excitement too much to be borne. Will he come? Even when he doesn't, she isn't disappointed. He exists. He desires her. He will come again.

And when he did come! She holds him and strokes him all over — his arms, his legs, his belly — reveling in the wonder that is *him.* The world recedes. Nothing exists but the two of them in the soft bed. Even the pillows and sheets and blankets are discarded, not necessary. What is necessary? His hands. His mouth. The length of his body, pressed to hers, arm to arm, thigh to thigh, face-to-face. No space separates them.

What of Alma, then? What role does she play in this? Jane doesn't care at first. Alma is incidental. Collateral damage. Then she bumps into Alma on the street, right after one of her pilgrimages to Edward's office. For they were pilgrimages, daily journeys to a sacred object.

Jane! I haven't seen much of you lately.

I've been busy. Jane is trying to control her face, trying not to smile so much. She is certain everyone can see into her and see that she has come to life again.

Oh, it's my fault as much as yours. It's

midterms, and the students are demanding attention.

Jane smiles. She can't think of anything to say.

Why don't you come to dinner this weekend? I'm sure Edward would be delighted.

Even at the sound of his name being spoken aloud, a thrill runs through Jane.

Yes, of course, she says. Alma is as gracious and charming as ever, but did Jane detect something else? Something more intimate? More knowing? If possible, more affectionate? Jane doesn't care, not one bit.

Edward doesn't come to Jane on Thursday. He doesn't come on Friday. Then, on Saturday, Jane rides over to their house. Deliberately a little late. Trying not to show how desperate she is.

Edward opens the door. He looks pleasant, although not necessarily pleased to see her. Or not as pleased as she'd expected. As if welcoming any guest. She supposes that is to be expected. But it hurts nonetheless.

He ushers her in. The table is set as if for a formal dinner party. No, a romantic dinner. For three. The plates are white, there are glasses for wine and glasses for water and multiple forks and knives arranged around the plate in a way that had always bewildered Jane. A tablecloth. Candles. Flowers. Music is playing, piano music, something precise, almost mathematical, the cadences surprising, not soothing. Jane doesn't recognize it. Not elevator music. Real music.

Delicious smells. Edward disappears into the kitchen and brings back a glass of champagne for Jane. She is terribly self-conscious of the way she is dressed. She changed from her work clothes, so she is clean, but only just. She hasn't showered since that morning. She wears no makeup, only jeans and a T-shirt. She expected something informal like their previous lunches. But clearly they have something quite different in mind this time.

She sips her champagne too fast, and her glass is empty. Edward comes in with the bottle and fills it up. He's got a glass of his own in his other hand.

Alma will be with us in a minute, he says. Jane expects him to exhibit some sign of their intimacy, but there is none. She is melting. She is nearly in tears of joy at seeing him again, at being in the same room as him, and despair, that he is not acknowledging her. It takes all her willpower not to reach out and stroke his arm. He is wearing pressed trousers and a long-sleeved white shirt.

Alma, when she comes out of the kitchen, is wearing the proverbial little black dress. She puts a plate of paté and bread on the table. As she turns around, Jane can see that her dress is backless, showing her straight spine, her slender shoulder blades. Her dangling earrings sparkle.

Unlike Edward, Alma is effusive.

Jane! How lovely! She kisses Jane on either cheek. Jane still isn't used to that, and wiggles awkwardly when she should submit. Alma's perfume is faint but lovely. Rosewater, Jane guesses.

Jane is on her third glass of champagne by the time they sit down.

No, you here, says Alma, guiding Jane to the chair at the head of the table. Edward and Alma are sitting on either side of her, Edward to the left, Alma to the right. Alma hands the salad around the table.

Jane by now is quite tipsy. She spears a piece of lettuce but is not hungry. She is confused. She is bursting with her, their, secret.

Alma clears the salad dishes away and brings in a roast chicken with potatoes arranged around it. Jane realizes there is no way she can eat it. She looks with dismay as

Edward carves thick slices of breast meat and puts two on her plate, along with some potatoes.

Jane, you seem a little anxious. This from Alma, who has sat down again. *What's the matter?*

I'm sleeping with your lover, that's the matter, thinks Jane. She cuts off a tiny piece of chicken, puts it in her mouth, and chews.

If you're worried about your relationship with Edward and about how it affects me, please don't, says Alma. She is calmly eating her chicken.

Jane stops chewing. She stops breathing. She stops everything. She suddenly feels nauseous. She pushes back her chair.

What do you mean? she asks.

She means that whatever happens between us doesn't affect her, says Edward. He and Alma are holding hands under the table, Jane can see from her vantage point. She feels even more ill.

That's right. What's between you and Edward stays between you and Edward, Alma says. *What Edward and I have is what we have. Nothing can affect that. We thought perhaps we needed to be clearer about that.*

Jane doesn't know whether to laugh or cry. She does a little of both, and to her shame, it comes out as a rough snort. She wipes her eyes. As Edward had suggested, she'd wondered how much of the excitement of her relationship with Edward had to do with the illicit aspect of it. That it was a secret. Her and Edward's secret. Now she'll find out.

As if reading her mind, Alma reaches out and takes Jane's hand with her free hand, the one that isn't being held by Edward.

It will still be a secret, she says. *I don't think the good people of Half Moon Bay need to know anything about this. I don't think they would understand.*

Edward leans forward and blows out the candles. It gets suddenly dimmer in the room.

I'm not sure I do, Jane says.

A *ping* sounds from the kitchen, and Alma leaves the table. Then Edward, who has been quiet until now, says, *We don't have anything to lose from Alma knowing, and we have everything to gain.*

But Jane doesn't agree. She is familiar with loss. She knows there is always something to lose.

Alma comes back from the kitchen holding a frothy concoction. *Baked Alaska,* she says. *Always a complicated endeavor.* She removes the main plates from the table, Jane's still full, and spoons out the dessert.

I know you're worried, says Alma. *But I assure you everything will be all right.*

Has this happened before? Jane asks. Whether she leaves or stays depends on the answer. Actually, she thinks she might leave either way. This is too much, too weird. In Berkeley, you heard about these arrangements. But they usually involved a marriage that was dead or sexless yet keeping the existing ménage intact made sense, because of kids, because of property. That was clearly not the case with Alma and Edward.

You mean, has someone else ever been allowed in? No. Never, says Edward.

Allowed in? asks Jane. *That's a strange way of putting it.*

It's how we think of it.

You've discussed it, repeats Jane. She plays with her baked Alaska. The white meringue has been sullied by the chocolate ice cream. It's a liquid mess on her plate. She puts down her spoon, nausea rising again.

No one answers her. Jane looks up to see both Edward and Alma watching her.

We've discussed what's good for us, as well as taking your well-being into account, says Alma.

Jane has to laugh. *My well-being!*

Yes, Edward says, then adds, in a normal voice, but Jane gets the impression that he's quoting. *Days and hours withered in the scarcity of love.*

You shouldn't accept the waste of even one moment of your precious life, Jane, he says. *Love is scarce. Isn't it our duty to pursue it when and where we find it? I don't personally refuse such gifts. You shouldn't either.*

Jane breaks down. She can't help it. Alma gets out of her chair and walks around the table. She kneels next to Jane. Jane finds herself crying into the crook of Alma's neck. Alma's hand rests on the small of her back. The pressure a surprising balm.

You'll see, it'll all be okay, Alma says.

The fourth girl is, like Heidi, the first one, five years old. Only this time she's from the town. She's the second daughter of the Schroeder family, who had bought the frozen yogurt shop last year, right before Jane moved to Half Moon Bay.

They lived in a small ranch house with six kids, three girls and three boys. The oldest and youngest girl shared a room, but Susan had her own. The windows had been locked, as all windows in all children's rooms — especially girls' rooms — are locked these days. But the kidnapper used a diamond-tipped blade to cut a square opening in the glass, reached in and flicked the lock, and came through the now-open window.

The town has gone mad. One of their own has been taken. No need to put up pictures. Everyone knows what little Susan looked like. She was frequently at her parents' yogurt shop after school, coloring or drawing in the corner with her two sisters.

Police and sheriffs from all over San Mateo County amass at one end of Main Street. Roadblocks are set up going in and out of town. Even more press arrive, if that is at all possible. Four girls!

There's no way he's getting away with this one, Jane heard one police officer tell Margaret in Three Sisters.

The *Moon News* runs articles telling parents of young girls to not let them out of their sight, even in their own houses. Parents walk or drive their girls to school. Recess is canceled, after-school sports cease, music and ballet lessons are abandoned.

Where will Susan show up? Everybody knows it will be in eight days. Everyone awaits that day with dread.

In Three Sisters, Jane is hailed by the same blogger as after Heidi's funeral.

One is a story. Two is weird. Three you'd got national attention. Four is an international sensation, says the woman. *Congrats, your little town has made the front page of* The

New York Times, *the* Guardian, Le Monde.

Edward had come to Jane the night that Susan was taken. It had been unusually tender. He never said anything as a rule, but that night he had called her *precious* and *dear heart,* words she had previously associated with Victorian novels. He brought her a glass of wine. Then he got up and poured her another one. He stroked her hair. He was even more attentive than usual.

When she wakes in the morning, he is gone. She has overslept and feels oddly tired and thirsty and hungover. Typically she wakes as he dresses, before dawn, but not this time.

Little Susan. Details are pried out of her parents, her teachers, her schoolmates. She was a little shy but excelled in math. She had a crush on a boy, David Dos, and was planning to marry him. She was obsessed with the bridal magazines found at supermarket checkout counters and would beg her mother to buy them, not for the dresses, but for the formal dinners and meals pictured. When she grew up she was going to be a fireman.

Angela had also gone through the fireman stage, followed by the usual rock star dreams, then doctor, then lawyer. She wore out all the possibilities by the time she was fourteen. After that, she had no idea what her future held. It held nothing.

The pattern breaks. On the seventh, not the eighth night, Susan is found. How the killer did it no one knows. But a group of schoolchildren visiting the Fitzgerald Marine Reserve discover her when they arrive in their boots and their waterproof jackets to seek sea urchins and starfish and snails. Sitting cross-legged against a rock overlooking the mussel beds is Susan, her brown hair carefully braided, dressed warmly against the chill she wouldn't feel. Someone had taken great care with her, as usual. A pail full of seashells was placed next to her, along with some digging implements. In her open hands, a starfish.

What does Alma say? It is the day after Susan was found. Edward and Jane are sitting in Jane's cottage, keeping themselves warm against a sudden chill that has enveloped the coast.
　She doesn't.
　What does that mean?
　It means I am free to do what I want.
　It's complicated.
　Not really. When you meet one of your

persons, you know it.

What does that mean, one of your persons?

There are only so many people for your inner circle. When you find one, you must grab her.

Not him?

Not for me. Not yet, anyway.

Must you have sex with your special person?

Absolutely. That's part of the beauty of it.

You are my first special person. The only one I've felt this way about.

You're lucky. Most people don't find any. I'm especially fortunate.

Jane is afraid to ask, but asks anyway. *How many do you have?*

A certain number. He smiles and gets up, begins to dress.

Even when he is gone, there is magic in the room. Dark magic. Jane has no trouble sleeping these days.

A week passes. Then two. Edward comes to Jane every two or three nights. No warning, only a knock on her front window at nine-ish, well after dark given that the clocks turn back the first week in November. Fall behind. Jane likes it. She can leave her house at 6:00 a.m. and the sun is already up and causing the eucalyptus and palm leaves to glow. The autumn light suits her. She used to think it cold, severe. But now she likes how it brings out the cooler colors in the ocean, the darker undertones in the pines. Night bringing dark delights. She purposely welcomes Edward into a house with no lights on. She prefers to make love with the curtains closed, only a faint hint of the streetlights glowing behind the material. Edward always leaves before dawn.

One day he sends her a text, a first. It says simply *Help out at the office tomorrow?* She gets permission for a half-day off on a Saturday, arriving at the YourBeaches.org office at half past ten. Alma is there. Even dressed in loose overalls over a man's flowered Hawaiian shirt, she looks enchanting. Jane feels shy and doesn't approach, but stays in the background until Edward gathers all the volunteers together to give them their instructions. It is about Dunes Resort, the five-hundred-bed luxury hotel to be built just above Secret Beach, ruining it.

"The builder at Dunes Resort is giving investors a tour tomorrow at noon. We just found out. We need to be there, in force," Edward says. He starts assigning roles to people.

Jane's job is to take posters and pamphlets and place them about town, in as many storefronts as possible. *It won't be difficult. Everyone is on our side,* says Edward. He tells Alma to accompany Jane. *No one will be able to refuse the pair of you,* he says, giving Alma a quick smile before turning to the other volunteers.

Jealousy stings Jane. Edward hasn't been by for five nights — the longest he's stayed away since their first night together. But Alma immediately approaches Jane, and the warmth of her greeting disarms her.

Jane! So glad we're paired together. We'll have fun. Alma's manner is so kind, without a hint of patronizing, that Jane puts aside her misgivings and even manages to relax. Walking beside Alma, Jane finds her head held high and her step light. Is this how men feel when they are accompanied by a beautiful woman? The admiring looks, the smiles, the nods? Jane doesn't imagine that her own happy expression might be contributing to the goodwill flowing to them from passersby.

It is a glorious day, the kind rarely seen in summer but common in the Half Moon Bay winter months: clear, sunny, the air blowing fresh and cool from the sea.

Jane and Alma make their way down one side of Main Street. By now, Jane knows all the storekeepers, by face if not by name, and those she has not formally met cordially shake her hand. They are understandably intrigued by Alma. Edward is a known quantity, but Alma spends most of her time over the hill, on campus. They direct questions toward her. Jane takes a backseat.

What do you teach at Stanford?

What does that mean, particle physics?

Where were you before?

What does that mean, adjunct?

They are surprisingly well informed. All willingly put posters in their windows, piles of pamphlets on their counters. They offer Alma and Jane coffee and cookies, show them the latest goods that have come in, introduce them to their employees. When they finish the west side of the street, Alma suggests they take a break. There's a sort of public plaza where the day laborers wait to be picked up by farmers and builders who need extra hands. On a bright Saturday like this, it's crowded with tourists. A bluegrass ensemble of guitar, bass, and violin is entertaining the crowd. They switch from a fast song to a slow one. The female violinist puts down her bow and sings mournfully, in contrast with the bright sun and ice cream–eating children.

Only a dream, only a dream
Of glory beyond the dark stream
How peaceful the slumber, how happy the
waking
Where death is only a dream.

Jane and Alma find seats. Jane finds herself surprisingly hopped up by the morning's canvassing.

This sort of thing usually exhausts me. But you make it easy, she tells Alma. She's still a little shy. A little in awe. A little envious at the abundance of charm. If Alma had been less . . . Alma . . . Jane would be more prone to jealousy. But she can't compete with her on any level. Whatever Edward sees in Jane, it must be so radically different as to make Jane almost an alien creature. Edward and Alma were right: Jane wasn't a threat to their relationship. How could she be? Surprisingly, this buoys her up rather than dampens her mood.

You don't know your power, Jane, Alma says suddenly, as if reading Jane's thoughts.

Me? Power? Jane has to laugh.

Your intensity. Your quietness. You don't let your energy dissipate in extraneous chatter. When you do release it, it packs a wallop. Alma pauses. *And, of course, you're so beautiful. That skin! That hair!* She pinches a strand of Jane's hair and holds it in her fingers for a moment before dropping it.

Jane shakes her head.

Yes.

Unspoken: *We would not let anyone but the beautiful in.* Yet Jane hears it. Still she doesn't believe. When she looks in the mirror, she sees only the too-pale skin, the eyes a nondescript brown and so large that they overwhelm her face, the unremarkable nose, the too-thick lips. Altogether unexceptional. The Jane Alma has described doesn't exist.

Jane had been carefully watching Alma in action as she charmed the storekeepers. Although she had played down her beauty with her clothes, her lack of makeup, her dark hair pulled back in a simple ponytail, she still took people in. A charismatic. Your eyes would rest on her and linger without knowing why.

In the stores, Alma would enter, and start with a simple *Hi.* She'd introduce herself. *And you probably know Jane.* She'd explain the mission, but the words were clearly less important than the smile with which they were delivered. Her complete absorption into the shopkeeper's expression, her wry look when she made her request. And the *Of course, feel free to say no* she added at the end of every request. No one says no. It is simply not possible to say no. The exact right amount of positive energy is used, the exact right amount of warmth. Nothing inappropriate. Sometimes Alma will reach out and touch a storeowner on the shoulder, but only when she judges it not intrusive.

In the middle of the pitch, Alma often breaks off, seemingly spontaneously, to remark on a scarf, or a lamp, or an arrangement of furniture in the shop. It seems utterly sincere, but Jane detects the pattern. Jane is less happy with that. It makes the storekeepers into patsies. Jane wonders if she too is being duped, if Alma is following a script with her too.

But when they sit down, Alma seems to let down her guard. Her shoulders slump. *Glad we're half done. That takes a lot out of me.*

But you're used to lecturing in front of a hundred students!

It's an act. It's all an act. I can only be myself when I'm alone. Then, with almost naive earnestness, *I'm so glad we found you, Jane! You do our hearts good.*

Jane can't help but wonder if this is the version of Alma's pitch tailored for her, Jane. After all, she has no scarves or pine sideboards to admire, only her Jane-ness. This is the praise that would go to her heart, for she has nothing else. She has been shorn of worldly goods and attachments. And she can't help it: she is undone.

Jane gets into the habit of stopping in at YourBeaches.org every day. She is drawn there; she can't help herself. She finds herself getting agitated as she approaches the door, but the desire to enter, to see Edward — and Alma, if she is there — is stronger than her desire to run away. Both emotions being equally strong. She is rarely herself by the time she actually enters. Edward is usually at his desk, writing or on the phone, but no matter what he is doing, he gives her a smile that assures her she is welcome. No, that she is special, that she has been awaited. Alma is often there too, sitting at a desk grading homework or tests or preparing lessons. She also seems delighted to see Jane.

An increasing number of others are also in the large space, creating posters, working on computers, talking on the phone. Volunteers, Jane knows, as Edward doesn't have the funds to pay salaries. But the prospect of Dunes Resort at Secret Beach has fueled a lot of local outrage and interest. Already, ground has been broken, and steel beams are being embedded deep in the earth to create the foundation. Cement is being poured. The land has already been despoiled. There is little hope, but the group is determined.

How are you holding up? This is Alma, who has closed her laptop and has come over to hug Jane and kiss her on both cheeks. Jane has become accustomed to this and no longer flinches.

I'm all right, Jane says, and, surprisingly, feels that she is. She gathers strength from Alma's presence. More than that, she craves it. It is a little like being in love. When she is with both of them, Edward and Alma, she feels whole again. When without, she is nothing. With them she is known, and accepted. This is reassuring. She considers Adam and Helen, and thinks, *But they don't really know. They don't really understand what's inside me.* She is accepted, but who have they welcomed in? It is not the real Jane, not the Jane Edward and Alma know.

Let's go get a cup of coffee, Alma urges. She beckons to Edward, and he nods and pushes his chair back. But at the Three Sisters he orders three glasses of chardonnay, even though it is barely 11:30 a.m. Jane is surprised at how pleased she is to get the cold glass with the pale yellow liquid in it. Magic elixir. She is drinking too much, she knows, a problem given her family history, but she doesn't care.

Edward leans forward and speaks softly so no one can hear.

You up for a little civil disobedience?

What does that mean?

It means we're going to get in the way of them getting supplies into the building site at Secret Beach.

How?

We're going to block the road. One of our volunteers has a set of keys to a bulldozer being used at the construction site. We're going to push debris onto the road. You with us?

Jane says, *What happens if you get caught?*

No big deal. Fines. It would be a misdemeanor. Maybe some community service.

But on your record.

Yes, that's the risk. Again he asks, *You up for it?*

Yes, Jane says. She is.

No moon. On top of that, fog. Cooler, now that it's well into November. Jane dresses in black, as instructed, with a hat and a scarf around her face and gloves on her hands. It's 2:30 a.m. She rides her motorbike to Edward and Alma's house. They get in the small, beige Toyota, the car Alma drives to campus — *less noticeable,* says Edward —

and drive to the construction site.

The bulldozer is parked at the edge of the building site. Beyond that, the sea. Jane is feeling that familiar twinge of doing something wrong — half excitement, half terror. It's almost a sexual feeling, the excitement. It almost equals, balances out, the inevitable pressure in her chest. She and Alma direct Edward as he climbs into the bulldozer, inserts the key, and revs up the motor. He is surprisingly competent with the machine, putting it in gear, backing it up, and going past them down the lane. It makes a terrible row. Jane is certain they'll be caught. But at 3:00 a.m., no one else is around.

He drives the bulldozer to a pile of construction materials and pushes it into the side road off Route 1 that leads to the site. He does this until the road is completely blocked. Then he parks the bulldozer next to a large stack of two-by-fours.

He takes something heavy out of his backpack. Jane sees that it is a can. He pours something on the pile of wood that is stacked neatly next to the bulldozer. He seems to be distributing it evenly over the wood and then over the bulldozer itself. Alma hurries up. A sharp smell.

Come on, she says. *We have to get back to the car.*

She grabs Jane's hand and pulls her back up the road.

Run! she says. Jane obeys. Something is happening that she doesn't understand.

Route 1 is empty, as before. They run across it and behind the fruit stand to the car. Alma gets in the driver's seat, turns the car on. They wait.

What is going on? Jane asks.

You'll see. Alma reaches out and takes Jane's hand. They sit, hand in hand, waiting. Suddenly Edward is there, falling into the backseat.

Go.

Alma floors it, taking off south on Route 1 toward Pescadero. They pass no one before they get to the turnoff to the house. Looking back, Jane sees a red glow coming from the construction site.

What have you done?

You mean we, Edward says. Alma takes her hand off the wheel, reaches over, and takes Jane's hand again. *You're implicated in this. If we go down, you go down.* He's laughing as he says this, but Jane knows he's serious.

They heard a loud explosion and through the back window see a spectacular burst of flame from the direction of the site

The bulldozer, Edward says. *One final* fuck

318

you *to the developers.*

Naturally, the first person the police came to about the fire is Edward. All of Edward's staff have iron-tight alibis — he must have warned them — and Edward had Alma to say he was asleep in bed all night. The police couldn't prove anything, but they are suspicious. They search the offices, pore over Edward's email. Find nothing.

After the bulldozer episode, Jane is more in love than ever. It is like nothing she has ever experienced before. The sky is spinning. It's not that she forgets about Angela. Angela will always be with her. But now there is music, some counterpoint, in Jane's life. She is doing what she has to do.

Jane is jealous of all the women who cast glances at Edward — of whom there are quite a few.

Except Alma. Alma is different. Alma is somehow part of it. Jane loves both of them. She wants to sleep with Edward, but she craves Alma's presence as well. The two together are magic. When she is with them both, she is satiated.

Night and day she yearns to be with them. They complete her. They understand her pain, they don't make it go away, but they make it acceptable somehow. She wants Alma as much as she wants Edward, but in a different way. On nights Edward doesn't visit, she lies there unsatisfied, the weight in her chest heavy. But when he does come! She is blissed out. And when she is with both of them together, she feels whole again.

A friend of Jane's from college suffered from a mild form of bipolar mood swings. Jane used to envy her friend her manic phases. She was under medical supervision, and on medication, but she still had her glorious ups. She would sing in the shower — you could hear her all the way down the dorm floor. She'd effortlessly study for and ace her tests, and was so charming and full of life that everyone warmed to her. Of course, there were the matching lows, when she would emerge right before dinner, pasty-faced, from her room, having missed break-fast and all her classes. For Jane, always middle of the road, she envied the wildness in the girl's moods. In the manic phases, she had magic at her fingertips.

Magical. That's how Jane feels these days. She not only smiles, she laughs. The first time she did so at work, she startled Helen and Adam. They were closing up the shop after a busy Saturday, putting the plants and flowers in order after they had been moved around by careless customers who changed their minds and left succulents in the rose room and chrysanthemums in the hummingbird garden. Adam was sitting cross-legged on the ground in the butterfly garden sorting out the pots when a gorgeous blue-throated hummingbird came up and nipped his ear. Adam's shriek and look of outraged puzzlement caused Jane to ripple with laughter, and when Adam recovered, he joined in with so much generous delight on his face that even Helen, who smiled often but rarely laughed, broke out too.

Oh, Janey, you know how to laugh! Adam says when he catches his breath.

Janey? Where did he get that from? Jane hasn't been called that since she was an undergraduate. A carryover from her youth. She finds she likes it. She gives him a hand to help him off the floor and nearly collapses on top of him, she is still giggling so hard. When it finally subsides, she realizes she is still clasping his hand. She lets go but with reluctance, she finds. How did she live so long without love? It nearly killed her. Now she is alive again.

Jane awakens alone. She is not bothered by this. She revels in her tangled sheets, stretches her naked limbs. Postcoital satisfaction.

It's 3:00 a.m. Jane is restless, the cottage is too small, it can't contain how large and expansive she feels. She doesn't want the sea tonight. It would be too much, her ardor, her euphoria, would dissipate. The greenhouse, with its heat and humidity and growing things, beckons her. She would get some work done.

She has never been in the greenhouse at night. The eucalyptus trees wave overhead in the wind, which has picked up. The warmth is a shock after the coolness of the night. She breathes in deeply. The earthy smells excite her. She does not think of the way she spent the previous hours. Such delights. She wants to save them, savor them over time.

She gets to work, pulls up a stool, and sits down. She takes off her shoes and is barefoot on the cement floor. She rubs her bare foot against the weathered oak of the stool and curls her toes in pleasure.

So engrossed is she in placing each tender shoot in a plastic container, gently cupping the soil around its slender stalk, she doesn't hear the door to the greenhouse open. She doesn't hear the footsteps come up behind her. She doesn't see the shadow that falls across her body and is insensible to another's presence until a hand is placed on her shoulder.

Jane starts so violently that the stool slips out from beneath her. It falls with a bang. Half the tray of seedlings goes with it. Jane barely catches herself from falling too.

I'm so sorry, says Adam. *I thought you'd heard me come in.* He's holding the hand he touched her with a little away from her, as if it has been burned.

No, says Jane, she is panting slightly. Her heart is still racing.

I'm really sorry, Adam repeats. He is still holding his hand out awkwardly. Then he reaches out again and touches Jane on her shoulder in the same spot, as if it were *home* in a children's game of tag. He rubs his palm on its curve.

I heard a noise, he says. *I couldn't figure out who would be here at four a.m.*

What are you *doing here?* Jane asks. She tolerates the warmth of his hand on her. It steadies her. This surprises her. She thought she would eschew all touch now except from Edward or Alma. She finds that Adam doesn't cause her to forget Edward's caresses as much as prove to her how much they matter. She is touchable again.

I sometimes crash here. It depends on

what's happening with the tides and my bud-dies, Adam says. *I keep a sleeping bag in the car and camp out in the break room, on the sofa.*

I didn't see your car, says Jane. *The chain was up across the entrance to the parking lot. I had to unlock it.*

Adam's grin is a little ashamed. *Yeah, I'm not sure Helen would approve. So I park behind the winery next door.*

Jane can still feel the warmth of his hand on her shoulder.

And you? he asks.

Couldn't sleep, Jane says shortly. She finds she wants to blurt everything out. She knows that would be a mistake with Adam. She is more convinced because he keeps his hand on her shoulder and moves closer.

You look so beautiful. In the dark like this.

Jane knows she has to diffuse this situa-tion, quickly. She moves slightly away, but he doesn't relinquish his hold on her.

Yeah, in the dark, she tries to joke. *When you can't see me.*

No, I mean the half-light. Like a sort of Madonna. Your hair down and straight. The way you were concentrating on your plants. The expression on your face. Like Mary just having been visited by an angel.

He's using language she doesn't associate with him. She has to remind herself that he got a J.D., then a Ph.D., from Santa Cruz, is a lapsed Catholic like her. They'd laughed and compared notes about it. *Once a Catholic, always a Catholic.* On Ash Wednesday, he'd anointed himself with dirt and left the smudge on his forehead all day. A private joke between them.

I certainly don't feel like that, she says, forcing herself to laugh. *I came here to calm down. I was agitated.*

He finally takes his hand away. Seemingly reluctantly, he places both hands in his jeans pockets. *Do you want to talk about it?* His voice is kind, patient. He has done what she wanted, which is to put his own agenda about her, whatever that is, on the back burner. So why is she disappointed?

She is bursting to talk. She finds she wants to tell it all: her loneliness, her guilt, her having been found by Edward and Alma, and then the gift of tonight. But she stays mum.

Just stuff, she says.

Well, let me help you with these, he says, and he pulls up a stool, and together they work until the sun's rays penetrate the windows. So there, companionably up to her elbows in damp earth, with Adam at

325

her side, Jane finds the tranquillity she had been seeking.

One day at the nursery when Jane is using Helen's computer in her office to do some research on a pest that had infested her *Heteromeles arbutifolia,* she decides to look up YourBeaches.org. A page comes up. Edward is a senior director, and it is based in San Diego, with offices in Charleston, San Luis Obispo, and Boston. It seems to be doing good work: a number of impressive beach saves are listed.

From there Jane googles Alma's name: Dr. Alma Godwin. To her surprise, a vast number of hits immediately return.

Tulane Professor Suffers Immense Loss

Carbon Monoxide Poisoning Claims Two Small Victims

Prominent Attorney Loses Children in Carbon Monoxide Poisoning Incident

Carbon Monoxide Deaths Deemed Accidental

Photos of Alma, some smiling professional shots, others showing her disheveled and tearstained, obviously in extreme distress. Others of a blond man, so bland you would overlook him in a crowd, presumably the husband. Two children, one fair, the smaller one as dark as Alma.

Carbon Monoxide Fumes Kill Two New Orleans Children

NEW ORLEANS — Gregory Bixby, noted attorney and arts patron, put his children in his car in the garage at his home at 116 W. Oak, then ran back inside to retrieve his cell phone. While inside, he got in a prolonged argument with his wife, Tulane professor of physics Dr. Alma Godwin, that distracted him. The older child, aged five, got out of her car seat and switched on the car. Both children died of carbon monoxide inhalation. The deaths have been ruled accidental by local authorities. No charges have been filed. Funeral arrangements are private.

Jane is in shock. Surely it couldn't be! But the many stories that she scrolls through convince her.

She is shaking. She is able to do nothing the rest of the day except attend to the plants in the outer field. She pulls viciously at the weeds, throws them on the ground. Sometimes she pulls up a plant too. She doesn't care. That evening after work, Jane goes over to Edward and Alma's house.

She doesn't call Alma and Edward to tell them she's coming. She doesn't knock on the door. She finds them hunched over a map spread out on the kitchen table, two half-full glasses of wine, some cheese and crackers. They look up simultaneously. It's the first time Jane has received anything but pure warm welcome, pure happiness, at seeing her. What she sees in their faces she's not sure. What's showing in her face? Confusion and fear and rage. Don't forget the rage.

Hello, Jane. Alma's voice is flat.

I know about the children.

Of course you do. It was only a matter of time. Edward's voice is soothing. His face is impassive.

How could you not tell me? Why tell me you'd left them?

Because I had. I'd left them for Edward. Greg was going to win custody — the divorce rules in Louisiana are archaic — that was it. I wasn't going to raise them. I wasn't going to be a real parent, not with visitation rights only twice a month.

Lots of people are good parents on weekends.

It wasn't going to work for me. We were planning to leave town anyway. They were already dead to me.

But this happened so recently! Just before you came here!

Two months after the deaths, we left.

But how can you hold it together? It's been more than a year for me, and I'm still a mess.

The grieving had happened earlier. It was over. I was done. Don't you understand? I don't wallow. I move on.

No, Jane does not understand. Not at all. But she finds she can't judge Alma. She is that enmeshed.

Despite the shock of the discovery, Jane finds herself spending more and more time with Alma. She sees her more than she sees Edward, in fact.

Jane doesn't sleep with Alma, but she doesn't have to. Her physical desire is all for Edward, but she finds herself yearning night and day for Alma. Alma's smile, her capacity for deep understanding of small things. As they walk down Main Street, passing a group of teenage girls that Angela would have fit into, Jane gets a stab of guilt and is pulled temporarily into a fit of despair. How could she have forgotten? She is not aware that a muscle in her body or face changed, but she suddenly feels a warm arm around her shoulder and a hug that bears so much affection and understanding that it brings tears to Jane's eyes. She immediately calms down and returns to the joyous, satiated state. Yes, that is the word. *Satiated.* Jane is getting what she needs, and even more. She is full. Any more would be too much. It is almost unbearable.

Jane wonders what Alma does on the evenings that Edward is with her, Jane. She imagines her sitting in the living room on one of the hard black-cushioned chairs, perhaps a blanket around her knees, as it is getting cool in the evenings. Grading papers. Reading a scientific journal perhaps. She does not detect any loneliness or regret in Alma when they are together. Just serenity and patience. Jane imagines that Alma would be a good teacher. Patient. Wanting to pull the best out of each student. She would be a good mother too. Jane still doesn't understand how Alma can deal with a loss that extreme. Losing her two girls. Is it buried? Is it processed, the way Jane's shrink used to say she needed to *process* things?

She feels toward Alma as she did at the age of seven with her best friend, Jenny, tied together with a blood vow on the play-ground after school. Safe in a world of their own. Even Edward was superfluous to this bond.

To Jane, Alma's best features are her hands. Expressive, they weave phrases of their own even when Alma is silent. Pale with long slender fingers, they are the hands of a musician or an artist. Alma laughs when Jane tells her this.

One evening they ride Jane's motorbike to San Gregorio Beach, like that time before, when they hardly knew each other. A long, long time ago. They sit on the edge of the cliff and watch the offshore fog roll in. Jane keeps a blanket in her saddlebag, and they huddle under it as the tide comes in, the waves heaving up and over and crashing onto the rocks.

Don't you think of your girls? Jane is amazed she is actually asking this question.

Alma is silent.

I mean on an evening like this. I always think, What would Angela be doing if she were here? But it doesn't hurt as much to think that as it used to. Jane is surprised to find out that this is true.

I miss them every day, every minute, Alma says. *I can never let go. I try to imagine what they would be like now, nearly a year older. I can't. I see them as they were.*

Her eyes close momentarily. Jane tentatively puts a hand over Alma's. Previously, Alma always instigated any touching. That seemed to be the unspoken rule. Jane feels the long elegant fingers tense and experiences a little thrill of panic. What has she done? Then Alma's fingers relax, and Jane gets pressure back. So Jane is now giving as well as receiving. She needs to know that. After being a mother, after suddenly having no one to give sustenance to, that was the hardest thing. No one to hug, to pick up, to kiss a knee or a finger and make it all better. Mother's magic touch.

Touching. So important. So many different ways to touch. Edward's touches evoke desire, wake up feelings and sensations. Alma's tamp them down, make the hurt go away, almost like the way a spider injects a fly with anesthetic to dull the pain before killing it. What a strange metaphor. What made Jane think of spiders and killing on this sunset over the beach? Alma's head is bowed, her eyes closed. Jane keeps her hand clasped tight around Alma's.

Minutes pass. Seabirds call. The surf rolls ever closer below. The sun is below the horizon now, but a glow suffuses everything with a gentle light.

Alma slowly comes back to life. First, her head raises and her eyes open. They are dry.

Her mouth is a little tightened, making unfamiliar lines on her face. Is she resolute or angry about something? Jane involuntarily lifts her hand, pulls away. She knows the signs of pending violence from her father. *But this is different,* she reminds herself. *This is Alma. And I'm a grown-up.* She is embarrassed that she has to remind herself of that. Sometimes she worries that she has grown infantile, her dependence on Alma and Edward. A sort of cult-like dependence. She dismisses these thoughts.

There are some places you don't want to go, says Alma. It is unclear whether she is referring to herself or Jane.

■ ■ ■ ■

PART IV
CHOICES

■ ■ ■ ■

Soup was a mainstay of Jane's childhood. Her father wanting to be in the kitchen, because according to his ethics, you kept the bottles in the kitchen cabinet. You never brought them into the living room where the television was. Which involved a lot of getting up and down, and Jane's father was essentially lazy. So he made soup instead. To be nearer the cabinet and the bottles. Made soup, and poured and sipped, and sipped and poured, and made soup. The soups were pretty good, as soups go, but Jane hates soup. She'd rather eat mud.

He eventually quit drinking, was sober for nearly a decade before he died, yet the soup habit persisted. Somewhere along the way, he acquired a ferret, a little furry bandit of a fellow that sat on his shoulder and bit him gently on the neck if anyone else got too close.

Jane thinks of him as she makes some pea

soup with ham. She remembers how the ferret would chew on her father's earlobe. Jane could never look. Right now, she can't bear to look at artichoke and sausage soup so popular on the coast, a poisonous green with pink chunks of flesh floating in it. That's how she thinks of it now, *flesh,* since Angela was taken.

Her father would pick these pieces of meat out of his soup and feed them to his ferret. Liberty was her name. She was devoted to him. He clipped her nails every week. He cleaned out her ears every other day (ferrets are prone to ear infections). They brushed their teeth together every night. Her father's toothbrush was red, Liberty's blue. First, Jane's father would attend to his own teeth, mostly intact. Then he would put a little toothpaste on the blue toothbrush and Liberty would bare her teeth (ferrets are very intelligent), and he proceeded to scrub them. Liberty would stick her tongue out to taste the toothpaste. Her tongue was long, and extended a full inch past the opening to her mouth (ferrets don't have lips). Jane shudders at the memory. Her father died last winter, five months after Jane's mother, his wife; six months after Angela. Good riddance. Jane didn't go to the funeral.

Jane was the third child of what her father

called *the litter:* a family of ten children: eight girls, two boys, all born within thirteen years. Her parents didn't get their first boy until Number 7. Then there was much rejoicing, *for unto us a child was born.* Jane's father purchased and consumed two bottles of wine, and of better vintage than his usual one, to celebrate accordingly. The Number 9 male was duly welcomed. An heir and a spare. Then a caboose, another girl of course.

To her younger siblings, Jane was a second mother. Someone had to do it. Their real mother wasn't up to the job.

As siblings, the girls were both extremely close and extremely cruel to each other. The affection was bountiful, and it was real. Cry out in the middle of the night from a bad dream, and a warm body would edge its way into your bed, an arm thrown around your shoulders for comfort. Have trouble with a bully at school, and that kid would have the entire O'Malley clan to contend with.

But the cruelty. That was real too. Perhaps because of the closeness, because you knew exactly where to thrust the knife to inflict the most grievous harm. Outsiders might say the boys were the worst — the worms in the cereal, the dog shit between the sheets — but there's a peculiar brutality between sisters close in age that, although nearly physically invisible, is infinitely more toxic.

Depending on the father's mood, punishment for misdeeds (eating an extra cookie, playing too boisterously near his bedroom window) could be quick and relatively harmless, or it could send a bloodied daughter to the ER. Back then, nurses and doctors weren't trained to look for such things; there were no social workers to alert. So all the trips to the emergency rooms went unremarked.

The house was bloody in other ways too. Once they reached adolescence, the daughters' menses were all in sync, and every month there was a run on the Kotex in the hall closet. Bloody towels, bloody messes in the toilet, blood everywhere. The girls would steal their father's razor to shave their legs and it would dull the blade. He'd pull it across his unsuspecting face and cut himself. Blood again! All in all, it was a violent household.

They were equally antagonistic to each other, of course. Alliances could form and be torn asunder in a millisecond. Jane did her share of being aligned with tormentors, of being a tormentor herself. But her alliances would dissolve, her allies would turn on her in half a second, at any opportunity to inflict pain. *Black Heart! Black Heart!*

Jane goes for long walks. She ignores everyone else in the nursery, does her work, and leaves as soon as the nursery closes for the evening. Adam is heartbroken, but she has no time or energy for him. She goes on long rides on her motorbike. She stops going into YourBeaches.org. By unspoken arrangement, she meets Alma in the morning for coffee. They don't discuss Edward. They don't discuss the children — any of them. The air is charged between them. Jane can barely keep her eyes from Alma's, she who is oh-so-beautiful. They talk about the weather. They discuss the quality of the coffee today, or the texture of the croissants. They speak in code. They don't sit on opposite sides of the table of each other, but right next to each other, their thighs touching.

Alma's and Edward's presences are now all Jane desires. Her beauty. Her scent. His way of laying a light finger on Jane's shoulder as she passes. One finger, as if pointing to Jane, claiming her. It's not necessary. Jane has been claimed by them both.

She starts spending all her spare time with them. She is like a besotted teenager with her first crush.

She even begins to spend the odd night at their house. Perhaps once a week. They've given her one of the many spare bedrooms. The same lacquered funereal furniture as the rest of the house, a huge bed with a shiny black headboard, a slab of what looks like plastic but which Alma tells her is lacquered teak. Jane feels like a child in her parents' bed.

It seems to be an unspoken rule that Edward will not come to Jane while Alma is in the house. Only when she is over the hill teaching or at a faculty meeting or seminar. It all melts together for Jane. She can't tell where the experience begins or ends. It is all one. She is engulfed. Now when she shows up at the Three Sisters for her morning coffee, she sometimes arrives from the opposite direction, from Pescadero. She wonders if anyone notices that her motorbike now faces the wrong way on Main Street. She finds she doesn't care. She nurses her coffee at a table by herself as usual, nodding in a friendly way at everyone but not committing herself to words. She has nothing but Edward and Alma. She is full to bursting.

At work she throws herself into planting. She takes a trip over to Berkeley and accepts as a gift from her former colleagues some cuttings of the rarer plants in the arboretum. The person who took over her job is happy to let her. They do it after hours so regular visitors won't get any ideas. Helen is delighted. Adam enters into the spirit of the things. He accompanies Jane on scouting expeditions to various beaches for cuttings of native flora. His hummingbird garden has now been deserted. The earth is going into hibernation. It grows cold. The walls of the greenhouses go opaque with condensation. While at work, Jane feels enclosed in a warm green bubble. She laughs and jokes with Adam without giving up any of her secrets.

One evening she and Edward are in bed together. They are naked. The lights are on, as Edward insists when they are at his house. *My rules,* he says. Jane has grown less shy about her body. His body. The surfaces, hard and soft, the feel of bone softened by skin, of muscles taut underneath. Jane could cry from the awesomeness of it all. Lips against skin, warmth, drowsiness, sleep.

Then the door to the bedroom opens.

It is Alma. *Class was canceled,* she says casually. She starts unbuttoning her coat, the red woolen retro one that Jane admires.

343

Jane shrinks, pulls the sheet over her body. Edward merely stretches out his long frame, completely exposed in the light, seemingly comfortable with that. He even rolls his hips and groin toward the ceiling. Jane recoils. He just as casually answers, *That gives you some extra time for that report.*

Alma finishes unbuttoning her coat and tosses it on a chair. She observes Edward, seemingly dispassionately. *You're looking better,* she says. *The running is slimming you down. Sitting at the desk wasn't doing you any good.* She sits down on the corner of the bed. For the first time, she looks at Jane directly. Jane has the sheet pulled up to her chin. She blushes.

Don't be a fool, Alma says. The words are harsh, but the tone is affectionate. Amused and not at all angry. Playacting. *Don't we all know each other better than that?*

Jane does not feel she knows anyone that well. She feels exposed and is uncharacteristically suspicious. Why are both Edward and Alma so calm? How are their words and actions so perfectly choreographed? Could they have planned this? Jane finds that she is frightened.

Edward reaches over and pulls Jane to his chest. He runs his fingers through her hair.

He does this while continuing to chat with Alma. *You look tired,* he says. Jane expects them to discuss the week's shopping. *Don't forget the toilet paper. The toothpaste.*

I am. And cold. Alma surveys them both. *You look so cozy. Do you mind?*

Jane decides she's gone into a state, a state when nothing makes sense, or else it makes beautiful sense. She watches, as if disembodied, as Alma undresses. Edward now has his arms crossed behind his head, like he's enjoying the view. A pasha with his women. Alma is as lovely undressed as she is dressed. Her skin so soft as she sidles up against Jane. Edward reaches over Jane and puts a hand on Alma's flank. He has both women encircled now. He reaches out with the other hand and fumbles for the light switch, turns it off. Nothing but slow measured breathing. Heartbeats. Hers or theirs? Jane can't tell. Astonishingly, she finds herself dozing, her eyes closing, she is so warm, so protected between the two bodies, Alma's slow breath against her neck, Jane's head under Edward's chin, her cheek on his chest. Jane sleeps, and dreams.

Jane is at home, which she rarely is these days, in between work and the time she's spending at Edward and Alma's. The place looks deserted. Lonely. She feels lonely when she's here. Bereft. It is only here that she thinks about Angela. Somehow she has managed to compartmentalize. For now, thoughts of Angela belong here in this dusty, forlorn cottage. Jane goes into a different space when she leaves here. She shuts the door on pain.

She takes a hot shower, turns on the heat, which grumbles before warm air starts coming out of the vents. She is in her robe and bare feet, wet hair, when the knock comes at the door.

It is the same FBI agent who interviewed her. Ms. . . . Tempe? Tompo? No, Thompson, accompanied by another, a rather short man. He barely reaches Ms. Thompson's nose. They are serious. No smiles. No niceties.

Ms. Thompson puts her briefcase on the coffee table. She doesn't ask permission. She has barely nodded hello at Jane. She seems angry. It seems personal.

What is this? She holds out a photo.

A car. Jane tries to remain calm, but her voice catches. She is embarrassed to be in her robe in front of these suited officials.

Just a car?

So it seems.

Ms. Thompson nods and fishes a piece of

paper out of her briefcase. She hands it to Jane. It is a printout from the DMV. At the top of the page is her name, Jane Mary O'Malley. It is a registration form for a car, a Subaru Outback wagon, ten years old. It shows serial numbers and license plate numbers. It has Jane's old Berkeley address on it. *Registration expired* is printed in red letters across the bottom of the paper.

It's funny. What you find when you pop a person's name into various databases, says the detective. *We were doing random searches on you. Call it a hunch. So we checked out the DMV database. Your motorbike is registered to you at this address. But we found this. A car. You listed the car as out of action and didn't pay for registration this year. But the funny thing is, we found it parked right around the corner.*

Jane is silent. There is nothing to say.

Why did you lie to us? This is the man, he hasn't bothered to introduce himself.

I didn't. I don't drive that car.

The neighbors say different. They say they see you getting into it and driving off. Or returning, sometimes late at night.

I'm only moving the car to avoid getting a ticket, Jane says, trying to sound reasonable *You get towed if you're parked for more than thirty-six hours on Princeton streets. So I have to move the car every three days.*

The man and the woman just look at her.

Sometimes I forget until it's late. So I move it then. I'm an insomniac. I have trouble sleeping. So sometimes that's 3:00 a.m. Sure. But that doesn't make me guilty of anything.

It means you not only had the opportunity, you had the means. You didn't have that before. We had eliminated you. Because of the motorbike. Because of the lack of a car. This is the short man talking.

What about motive? Jane asks. *Why would I kill four little girls?*

We figure we don't need one, says the man. *We figure we're dealing with an unbalanced individual. Someone who doesn't think or act the way everyone else does.*

By the way, he continues, *we've impounded the car. One hint of DNA and your ass is ours.*

The woman stirs at this. She points to the sofa.

Can we sit down? She doesn't wait for an answer, but settles herself on the right-hand side.

Jane doesn't move. She tightens the belt around her robe.

Jane. Please. Some of the warmth that Jane remembers from their past meeting has returned to the woman's voice. She smiles. Jane doesn't trust her, but sits down on the edge of the couch.

Isn't it better to tell us the truth? Her voice is soft. Jane can barely see her face. Dusk has fallen, and she hasn't bothered to turn on any lights in the cottage.

I have. Over and over. But Jane's voice sounds unconvincing. Of course she hasn't told them the truth. Why should she? She would only be punished.

Why didn't you tell us the truth about what happened in Berkeley?

What do you mean?

I mean we now also know about the girl. About what you tried to do to the daughter of the woman who killed yours.

I don't know what you're talking about.

Yes, you do.

Jane is agitated. *Those records were sealed. They cannot be used in court. There was an agreement. A legal one. Who has breached it?*

People's lips aren't sealed. They have a way of talking about things they shouldn't. Now the man has taken up the story.

Who could it have been? One of the lawyers? The woman? The police officers who were directly involved? Anyone. It could have been anyone.

So you know. So what, says Jane. *That had nothing to do with what's going on here. That*

349

was my problem, back then. We settled it.

Problems don't suddenly go away. There are aftershocks, temblors that continue rever-berating. Now it's the woman's turn.

Jane's voice comes out sarcastic. *That sounds positively poetic.*

Talk to us, Jane. The woman's voice still smooth, without edge. *Tell us your side of the story. What we've heard sounds bad. Maybe you can change our minds.*

Passing lights of cars flicker through the blinds. Jane feels lulled by the flickering lights, by the soft voice. She leans back.

I was distraught. I wasn't myself. Angela was gone. My husband had left. I was alone. You don't know what it's like to be alone in a house that should have other breathing people in it.

Like this one? the woman asks, motioning around in the darkness.

No. This place was never anything but empty. But in a house that was full, you're always waiting. For the door to open, for footsteps to come down the stairs. To hear Mom? *or* Honey? *But it never happens,* says Jane.

She continues, *I was on leave from work. I took to driving around, just driving. The Subaru is a tank, hadn't been damaged at all by the episode with that murderer's, Hope's, BMW. I found myself at the grammar school where her child attended kindergarten. How did I know? Because she was dumb enough to put her daughter's photo on her god-damned Facebook page. So I started showing up at pickup time. I found out that Hope always came at the half-hour. The kids are paraded outside at quarter past. One day I just did it. Because I could. I called the girl over. I told her that her mother was sick, and I was going to take her home. It was so easy. Classic. The thing they tell kids to guard against. You'd think she'd have been more on guard. But no.*

What were you going to do? The woman's voice is so soft that Jane can barely hear it.

I didn't know. It didn't matter, anyway, since I got busted. Right away. Suddenly I heard shrieking. Hope had come early that day. I knew the game was up. I got in the car and hightailed it out of there.

But you didn't get convicted.

No. I agreed to counseling and community service. Charges were dropped and the records sealed. The judge was sympathetic. She understood. Maybe she had kids herself, who knows.

What were you going to do? the woman repeats.

I don't know. Take her home. Feed her milk and cookies. Be nice to her. Nothing bad.

Were you going to return her?

I hadn't thought that far ahead. I suppose. I was thinking of reciprocity. An eye for an eye. A child for a child.

The woman's voice is softer still. Jane has to lean in to hear her.

A death for a death?

Jane doesn't answer. She's remembering finding little Amy dead in the tree. That nursery rhyme: Jane and Edward sitting in a tree, K-I-S-S-I-N-G. She remembers the playdates from when Angela was three. Many of the children still calling any woman in sight *Mom.* She had loved it. She had indiscriminately kissed them. She had planted a kiss on the little girl's blond head right before they were spotted.

I always treated my girl well, she says.

Yes? The voice is softer still.

I could never hurt her. Never.

Is that why you put makeup on them? Wrap them in blankets? To show you care?

Yes. I mean no! Jane is suddenly awake. *I didn't take those girls!*

The spell is broken. The agent sits up. The man sighs and reaches over and flips on the light. Suddenly everything is too clear, too visible.

The agent stands up. *Well,* she says in a matter-of-fact voice, *that's that.*

352

The next morning a Ford sedan is parked in front of Jane's house. The two men in it deliberately stare at her as she exits her cottage, makes a point of locking it, and gets on her motorbike. They start their car and follow her to Smithson's, staying right behind her all the way. They park in the handicapped zone, and the driver yawns and crosses his arms on his chest to indicate they are there for the long haul.

The police car waits all day at Smithson's. Jane wonders at the patience of the two watchers. Not to mention their bladders. At least once an hour, the man in the passenger seat, stocky build, blond crewcut, goes next door to the Half Moon Bay Winery, open for tastings from 9 to 5, and comes back with plastic glasses filled with water. At least Jane assumes they are water. She wouldn't have thought they would drink on the job. Adam is counting the cups.

That's three glasses each they've drunk in the last two hours, and they haven't peed yet, he reports to Jane. *Those guys are gonna bust out any minute.*

Helen doesn't consider it such a light matter.

Why are they here? she asks Jane. Jane ashamedly tells her about what she has decided to call the "misunderstanding" about her car. Helen doesn't respond the way Jane hopes, which is to shrug it off. Helen purses her lips. She crosses her arms across her chest and turns away from Jane, looks out the window at the two men who are sitting, looking straight ahead, not talking to each other. Even from here, you can feel their grimness.

They seem to be taking this quite seriously, Helen says. Jane tries to appear casual, although she is in fact deeply humiliated. She tries to think about when she has been quite this publicly ashamed. Because of course all the workers at Smithson's are curious about the men. It doesn't take them long to cotton on to the fact that people in authority — "responsible" people — clearly consider Jane a monster, think her capable of heinous crimes. Jane can feel her coworkers shrink away from her. Erin enters the break room at the same time as Jane to get coffee, only to leave hurriedly, her cup still empty. Peter doesn't meet her eyes when he bumps into her outside the unisex bathroom. She is a pariah.

Jane remembers being a pariah at thirteen. She remembers one particular winter day. It was only the second time she had gotten her period. She still didn't understand all the symptoms, thought she had a bit of a stomachache, felt some wetness in her underpants but didn't consider that it might be blood. Why should she? She'd put her first period firmly out of mind as an aberration. Her mother had simply handed her a sanitary napkin and a book entitled *Now You're a Woman!* Jane's two older sisters had snickered but offered no help. It had never occurred to Jane that it would happen again. She saw it as a onetime event, stepping over some unappetizing threshold that entailed discomfort and mess, but at least it was over.

It was raining that day, sleeting, really, so instead of going outside for PE, the kids in Jane's seventh-grade class were stuck in the gym playing dodgeball, the girls against the boys. Jane was bad at this game. She hated the smack of the ball hard against her thighs, the way the boys would jeer when they managed to hit a girl on her buttocks or breasts. The only saving grace was that as a sort of class scapegoat, she was usually targeted, hit, and out of the game early, so she could go and sit against the wall next to her fellow exiles and be ignored. But on this day, something odd was happening. Girls to the left and right of her were being hit by the ball and called *out,* but the ball never came close to Jane. One by one the girls were eliminated, until there were just a handful of them standing. Only a few of the boys had been declared out, which left a huge gang of them standing and leering at just five girls.

Jane was aware that not only the boys but the other girls were openly snickering and pointing to her. She couldn't figure it out. What was so wrong about her today that was different than what was generally wrong with her? She even saw her gym teacher, Miss Coutts, stifle a grin. Miss Coutts was famous for being easily baited during sex education classes. She asked for anonymous questions to be written down on pieces of paper, thinking this would encourage the girls to ask things they'd be embarrassed to ask in front of the group. But the girls would prank her and giggle when she read their questions out loud and treated them as inquiries for serious knowledge. One memorable day she had replied *Salty,* to *What does a boy's penis taste like?*

Suddenly Jane realized she was the only girl left standing on her side of the gym. Whatever gross humiliation the boys were planning for her — for there were laughs and whispers coming from the other side of the room — she wanted it to be over. One of the boys, clearly nominated by the rest, took the ball. He came almost up to the line separating the girls' side of the gym from the boys' side. He took careful aim. Jane simply stood there, her arms at her sides. She wasn't going to fight this. She wasn't going to scurry back and forth like a trapped rat. She closed her eyes and waited. The ball hit her squarely in the stomach. The blow was cruel and hard. It knocked the breath out of her. Jane fell to her knees, gasping. It was then, as she knelt taking deep painful breaths, that she noticed the blood. Her gym socks were stained crimson. Surrounding her, the polished wood floor was covered with drops. Had she been hit that hard? Was she bleeding internally? It wasn't until Marcie Banks, not a friend exactly, but not an enemy, tiptoed over and helped her up and led her to the bathroom that she dimly grasped what was happening. No wonder they called it the curse. The three days of bleeding and pain she had experienced the previous month were just the beginning.

Just the beginning. Jane dimly realizes from the looks from Helen and her coworkers that something bad is just beginning. Another sort of curse. Where would it lead?

Jane hadn't realized how important it was

to be a part of the Half Moon Bay community until she is excommunicated from it. Suddenly, everyone knows everything. No friendly nods at the Three Sisters — even Margaret serves her coffee without a word. In the street, people either stare, openly hostile, or avert their eyes. Even her cottage, formerly a safe haven, is assaulted. Eggs thrown. She wakes up one morning to find her shrubbery, mailbox, and window shutters wrapped in toilet paper.

Jane doesn't even think about it. Instead of driving to the nursery, as usual, she heads toward Pescadero, toward Edward and Alma. At this hour of the morning, both should be there. She needs both of them.

The gates to Edward and Alma's house are open, as if she's expected. She feels expected. And indeed the door opens before she even knocks and Alma is standing there, then taking her arm and leading her to the kitchen, putting a glass of cold water to her lips.

I . . . Jane begins, but can't come up with words. She has not yet looked Alma in the face. *Where's Edward?*

In the shower. He'll be out soon.

Jane needs him. She needs them both.

Alma . . .

Yes? Alma's voice is curiously devoid of

feeling. After handing the glass of water to Jane, Alma has stepped back. She is now leaning on the kitchen table.

You believe me, right? You know I wouldn't hurt those girls.

Silence. Jane slowly lifts her eyes to Alma's face and is petrified by what she sees there. Nothing. The lovely features are just as lovely, but there is no warmth in the expression. There is nothing in the expression.

Alma?

Edward strides into the room wearing a bathrobe. He does not look friendly.

What is she doing here? he asks Alma.

She came here before work. I knew she would come one of these days. I was expecting her. They discuss her as though she isn't standing next to them.

Jane feels her world sliding away from her.

Please, she says, knowing how feeble and weak she sounds. *Please, not you too. I need you. On my side. You don't know how badly I need you.*

Edward shakes his head. His face is composed, his eyes steady.

Out, he says.

November limps to a close. The weeks pass, cold and bleak. Jane's hands freeze as she rides her motorbike to Smithson's Nursery, but she refuses to put on her gloves. A punishment. *If thy hand offends thee, cut it off.* The back greenhouse contains the tattered remnants of her shrunken world. She hadn't known how much she depended on her bland anonymity, on the general goodwill she'd earned in Half Moon Bay, until she didn't have them any longer. More than her fingers are chilled. The unmarked police car conspicuously follows her when she leaves her cottage until she arrives at the nursery, and it's there waiting for her when she locks up in the evening. Jane finds she doesn't care. She goes home and consumes cans of chicken noodle or tomato soup, hardly bothering to heat them up, anything to spoon calories into her uncaring body. But deep down is still a flicker of hope. They will come back to her, Edward and Alma. They will rescue her.

The last week of November, the weather takes yet another surprising turn. Each day dawns cloudless and warm, mocking Jane with blue sky and beckoning azure sea. She keeps going to work. Helen doesn't say anything as Jane stays in the back greenhouse, hiding from customers and other staff. Hostility lurks even there: her plants are wilting, mites have eaten her stock of spring seeds, and the hummingbirds have all vanished from the garden. Jane anguishes at the loss of Edward and Alma. They are drugs she has unknowingly become addicted to. She sits outside her greenhouse and tilts her face to the sun, but still feels cold. *Black Heart.*

She listens to Bach with her earphones, absorbs the mathematical precision of the cello suites, the hidden repetitions in the cantatas. She is reading *No Exit* again, it is a comfort.

Anything, anything would be better than this agony of mind, this creeping pain that gnaws and fumbles and caresses one and never hurts quite enough.

Helen, after one talk, remains coolly friendly. Only Adam stays loyal. He brings Jane his tea. He comes, holding out dolphin-free tuna fish sandwiches, organic falafel, as if such delights could tempt her. He hasn't tried to touch her since the night in the greenhouse. He has taken to calling her Janey, the way her sisters did when she was young. When did this start? She doesn't know, but hearing the way he pronounces the two syllables is the only relief she gets. Her phone remains silent.

Still, Jane endures and does not break.

She does not break until Wednesday, November 30, comes, another startlingly beautiful day. Again the unmarked car following her, again the retreat to the back greenhouse of the nursery. Adam greets her with his customary cup of tea. Today she drinks it down. Adam is startled but pleased.

This too will pass, Janey, he says.

I don't see how, Jane says. *I can't leave town. I can't escape it.*

They'll catch the real murderer. He'll make a mistake, you'll see. And you'll be cleared.

After he leaves, throwing reluctant glances backward, Jane hugs herself. The loneliness is unspeakable. The pain creeps into her bowels, giving her feverish chills, dreams where fantastical things happen, dark horrors worm into her consciousness, and she wakes gasping. She becomes fearful of sleep, previously her last resort of comfort.

She is fitfully watering her plants when she hears, as if spoken out loud, her daughter's name. *Angela.* She realizes it has been weeks since she has thought of her by name. What has come over her? She waits. Again: *Angela.*

Yes, she thinks. *Angela, I'm coming.*

She waits until Adam is engaged with a customer. She moves swiftly to the break room and puts her hands into his jacket pockets, filches his keys. At first she's afraid that the aging Volvo won't start, but then the engine turns over with a groan. She's also appropriated Adam's hoodie and hidden her bright hair under its peaked cap, so the cops sitting in their car next to her motorbike don't even look up as she drives out of the parking lot. Once she's heading north on Route 1, she relaxes. She's going to make it. There's a way out for her after all.

She reaches the entrance to the old road to Devil's Slide, now a walking and biking trail since it was deemed too dangerous for cars. She pulls into the parking lot right off the entrance to the tunnel. She doesn't bother hiding it — the sooner it's found, the better.

She walks onto the abandoned road, now newly tarmacked. It's only three in the afternoon, but the fog has already started to drift in from offshore. The trail is largely deserted. Jane can see some joggers farther down the road, but they're moving away from her. The surf pounds the rocks nearly five hundred feet down. It's a truly spectacular view. The sides of the hill have kept eroding since the road was closed, and cement blocks line the edge to keep people safe. Jane sits down on one of the blocks and swings her legs over. Now nothing is between her and the jagged boulders and water except air. The precipice is dizzying and alluring. She feels the inevitable pull to the edge. She remembers that day with Alma, years ago, it seems, down on the bluffs in Half Moon Bay.

She imagines what it will feel like. A few seconds of terrifying free fall, then the end. The pain would be brief. Much more manageable than what she feels like. *Pain management.* That's all she's doing.

She hears a noise. Two cyclists pull up behind her, on the other side of the cement barrier.

Awesome, isn't it? says one of the women.

Yes, says Jane, when she realizes the woman is talking to her. The woman is wearing a helmet with a tiny mirror attached to it that always makes Jane think of the horrors of the dentist's office.

Move back a little. You're making me nervous, says the other woman.

I'm fine, Jane insists.

The women look at each other, then wordlessly come to a decision. Jane knows that phones will be pulled out of pockets as soon as they've moved away. Calls will be made. She doesn't have much time.

Well, enjoy your day, the second woman says.

You too, Jane says, and turns back to the ocean. The fog is coming in thick now, larvae-like tentacles snaking around Jane's feet. She retreats into her dreams. Nothing is real. Soon unsavory things will emerge from the crevices and the sun will darken and it will be time. It is almost time now.

The sea below is now invisible, shrouded by fog. If she jumps now, she will land on its soft pillow. It will be like going to sleep. Still she doesn't move. She wills her feet to step forward. One step. Another. Yet another. It will only take one more. A pebble dislodges itself from under her shoe and rolls soundlessly over the edge. You cannot hear it land, it is so far down, the crashing of waves on rock below so loud. Another pebble follows. She can feel the earth give a little when she presses her toes into the ground.

She tells herself to take the final step. She can almost do it. She will step onto nothingness, and that will be the end. Jane closes her eyes.

One step. That's all she needs.

But finds she can't do it, after all. Sartre would have understood.

I can't go on, I'll go on.

Oh dear God.

Jane most definitely does not want to be early for this meeting. Funny, to think of it using that term, *meeting,* like an office function, formal and cold. To consider Edward and Alma in such terms. Alma had sounded casual enough on the phone. But when she said, *No, not our house. How about the Sisters?* Jane knew that whatever they wanted to say to her, safe — or at least neutral — territory was necessary.

So Jane waits until five minutes past the hour before leaving her cottage — three hundred excruciating seconds. She counts every one. This is against every grain of character she possesses. She never permits herself to be even a minute late. What did her mother used to say? *Early is on time, on time is late, late is unacceptable.* She walks from kitchen to bathroom and back to the kitchen again. She unloads the dishwasher. Finally she allows herself to get on her motorbike and head toward downtown Half Moon Bay. It's a cloudless and fogless night for once. The stars seem ominously near, the moon too large, as if it could crash into the earth's orbit. Jane feels small and vulnerable as the wind rips past her face.

She arrives at the Three Sisters fifteen

minutes late. Still, Alma and Edward are not there.

She sits there four minutes, alone. Margaret doesn't come to ask her what she wants. The place is deserted except for two regulars at the counter, so it's not that she's too busy. Jane is toxic, even here. Nine-fifteen. They'll be closing up in another fifteen minutes. Five minutes pass. When the second hand of her watch ticks off the sixth minute, the door opens.

She can't tell from their faces what they might be thinking. Neither looks in her direction. They take their time winding their way to her table.

Jane. Edward pulls a chair out, takes his coat off, and hangs it on the back. He sits down. His eyes had passed over her when he said her name.

Alma takes more time, unwinding a large scarf from around her neck and looking around the café to see who is there. She smiles and waves at Jeff Stone and Jerry Rigg at the counter, neither of whom had acknowledged Jane when she came in. They smile and wave back.

Then Alma turns to Jane. She holds out her hand. Jane automatically extends hers. She remembers that first day, in the flower market, this was how Alma had been introduced to her, with a semiformal handshake. Then she had thought it charming. Now it seemed calculating.

How are things? Jane asks, addressing both of them. Her feeble attempt at casualness. Alma drops her hand almost as soon as Jane takes it.

We're good, Edward says. *But how are* you? His voice stressing *you.* It sounds sincere, perhaps even caring. Jane sits a little straighter. But Edward still hasn't looked directly at her. Now he's taken a napkin from the holder on the table and is wiping his leather jacket at a spot on the sleeve, real or imagined, Jane can't tell.

Fine, Jane says first, automatically. Then she corrects herself. *Actually, no. I'm struggling a bit,* she says. Her voice breaks in the middle of *struggling. Strug. Gling.* She sounds like she is attempting to speak an Asian language. She is chagrined. Edward simply continues polishing his jacket. He's moved on to another spot. Alma is sitting poised and alert, smiling serenely.

How beautiful they both are. Jane can hardly stand to be so close to them.

What is it? Why are you shunning me? She hadn't meant to be so direct. The words burst out.

Edward finally finishes with his jacket. He

looks straight at Jane for the first time.

You look pale, he says.

Jane finds herself blushing deeply. He has addressed her personally. Even now, she feels the full force of his *Edwardness.* How could she have ever thought she could claim him, even temporarily?

Edward reaches across the table with his hands. It seems as if he might take one of Jane's hands into his, but he stops short. He is only flexing his shoulders. *Too much office work,* he says.

What is going on? Jane says, louder than she intended.

I'll tell you, says Alma. Her smile is as warm as ever.

Jane waits like an obedient child.

We are disappointed in you.

Clattering comes from the kitchen as one of the twins drops something. Margaret chooses that moment to come over to the table.

A bottle of your house red. This is Edward.

Jane shakes her head. *Just water for me, please.*

Three glasses, Edward says, raising three fingers, as if Jane hasn't spoken. Margaret hasn't looked at Jane. She nods and disappears behind the counter, returns with a bottle of a local merlot, uncorks it, and offers a splash to Edward. He waves it away and gestures for her to pour. Once Margaret is gone from the table, Jane picks up where the conversation left off.

You're disappointed? Jane asks. *In me?* Despite her intentions to keep her head clear, she drinks her wine. Half the glass is gone before she realizes it. *What the hell.* She drinks the rest and pours herself another glass.

Edward and Alma watch her in silence. Neither has touched their wine.

Perhaps disappointed *isn't strong enough,* continues Alma. She is still smiling. Jane feels herself shiver.

What then? Jane tries to get a grip on herself. She tries to summon a sense of outrage. Who are they to lecture her, a grown woman of forty? But all she feels is shame. They have the right. Everyone has the right. Not for what they believe she's done, but for her real sins, of which she is all too aware.

Betrayal, Edward supplies. He's back to looking at everything but Jane. His glass, Margaret as she begins cleaning tables in preparation for closing. She's turned up the lights, making everything harsh, even Alma's dark eyes.

Jane stands up and, for lack of a better

thing to do, wanders around the Bong Wall, reading the various rejections.

We're sorry, but you do not fit
our requirements for this job.
We regret to say you were not chosen
to be one of the class of 2019.
Please collect your belongings
as soon as possible.
We must ask you to refrain from
contacting your ex-wife in any way,
whether in person, by telephone,
or electronically.

Rejection. She'd experienced it before. Multiple times with Angela. But then there were the second chances. Weren't there always second chances? With her sisters, alliances could shift within a moment, a friend could become an enemy in the blink of an eyelash. But then it could change back equally quickly. Which made Jane into someone who always hopes. A hoper. Also a wiper of boots, a licker of bottoms.

How would it appear on the Bong Wall? *We regret that you no longer fit our requirements as a lover.*

Was that it? Was it the sex? The withdrawing of it? No. Yes.

But she hadn't felt that way with Edward

and Alma. She'd felt . . . cherished. Valued.

You're like a unicorn, a mythical beast with magical powers. Had she imagined Alma saying this?

The sex was the least of it, she tells herself. And yet she's suddenly overcome with physical longing. She recalls the morning she woke up, Edward on one side of her, Alma on the other. How warm. How protected. How delighted to have all this without having to pay for it. Hadn't she paid dearly enough already? Hadn't she?

She makes her way back to the table, sits down again. Alma continues as though there had been no interruption.

Yes, that word works. Betrayal. *We were betrayed. How could you not tell us about Berkeley? About the girl.*

I told you what mattered.

Edward raises his eyebrows but remains silent. He's letting Alma do the hard work. He lifts his right arm and places it along the back of Alma's chair. Jane aches to see it. She wants that arm, that hand, close to her. Even now.

Yes, but you left out a very significant part.

Can you blame me? With everything going on around here?

But not to tell us. *We really felt that lack of trust.*

Is that all? Jane asks. She has stopped shivering.

All? Edward addresses her for the first time. *In our book, betrayal is pretty serious.*

But you don't think I'm responsible for all this. Jane waves her hands at the posters on the walls.

Of course not.

Jane goes limp with relief. *That's not why you've been avoiding me, then?*

No. It was the lack of trust you showed in us. As if we wouldn't understand.

Margaret begins stacking the chairs on the table next to theirs.

Time to wrap up, she tells them.

Jane remains seated. *No one else believes in me,* she says. *But I really need you two on my side.*

Alma reaches out then and holds out her hand. Jane slowly puts her own into it. Alma clasps it tight. It is a lifeline for Jane. She is nearly weeping with gratitude. She has never felt such relief. Why is their goodwill so important to her? She doesn't know, but it is.

That's why you have to be careful with those who do. *Believe in you, I mean,* Alma says. *You have to treat them well. With respect. Even obedience.*

Yes, says Jane.

Guys, really, you've got to go, Margaret tells them.

Slowly they all get to their feet.

Edward asks for the check and hands over a twenty-dollar bill. *Keep it,* he says. Margaret looks pleased.

He pauses right outside the door. Looking carefully up and down the street, he says in a lower voice.

We need you to do something for us.

What? Jane says. She is ready to walk to the ends of the earth, she feels so grateful. She has her world back.

It's a little dangerous.

What? Jane asks again.

We need to send another strong message to Dunes Resort.

How can I possibly do anything? Jane says. She points to the car parked on the next block. *My constant companions,* she says.

This too will pass, says Alma.

Yes, says Edward. *It's actually a good thing they're keeping you in sight all the time.*

How on earth could this be a good thing?

Sooner or later, the real murderer will strike again. And you'll be in the clear, Edward says.

That means hoping for another killing. I can't do that, Jane says.

Take my word for it, there will be another. And once it happens, you owe us.

Jane gets on her motorbike and drives home, closely followed by the police. One of their headlights is out, she notices. She smiles. Her heart is much lighter.

It happens as they predict. A fifth girl goes missing. The oldest yet, ten years old. Megan Hayes. The dentist's daughter. She left school on Wednesday but never arrived home. Her young friends saw her talking to someone in a silverish or grayish car, of a make they couldn't identify. Just a *car,* they said. Jane is at the nursery when the town tsunami alarm goes off.

Oh no, Jane says. *Oh God, please no.* She is in the break room eating a sandwich, Adam nearby, as he nearly always is these days. Jane reaches out and grasps his hand. She feels as though she is going to be sick.

Helen strides into the room. She is pale and has a stricken look on her face. She goes right up to Jane and embraces her.

I am so sorry, she says.

Why?

Because I doubted you. Because I thought it was a possibility.

Jane doesn't get it. The siren continues to wail.

Adam sees Jane's bewilderment.

Janey, don't you understand? This is a ter-

rible thing, a horrible thing . . . but it gets you off the hook, he says. *You were here, with us, all day. You finally have an alibi.*

Helen says, *The police car zoomed out of here when the siren went off. You've lost your tail, Jane.*

Jane puts her hands to her head. *Who will it be this time? Poor little girl. Poor parents.*

Adam is checking his smartphone. *Yeah, oh man, it's bad,* he says. *Dr. Hayes's kid.*

My dentist, says Helen. *Oh my God, I know him. Her. Megan. He brings her to work sometimes. Nice kid.*

Poor thing, says Jane, but her heart, she can't help it, is lightening. She is exonerated. She will no longer be an outcast.

Then she remembers Edward's words.

You owe us.

Excuse me, Jane says. *I have to make a phone call.*

Jane is at the nearly completed Dunes Resort. It is 2:00 a.m. It has been one week since Megan Hayes disappeared. Child Number 5. No, that's not exact enough. Girl Number 5. Daughter Number 5. Megan. Surely those were more accurate descriptions. Despite the horror of what that means, Jane is still grateful to be off the hook, to be greeted by smiles and her name again when she walks into the Safeway, when she gets her coffee at the Three Sisters.

The fog touches everything with damp fingers, so densely that when Jane walks, a fine mist envelops her face and hands, the only parts of her exposed. The can is heavy in her right hand.

Go down the beach path, Edward had told her. *Climb up the hill. You'll see that the fence doesn't go all the way to the edge of the cliff. You'll find it easy to get around.*

Jane clambers the final few steps to the top of the cliff. She heaves the can up and places it next to the fence. The surf is high, shimmering palely down below. The eight-foot chain-link fence goes nearly to the edge of the cliff and stops. Edward is right. It should be easy to swing herself around, from one side to the other. Easy, that is, for someone with no fear of heights. The cliff is a straight vertical drop of sixty feet. For a brief moment, she would be hanging over a sheer drop onto rocks, her grip on the fence the only thing keeping her from what would be major injuries or even death.

Jane puts her hands on the fence post. She counts one . . . two . . . three. Then she closes her eyes and swings herself out and around. A heart-stopping moment when her feet can't find ground, but suddenly she's safe on the other side. She reaches around for the can, manages to get that onto the other side of the fence with her. There. So far, so good.

Jane turns to look at Dunes Resort. The frame of the massive building is completed, and the exterior walls of the first floor have been constructed. The crew must be in the process of putting down flagstones surrounding the hotel. Huge pieces of multicolored stone are stacked up to her right, and the surface where they are going to go has been prepared. It's flat and damp, so damp that Jane has to extricate her shoes with each step with a slight sucking pull downward. The walls of the hotel seem to be made of stone, but that can't be, not in earthquake country. A more flexible material would be needed. The stone must just be a facade. An illusion.

Find the equipment, Edward had said. *The closer to the building, the better.*

Jane does exactly what she had been told. She has always liked the smell of gasoline; it doesn't bother her the way it did Rick. He was fastidious, refused to fuel up the car so left it close to empty rather than risk getting gasoline on his hands or clothes.

Edward had briefed her at the house in

Pescadero earlier that evening. Alma had not appeared. Jane had had no idea what would be asked of her. But she was a woman of her word: Edward and Alma had agreed to come back into her life, and she was determined to pay the price of that, whatever it might be.

Here, Edward had said, handing her a twenty-five-gallon can. It surprised her with its weight. *Gasoline,* he said. *And you'll need this.* He held out a disposable lighter. He'd already made her put on a pair of gloves and lent her a long black windbreaker. Her bright hair was tied back and hidden under a black cap.

But how will I get there? Jane had asked. *I can hardly carry this can on my motorbike.*

You'll take Alma's car, Edward said, handing her the keys to the Toyota. *Mine is too easily recognizable. If someone happens to see you . . .*

. . . but they won't, he had quickly added, catching Jane's alarmed look.

I just got cleared, she reminds him. *The last thing I want is to get back into trouble again.*

You won't, he reassured her. *We'll tell anyone who asks that you were with us all night.*

So far, it had all gone according to plan. The guard, as Edward had said, was in the trailer at the front of the property. The light spilled out into the darkness, and Jane could see the guard, young, bearded, and wearing a baseball cap, sitting at a desk, looking at a computer screen. *He's supposed to keep moving around the property, but he rarely does,* Edward had said. *You won't have any trouble from him.*

Jane walks around to the front of the hotel. The entrance is clearly going to be grand, with two-story columns and huge glass doors. A sea of dirt that will eventually be more flagstones. Trees with their roots wrapped in burlap lined up in a row against the fence.

Around the corner from the entrance she finds her target: a motley collection of equipment, ranging from small golf carts to bulldozers, to a strange crane-like machine with a pulley and sharp iron jaws. There are perhaps a dozen vehicles in all. The fog wafts between them. Despite her jacket, Jane shivers.

Jane takes the can and begins pouring the gas over the machinery. She makes sure, as Edward told her, to soak the seats and the tires. She leaves a thick trail of gasoline between each piece of equipment and onto a large pile of two-by-fours stacked next to them. For good measure, she also pours gas on what looks like a generator, a large iron box placed close to the faux stone walls of the hotel.

She backs away from the equipment, still pouring until she's back to the front of the hotel. She takes the lighter out of her pocket. She finds she can't operate it with her gloves on, so she takes her right glove off and flicks the starter. A small blue flame ignites. She bends down and holds it to the wet trail of gasoline. It catches so fast and with such heat that she jumps back. She drops the lighter in surprise. The line of flames snakes rapidly away from her and around the corner. She hears a loud whoosh and a flame shoots up, so high she can see it from where she's standing. The two-by-fours, she figures. The light is blinding in the midst of the dark and fog.

The guard, she remembers. She's been standing paralyzed for at least a minute, watching the flames grow higher and louder. There's an additional roar as each piece of equipment catches on fire. *Get out of there before it's hot enough for the gas tanks to explode,* Edward had said.

Jane hears shouting. A bobbing light is coming at her from the direction of the guard's trailer. She turns and starts running away, only to remember that she'd left the gas can, her right glove, and the lighter behind. She returns and in a panic can't locate them at first, even though the scene is now bright as day. She can now see the figure of the guard clearly as he races toward her. She thanks Edward for her dark clothing and her hat as she retrieves the items, and runs back the way she came. Out around the huge building, to the edge of the cliff, and swinging around the fence, going too fast to be afraid. She keeps running until she reaches the clump of bushes where she'd parked the car. After a false start she manages to get it going and is off as Edward had instructed, not north on Route 1, the direction that the fire trucks would come from, but south to San Gregorio and then east on 84 and through the rough back roads to Pescadero until she arrives back at their house.

It is now nearly 3:30 a.m., but she is exhilarated rather than tired. She has proven herself, has she not?

The gate to the house is locked, so she has to push the button at the entrance and wait for someone — Edward or Alma — to buzz her in. The gates close after her. She hears the click of the automatic lock. She supposes it would stop the police from making any surprise visits.

She pulls up and parks behind the Mercedes. The house is dark, but as Jane hurries up to the front door, it opens and she is pulled inside by Edward. He closes the door quickly behind her.

How did it go?

Okay, I think, Jane says. *I didn't stick around to check. But I did hear some spectacular explosions as I drove away.*

Good, good, says Edward, but his attention is clearly elsewhere. She is disappointed. She did this for him, them. Shouldn't she be rewarded? Jane realizes she is waiting for approval and affection. She thought this meeting would provide more satisfaction than she is getting.

As if sensing this, Edward pulls her to him. He holds her tightly, his cheek against her hair. *What would we do without you,* he says rather than asks. Alma appears out of the dark of the hallway.

Is it done? she asks. Jane is startled by her appearance. She looks as though she has been crying. Even in the dim light, Jane can see the wet tracks down her cheeks. Her hair is disheveled.

She passed, says Edward, not letting Jane go. She absorbs the warmth after the chill of the November night. Thinking she sees something in Alma's face, Jane makes an attempt to disengage herself, but Edward prevents her. *Stay,* he says, holding her closer.

Edward. Jane is startled by Alma's tone. Steely angry. Whatever troubles she is experiencing, whatever the source of her tears, they aren't making her weak. Quite the contrary.

Alma, just give me a minute.

Edward, it's time.

I don't think so.

She's one of us. She's proven it.

Not yet.

What else do I need to prove? Jane is angry. She pushes Edward away. *Look what I've just done for you. It was a huge risk. I could have gotten caught.*

But you didn't. This is Alma, an edge to her voice.

No.

So don't whine. Jane recoils from Alma's harshness.

Alma says to Edward, *We have to talk.*

Alma turns and goes back into the darkness. Edward looks at Jane, and shrugs, and follows Alma. *Stay here,* he says over his shoulder.

For a moment Jane does as she is told.

Then she thinks, *Fuck it.* She can just see movement up ahead in the dark. She is tired of being treated like a child. She follows Edward out of the room, perhaps ten feet behind him. She wants to hear what they will be saying. About her. It's about her. She follows Edward through a door. It leads down a corridor to yet another hallway, one she had never before seen. But the hall is empty. Numerous doors. But only one has a faint light shining from under it. Alma opens it. It leads to a flight of stairs going down. Jane can hear a faint *boom boom boom,* a rhythmic, almost hypnotic beat, as of a distant muffled drum.

Jane pauses, then starts down the carpeted stairs, taking care to hold on to the handrail so she doesn't trip.

The light comes from a candle burning on a table at the bottom of the stairs. Jane turns the corner and finds herself in a fully finished basement, with paneling on the walls and more deep carpeting on the floors. No windows. It is empty except for a washer and dryer in the corner, the latter the source of the muffled *boom*s. No Alma. Nothing but the sound of whatever is in the dryer going around and around. Then Jane sees a sliver of light coming from under a door on the far side of the room.

Jane crosses the room. The carpet muffles her footsteps. She tentatively opens it. Light shines into her eyes, and at first, she can't comprehend what she is seeing. All her senses are assailed. A beautiful room, smelling sweetly of hydrangeas, Alma's favorite perfume. Candles lit on every surface — on the floor, on white tables, on a dresser. Walls painted a soft peach. Stars shining down from the ceiling, presumably of some sort of reflective paint because they glow, reflecting the candlelight. A replica of the moon shines from the center of the room. This moon has a face, loving, wise eyes, and a smile looking directly down below. Jane shifts her eyes. She can take in only one thing at a time. She sees first the princess bed: white four-poster, a girl's dream of a bed. The thick fluffy white linens. Then a dark-haired girl, tucked into the pristine covers. She appears to be asleep. Victim Number 5: Megan.

She *is* asleep. Next to her on a tray are a syringe and several small vials, one of them empty, two full. A cup of milk. Cookies on a plate.

She'll be waking soon. Jane spins around. Alma is standing in the doorway.

So it was you, Jane says. The horror is just beginning to seep into her consciousness.

Yes.

But how can this be? Jane asks. She is bewildered. *You weren't even in town when the first girl . . . what was her name? . . . Heidi . . . was taken.*

We'd flown in from Denver. We bought the Toyota for cash from a used lot in South San Jose. We drove back to Denver in time to pick up the Mercedes, turn around, and drive both cars back. Heidi had a great time. They all did. You don't have to worry about them. They were happy. We were happy.

You don't seem happy now, Jane says. It is a statement of fact. Alma still looks as distressed as when she first appeared upstairs. Her usual air of calm assurance is gone.

The remembering. It's hard.

Remembering what?

Alma walks across the room and sits on the edge of Megan's bed. She picks up a small white hand and begins stroking it.

Of what it was like to be a mother. Come on, Jane, you feel the same way when you see Megan, don't you? You remember Angela. And it is killing you.

Jane gazes at Megan's face. How many times had she watched Angela sleep like this? Insensible to the world. Timed her breaths so they were drawing in and releasing air at the same time, as if with the same pair of lungs. Listening to the small heart beating.

You're also torn because you love us so much. I know all this is hard to take in, difficult to reconcile. But I'm confident you can do it. Because of how much you love us.

Love. It always came back to love. And loss. The two were always inextricably entwined.

Jane doesn't see Megan or the princess scene anymore. She is thinking of the night the three of them, she, Edward, and Alma, slept together. Waking up in the middle between them. The sun from the window picking up on the gray glints in Edward's hair, on the curves of the sheet covering Alma's naked body. Feeling so safe. So cared for.

What do you want me to do? Jane asks.

Put her to sleep for good. Give Megan some peace. Give Angela some peace.

Mesmerized by the flickering candles, Jane approaches the sleeping small figure. She has been expertly rouged. A natural color applied to her lips. Alma gets up and steps away to make room for Jane.

Jane reaches out and touches Megan's arm. It is warm. Angela at this age went through a period of night wandering, end-ing up in bed with Rick and Jane almost every night. Jane would wait until she was asleep and then carry Angela's unconscious body back to her bed. And then would sit and watch over her, sometimes for minutes, sometimes for hours.

Don't you wish they would stay this way? Alma says in a low voice. *It's a shame they have to grow up, isn't it? Sad for them, sad for us, the mothers.*

Jane listens as she strokes the little girl's hair. She is falling under a spell.

We knew you'd understand. We knew you would want to be part of this. You've felt the pain. Why should they live when your child hasn't? Why shouldn't other mothers go through what you've gone through?

A kitten is sleeping in bed next to the child.

They even get a kitten. Ice cream. As many bedtime stories as they want. Whatever they want. It's very gentle, in case you're wondering. They just gradually stop breathing. There's no pain. No awareness. Just sweetness and love until the end.

Jane sees Angela in the sleeping girl. What grieving mother wouldn't? Can't you feel the tenderness and pity Jane experiences as she watches the unconscious form? Can't you feel the rage that erupts inside her, all the stronger for having been contained?

Since Jane became involved with Edward and Alma, her bereavement, although never gone, had been muted. Now it comes back full force. Why should this girl be alive when hers isn't? Jane's longing for Angela, for her girl, for her darling, is stronger than ever. She feels tears stinging her eyes. But they will not come. The anger does. The murderous anger that caused her to obliterate the sea of roses of Angela's murderer, to crash her car, to attempt to steal her daughter. She looks down. Her hands are shaking.

You feel it too.

Jane nods.

The unfairness of death.

Is that why you do it? To make it less unfair? A deliberate act?

Spitting in the face of the gods.

Jane reaches out again to put her hand on the girl's perfect arm. Peach-colored with tiny brown hairs. The girl stirs, murmurs something, then settles down again. When Angela was a newborn, Jane would take her to bed to nurse for the midnight feedings, the tiny mouth sucking at her breast as Rick slept, oblivious to the miracle happening in the dark right next to him. Shifting position to move Angela to the other breast, the bundle so small she could easily hold it in one hand. And then sometimes dozing off, to awaken with a start and find Angela sleeping, her soft cheek against Jane's breast, her milky mouth open as she breathed sweetly. Jane was dismayed by every passing day, by the fact that this creature was growing and changing so fast, beyond recognition. *But she's so old now!* she'd cried to Rick when Angela passed her third week on earth.

I knew you'd understand.

I do. I do.

We take them. We pamper them. We treat them like the princesses they are. Like my princesses. Like yours. And then we put them to sleep.

Jane nods.

A phone starts ringing somewhere in the house. An old-fashioned ring, not a modern cell phone ringtone. It partially wakes Jane up. She sees Alma's attention has gone from her and Megan to something else.

The phone stops ringing. After a few minutes, they hear Edward call. *Alma! Can you come here? They need to hear both our voices.*

Watch over the angel, Alma says. *It's almost time. It'll be light in a couple of hours. We'll need to work fast.*

Alone with the sleeping girl. Jane watches

391

the small chest expand and recede from the shallow breathing. Megan is dressed in a frothy pink dress, the kind any girl her age would pick out for a party. Jane gazes with almost hunger at the bows on the front, the ribbons crisscrossing in the skirt of the dress. How she misses Angela! Oh, how she misses Angela! Jane likes the idea of giving Megan the gift of eternal sleep. Isn't that what Jane really wanted, after all? To drift into oblivion? To be free of the worries, the responsibilities? The pain. She can see the logic of what Edward and Alma are doing, really she can. They're just saving these girls, and their families, from the inevitable misery that awaits them in this world. Love and loss. Loss and love. Like that old song. *You can't have one without the other.*

Jane is vaguely aware that she has a choice to make. Although it seems less like a choice than an inevitability. And afterward? Will things be the same with Edward and Alma? No, she realizes. They could never go back. They would be closer, bound by a deeper, darker bond. One of absolute trust and an even richer and more robust love than before. Because didn't they trust and love her? To make the choice of their own to tell her, Jane, their secrets?

Megan stirs on the bed. Her eyelids flutter open for a moment.

Mom? she says, and then goes back to sleep.

That one word. That does it. It wakes Jane up. The full horror of the scene hits her. What had she been thinking?

Jane wastes no time. She gathers Megan up in her arms. Although small for her age, the girl is heavier than she appears — perhaps seventy-five pounds. Jane runs, almost tripping on the deep carpet. Up the stairs, thankful for the thickness under her feet that dampens any noise. She can hear voices coming from the kitchen, where the landline phone is apparently located. She moves quietly and swiftly to the front door.

She forgot the gate. How can she get out? She sees the intercom near the front door. A number of buttons are below the speaker. She pushes all of them, and then once again to be safe. The keys to the Toyota are still in her pocket. She fishes them out. Then she's out the door, depositing Megan into the backseat of the Toyota and jumping into the driver's seat. The engine almost catches, and for one heart-stopping moment she worries she's flooded it. Then it starts, she puts it in reverse, and roars backward down the driveway just as Alma and Edward burst out of the front door. She makes it to the gate just as it is starting to close. It catches on her front bumper, and she thinks she won't make it. Then, with a crunch of metal, she's free.

She turns the car around, steps on the gas, and roars toward Route 1. But just half a minute later — how could they have been so fast? — she sees headlights behind her in the rearview mirror. She presses harder on the gas pedal. Turns the corner and she's heading north on Route 1. The police in Half Moon Bay. Her best bet. Could she make it?

Her cell phone rings. She looks. *Edward,* the display says. She ignores it. After four rings it stops, goes into voicemail. Then it starts ringing again. And again. And again. She turns off the ringer, but it buzzes. Finally, she reaches over and presses speaker. The headlights are gaining behind her. She passes a road sign. Twelve miles to Half Moon Bay.

Alma's voice crackles over the phone.

Route 1 isn't very safe at night. So many twists and turns.

Jane concentrates on driving.

You can't outrace us, Jane, not in the old Toyota.

She could see the headlights getting

closer. They were right, she couldn't outrun them.

Jane, don't fight us. Without us, you're nothing.

Jane is getting closer to Martins Beach. A dot-com billionaire had bought it and promptly forbade the surfers to go there, but they merely climbed over the fence and went, anyway. There was no way to fence in the ocean.

She can see the headlights of the Mercedes behind her.

Jane, come on. Give us the girl.

Jane presses on the accelerator and barely misses wrapping herself around a eucalyptus tree. Megan murmurs behind her. She is waking up. Jane is having trouble focusing. The yellow line in the middle of the road is elusive. Sometimes on the right of her car, sometimes on the left. Trees loom. The streetlights throw out pitiful showers of beams into the inky black. The lights behind her close in.

You will not get away, Jane.

Her mouth is dry, and her jaw is clenched.

She makes a sharp right onto 92. Now she's heading toward Smithson's Nursery, the only place she knows as a possible refuge. She has the keys. She can go inside and lock them out. Retreat to the break room, which has no windows. Barricade the door until help comes. She makes a sharp right and snaps the chain to the parking lot.

That was unintelligent, Jane. We're right behind you.

They are. There's no time to get to the door and unlock it, much less get Megan inside. Jane brakes and stops. She has nowhere else to go. Looking in the rearview mirror, she sees Megan's eyelids flutter. The doors! She scrambles to lock them, but the automatic lock button doesn't respond. Only a feeble click, but nothing happens.

The Mercedes pulls up beside her, and Edward and Alma get out. They approach the Toyota. Alma has the needle and an ampule in her hands.

This won't take a second, Alma calls.

No, Jane tries to say, but her jaw clenches up. She scrambles out of her seat and into the back. She pushes Megan away from the open door.

Please, she says.

Jane, this is unworthy of you. This is Alma. She has now opened the back door, is pulling Jane out by the arm.

To be disappointed again. This is Edward.

I'm calling the police, Jane says, but remembers her cell phone is on the front seat. Edward opens the driver's door, reaches into the car, and easily captures it.

Here. I'll dial it for you, he says, and taps 9, then 1, then 1 again. His finger hovers over the green *call* button.

Do you really want me to do this?

Yes, says Jane. She nods.

If we go down, you come with us, he says.

Jane doesn't answer. Megan's eyes are now open, but she's not yet fully conscious. Jane strokes her hair.

We mean it, says Alma. *You will be implicated. We'll say it was your idea. That you masterminded it.*

Jane shakes her head. *Megan will live. That's all that matters.*

Edward drops the phone and lunges at Jane. He throws her onto the ground. Megan half tumbles out too. Her head hits the car door, and she lets out a small cry.

No! cries Jane as Alma hands the syringe and the bottle to Edward. He inserts the needle into the neck of the ampule and extracts the clear liquid. Megan is sitting up now on the edge of the car seat, her eyes fixed on Alma with bewilderment. *Mommy?* she asks. Edward moves in with the syringe in his right hand. He squats down to get to Megan's level.

Jane makes a superhuman effort and grabs a large eucalyptus branch that is on the ground next to her. She swings it up and around with all her strength and hits Edward in the neck. He gives a surprised yelp and misses Megan's arm. The branch tears a gash in the shoulder of his shirt. Blood seeps out. Edward clutches his arm, then turns savagely toward Jane. How could she have thought him beautiful? He is poisonous.

You can't stop this, Edward says.

Oh yes I can.

Jane lunges from the ground, pushing with her feet against the ground with all her might. She manages to tackle Edward right above the knees. His legs collapse and he falls, hitting his head on the side of the car door. So much blood! The syringe lies broken amid the dirty crabgrass.

Edward gets up on his knees slowly. Jane is lying in the dirt.

That's unacceptable, he says.

But we are done, says Jane, pointing to the broken syringe. Alma is standing off to one side, her look calculating. Jane knows she only has so much time to get Megan away, to raise help.

What the hell? A different voice, called from a different direction. Jane turns her head painfully. Adam. Running toward the car, wearing his Grateful Dead boxer shorts and nothing else.

Hey, man, stop right there! Leave her alone! He moves swiftly over to the car.

Jane slowly pushes herself up, sits down heavily. She is only inches away from Edward. She can smell him. Blood is trickling down his face.

Jane, he says, and her heart shatters.

Janey, says Adam from behind her. He leans down and helps her to her feet. He tries to put an arm around her, but she manages a smile and says, *No.*

I'm okay, she says.

Flashing lights and sirens. Cars pour into the parking lot.

I called the cops, Adam says, unnecessarily. Then, uncertainly, *Will you be able to explain this? Because I certainly can't.*

Megan emerges from the car, shrinking away from Edward. Jane steps forward and puts her arms around the girl, leans down to whisper in her ear.

It's going to be all right. This time it's all going to be all right.

ACKNOWLEDGMENTS

I would like to thank my editor at Scribner, Roz Lippel, for her insightful editing of the manuscript, and Julia Lee McGill for her skillful guiding of the book through the publication process. My agent, Victoria Skurnick at Levine Greenberg Rostan Literary Agency, was, as usual, immensely wise in her advice and extraordinarily energetic in her efforts on behalf of my work. And, as always, my love and gratitude to David and Sarah, the rocks of my world.

The lyrics on page 176 are from the song "Draw Me Close" by Kelly Carpenter. The lyrics on page 311 come from "Death Is Only a Dream," a traditional hymn.

ABOUT THE AUTHOR

Alice LaPlante is an award-winning writer whose bestselling books include *Half Moon Bay, A Circle of Wives, Method and Madness: The Making of a Story,* and the *New York Times* bestseller *Turn of Mind.* She taught creative writing at Stanford University where she was a Wallace Stegner Fellow and in the MFA program at San Francisco State University. She lives with her family in Mallorca, Spain.

The employees of Thorndike Press hope you have enjoyed this Large Print book. All our Thorndike, Wheeler, and Kennebec Large Print titles are designed for easy reading, and all our books are made to last. Other Thorndike Press Large Print books are available at your library, through selected bookstores, or directly from us.

For information about titles, please call:
(800) 223-1244

or visit our website at:
gale.com/thorndike

To share your comments, please write:
Publisher
Thorndike Press
10 Water St., Suite 310
Waterville, ME 04901